Bloodmines

Volume Three of
The Blue Dragon's Geas

by

Cheryl Matthynssens

To
Pat and Sarah
May 2016 Bless
You as You have
blessed us!

11-23-15

ISBN: **1505863449**
ISBN-13: **978-1505863444**

ACKNOWLEDGMENTS

I wish to give special acknowledgment to Katherine Roos and Alex Hunt, my editors, as they contributed a lot of suggestions and questions that helped this novel to flush out and kept me going throughout Chemotherapy and its side effects.

Also to Heather Scoggins that labors over my cover art to make it fit the feel and tone of the book. I love her rendition of Keensight on this cover. You can find more of her work at:
ursatomic.deviantart.com

I also wish to acknowledge my ***readers***. It is through your feedback on my Blog, Goodreads and Amazon that I have been able to improve my storyline and writing skills.

Independent writers rely on word of mouth and reviews by you, our faithful readers. We do not have a large publishing company promoting our work. It is all by word of mouth and social media work that our names are known at all. Please support Independent Authors by posting your reviews. I welcome all review be they negative or positive. It helps me refine my skills and take a look at sections of my work from a different perspective.

I look forward to hearing from you.

Chapter One

"The Trench Lord has arrived, High Minister. Should I show him in?" The servant bowed low then waited for the High Minister, Luthian Guldalian, to respond. His hands were clasped behind him, knowing that more words would be met with irritation at best, or punishment, if he was less lucky.

Luthian considered carefully how to approach the Trench Lord, Aorun, on the matter of his missing nephew, Alador. The man had not hidden his distaste that Luthian's nephew was a half-breed. "Yes, send him in, and bring a tray of sweets and cheeses," he answered, his back to the servant.

"As you command, my lord…" The servant left swiftly, silently shutting the door behind him.

Luthian drained his cup and eyed the failing light outside. The mist swirled in gauzy, dancing curtains, muting both the lights and sounds of the city below. He moved back to his large, wooden desk and set his wine glass down. He shuffled through the parchment notes as he slipped back into his chair.

Luthian knew he was missing something, but he was not sure what. How did a half-Daezun just disappear in a city full of guards? He glanced outside at the swirling mists and back to the reports. It was but one of the issues he would need to discuss with Aorun. The room had taken on a chill from the insidious dampness of misty sea air. Luthian waved his hand casually to the fire place and the fire roared up in response.

There was also the matter of the breeding stable that he needed to address with the Trench Lord. Someone had killed the Stablemaster, and he had conflicting information as to who was responsible. Some of those reports indicated that the men were Aorun's; but the Trench Lord had earned a great number of slips supporting the stable. It did not make sense that he would destroy a consistent source of income.

When the door opened and a man was shown in, Luthian rose in confusion. It was not Aorun, but his right hand, Sordith. "What is the meaning of this?" The outrage in Luthian's voice was palpable. "I sent for the Trench Lord. He does not deign to answer a summons now?"

"And so you have him." Sordith gave a dramatic bow and rose with a hint of flourish. "Aorun is dead," he said, his manner flamboyant, and his tone holding no remorse.

The High Minister blinked a few times. He knew little about Sordith. Aorun had commented on the man's brilliance when dealing with matters of business. In his simple statement, Luthian recognized that he had to be both intelligent and deadly. Aorun had been a highly skilled swordsman...

He eyed the man. Sordith was simply dressed in black and gray: hardly an outfit of status, and yet, as Luthian rested a studied eye on the other man, he noted that the material and work were exquisite.

Luthian slowly sat down and indicated a chair on the opposite side of the desk. "Please sit."

Sordith slipped gracefully into the chair. "You have a need that the trench has not met, Minister?" Sordith crossed his arms over his chest.

"I have…" he corrected his verbiage, "...***had*** many matters to discuss with Aorun." He eyed Sordith, the assessment in his gaze not hidden.

Sordith smiled. "Then let us discuss them. There were few matters of Aorun's that I was not completely privy to."

Luthian frowned. He would not give an ounce of trust to this rogue with the easy, charming smile. He had learned long ago that a man with a charming voice and easy smile often had much to hide, especially since that smile did not reach the new Trench Lord's eyes.

"Let us start with the stables. I have reports that Aorun was responsible for the death of the Stablemaster and the loss of many of my breeders." Bluntness, even to the point of crudeness, Luthian decided, might rock the other man's too-relaxed composure.

Sordith sat back with that easy manner, his elbows rested on the armrests as he tapped his fingers together. "Alas this is true," he said. "Aorun had become increasingly unstable in his last few weeks. His fixation on the destruction of your nephew became…" - Sordith paused looking for the right word - "…an obsession; and with it, he adopted a total disregard for the duties of his station. When he learned that your nephew had been accepted into the stable with open arms, I fear he flew into a rage and ordered the death of the Stablemaster." His eyes met Luthian's evenly.

Luthian picked up his glass and stood to move to the wine decanter. "I see," he said as he filled the glass. He hadn't known Alador had visited the stable. The dates did line up with the evening that Alador had been stabbed from behind.

Luthian stared into the wine glass, lightly swirling the contents. Had Aorun tried to kill Alador that night, before he went to the stable? Realizing a heavy silence had filtered into the room, he turned. Keeping his eyes on Sordith, he moved to his chair and softly broke the silence. "I had considered the man more reliable than that," he admitted.

"I do not think any Trench Lord is completely sane - a consequence of the position..." He winked at Luthian, his manner still light.

"What of you?" Luthian asked with no trace of an answering smile. Luthian did not like things being wrested from his control; this necessitated a shift in his planning that he had not anticipated.

"Oh, I am hardly sane. It is what makes me so efficient. Those around me never know what I am capable of doing." A note of seriousness crept into Sordith's voice. "And before you consider removing me from the position, do your research. There is currently no one nearly as capable as myself. Remove the pan and you may find yourself in a fire that could consume a considerable section of the city." Sordith was issuing a warning, of that there was no doubt.

Luthian sat back in his chair, his hands steepled before him. "How did Aorun die?" he asked, suddenly shifting the conversation.

The direct question brought a frown to Sordith's face. He took a moment to consider his wording. "He fell upon a dagger and drowned. Which action actually caused his death is debatable." A deadly tone crept into his words.

"In the back then…" Luthian looked disappointed.

The Trench Lord rose to his feet. "How dare you insinuate such a thing. He saw the blow coming all right, ***and*** had time to get in one or two of his own."

"Sit, Sordith," Luthian commanded, waving at the man to sit down. When the other man did not sit, the High Minister added softly. "I apologize for the slight. I have another two matters that need your direct attention."

Sordith appeared slightly mollified and sank slowly into the chair. Luthian realized that if his words were true, this was a man with some notion of honor. His offense had appeared genuine. Luthian watched him before speaking further, weighing again how to approach his concerns.

"My nephew is missing. He left the caverns with another guardsman, and neither has returned. It is imperative that I locate him." Luthian frowned. "The only thing I can think of is that they left through the trench gate. I know you keep track of comings and goings; has there been any word of Alador Guldalian?"

Sordith crossed his arms and frowned. "I am hardly your babysitter, Lord Minister," he snapped sarcastically.

Luthian's eyes narrowed. "You are trying my temper, Sordith. Do not forget that the Trench Lord still answers to The Council, and therefore, to me." Luthian's low growl had been meant to intimidate, but he noted that it had not shaken the man at all. "I am not asking you to watch him; I am asking you for information on his movements out of the city, which is a function of your office."

Sordith smirked at the noble. "Well, then, let me please you. Your nephew is not missing. He is in my protective custody." Sordith leaned back, arms crossed. That easy, roguish smile and the smooth manner were gone, and for the first time Luthian saw the real man.

"In your custody…?" Luthian blinked a few times in genuine surprise. "Just why is he in your custody?"

"Aorun had him. I had not planned to remove Aorun yet, but the man forced my hand. I found your nephew strung up like a fresh prang, and Aorun had been at him for a while. He was near death when I finally got him down." Sordith's tone was factual. His arms remained crossed as he eyed the powerful man in front of him.

"Release him to me; I will see he gets proper care." Luthian's face showed actual concern. His mind was racing. Aorun had not only made an attempt on his nephew's life; he had been torturing him. He had thought the man smarter than that.

"No." Sordith met the High Minister's eyes levelly. "He is safer with me, at this time, as I don't know who else is seeking his life. I actually like the boy. Obviously, I am doing a good job, as you did not even know where he was."

"You think I cannot protect my own nephew?" Luthian rose, now the one to take offense.

"I would point out, my lord, that if not for me," Sordith argued, refusing to rise, "your nephew would be dead at this very moment. Might a moment of gratitude be appropriate? Did you not say you were worried about the poor boy?" Sordith plucked at some lint on his pants before he looked back up to meet the eyes of the High Minister.

Luthian's cold gaze rested in Sordith's for a long tense moment before deciding not to argue the point. He sighed, and asked instead: "What of his companion?"

"Betrayed him, and now dead as well. I made sure that no one but Alador walked out of that room."

Sordith's level answer brought Luthian back down into his chair.

"How is he?" Luthian asked with genuine concern. "I can send healers." He needed that boy. Many of his plans rested on the potential magic that Alador seemed to possess.

"I have already seen to that. The damage left seems to be of the soul. The healer stated she can't undo what his mind has done. Only time will tell if this will heal at all." Sordith glanced out the window past Luthian. "She suggested someone that he trusted might be able to return him to a level of… awareness." Sordith's eyes returned to the High Minister solemnly. "I will send word when he can communicate again. If you want to help him, I suggest you send for his father."

Luthian's face fell farther. He had purposely cast doubts into the boy's mind as to the trustworthiness of his father, Luthian's own brother. It was doubtful that, if Alador's mind was damaged, Henrick would be able to help. However, Henrick might know who the mageling did trust.

"I will do that." Luthian gulped down the rest of his wine. He moved to the side board to refill his glass.

Wisely Sordith did not make a sound. The door opened, drawing both of their attentions, and the servant brought in the tray of food that Luthian had ordered. Luthian indicated to set it on the desk, then turned to look at Sordith.

"May I get you a drink?" he asked.

Sordith grinned widely. "I was afraid you'd never ask. Whatever you are drinking will be fine."

Luthian eyed him. They both knew that his preference was for a very old, fine vintage. There were few bottles left, and they were expensive, when he could find them. The Trench Lord had found a source, but Luthian paid dearly for it. Aorun had always wanted a hard, bitter brew that burned one's very stomach. Odd, Luthian thought, to find culture in a leader of the trench. In the past, such men were usually hardened and unrefined.

Luthian filled two glasses and turned to hand one to this new player. He handed the glass over as Sordith was popping a chocolate into his mouth. The High Minister returned to his seat, his mind having to calculate swiftly, given the turn of events. He was relieved that Alador was in the city, but disturbed to find out he was in the custody of the Trench Lord.

"I will want to see my nephew, if nothing more than to assure myself that you have been honest and forthcoming." Luthian sat down as he spoke.

"As long as you understand that he won't be leaving my custody until I am sure he is safe. I will protect him as if he were my own blood," - Sordith eyed the High Minister coldly - "…even from his own kin."

Luthian studied him. He was fairly certain that he had just been threatened, but the matter-of-fact way it had been delivered left him with at least two clear choices: kill the Trench Lord or remain silent on the issue. He chose neither.

"I understand your position if you have taken a liking to the boy. However, Sordith, do not forget my authority. You dance around what is proper like a weasel in a hen house." Luthian's tone made his own point clear. "You just inferred I would hurt my own nephew."

"I assure you, my lord, your authority was not in question." There was a dramatic pause, raising the tension between them. "But you and I both know that keeping murder in the family is commonplace within these walls." Sordith toasted the High Minister. "Now that we understand one another…," - Sordith paused to pop a piece of cheese in his mouth - "what is this other matter that you specifically need me to address?"

"I need you to kill my brother, Henrick." The simple statement lay between them.

"Speaking of murder in the family..." Sordith mumbled. The rogue slowly set his glass down. "Do you realize what you are asking? You want me and my men to kill one of the most powerful mages in the city: a fifth tier mage known to wield fire with a great deal of skill. We hardly have the skills to take on a full blown mage without severely damaging the city." Sordith leaned on the desk, tapping thoughtfully.

Luthian watched the man calculate. He knew that murder was just as commonplace within the trenches. If there was a way it could be done, the Trench Lord would know it.

"It is going to come with a high price."

"I will pay what you ask, I do not care about the price." Luthian frowned. "I would prefer, however, that it looks like an advancement attempt by a fourth level mage. Frame one, for all I care." The High Minister paused. "Given this recent development with Alador, waiting until you feel the boy is stable should give you enough time to plan something subversive enough to catch my brother off-guard."

Sordith eyed the mage. "You will pay whatever I ask?" Sordith tipped his head and stroked his chin, considering the High Minister's words.

"Yes, yes. The price is of no concern to me." Luthian waved his hand dismissively. "Henrick is moving against me, and he is sufficiently skilled in politics to make me uncertain of his next move. I prefer removing the head of a snake before it strikes."

Sordith slowly smiled. "Agreed! I will see to his removal after Alador is hale again." Sordith took a slow sip while noting the relief on the High Minister's face. "Tell me, my lord, why don't you see to your brother yourself? If tales are true, you are the stronger."

Luthian sighed. "I, like you, have a concern for the city. Such removals are punished if done too obviously. Two fire mages battling it out is not likely to go unnoticed. In addition, my position with the council would be weakened if they believed I had attacked Henrick outright. He is, unfortunately, well liked." The fact clearly exasperated the mage.

Sordith frowned. "Why don't you just poison him?"

"I have made three such attempts, and yet, as you know, the man still walks freely. He must have some spell of protection against such strategems." Luthian frowned. Try as he might, he had yet to detect any active spell when he had made such attempts. It did concern him that there was never any sign of active spells in his brother's presence. Henrick's hair also did not bleach from his use of magic: he maintained the same dark hair with which he had been born. If Henrick had found a rejuvenation spell, then he was not sharing.

Luthian had found ways to slow the ravages of time, but Henrick seemed to be completely immune to their taint, a fact that added an additional concern for Luthian. How many other skills had Henrick managed to harvest that Luthian remained unaware of? The one disadvantage of getting his brother out of the city and underfoot was that he then had first pick of the bloodstones from the villages with miners.

Sordith tone became casual. "Most puzzling that the High Minister is unable to remove such a spell. Don't you think that a bit worrisome?"

Luthian's eyes came up swiftly to Sordith. His whole body stiffened at the inquiry. He saw no animosity or disrespect on the man's face, yet the High Minister heard the verbal stab that definitely felt as if there was intent. "Give me the trench reports," he snapped.

Sordith gave a swift nod and launched into what was coming in and out of the city. His report was far more thorough than Aorun's had ever been. The mage was suddenly aware of a second reason why he would have to watch this rogue: Sordith was shrewd enough to know that it never hurt to give the enemy a reason to keep you.

Chapter Two

Sordith strode into the hall, taking no note of the men who saluted or nodded to him. He already knew that any sign of weakness, especially in these early weeks, would be an invitation to those with higher ambitions. Having served under Aorun, he knew many of those that he would need to watch. He had no intentions of becoming Trench Lord only to die with a dagger in his back. There was often a flurry of attempts when a reigning Trench Lord fell.

He entered his office, and Owen jumped up from behind the Trench Lord's desk with a sheepish look. The chair banged down onto all fours as the man found his feet. "Sorry boss," he mumbled as he hurried out from behind the red, wooden behemoth.

"I don't really care where you sit, Owen. Just keep your feet off of it," Sordith absently warned, his mind was still in the meeting with the High Minister. He tossed his gloves down and moved around the desk to the chair that Owen had just vacated. With a sigh, he brushed dirt off the desk, flashing Owen a scathing look.

Owen's eyes darted away, and he tugged at his jerkin as if needing to be a bit neater. "How'd it go in the top house?"

Sordith sighed at the boot heel on his latest acquisitions invoice. He held it up pointedly to Owen with a frown before speaking. "Well enough. I think we won't see the High Minister in too much of our business. However, he will be coming to inspect the condition of his nephew. I expect him to get a receptive welcome from all of my people. Understood?"

"Got it... No robbing the High Minister of all his slips."

Sordith unlocked a drawer with the keys he carried and pulled out a pouch, which he tossed to Owen. "I want those spread to any that live on the path that he will take. I want no tossing of garbage or shite. Tell them if the man makes it to my hall and out again with no harassment, I will be generous after, as well." On the surface, Sordith knew that it would look as if he was bribing the people to fool the High Minister. In truth, the last time a protest from the inhabitants of the trench had broken out, many had not lived. It had taken Aorun and the trench's men hours to put the fires out.

Owen caught it deftly and the big man turned for the door. Sordith caught a look of greed in the man's eyes. He looked down at his papers, but he called out loudly.

"Oh, one thing, Owen..."

Owen turned back for a moment. "Yeah...?" He saw the look that Sordith shot him and swallowed. "I mean, yeah SIR?"

Sordith picked up a quill to answer a message on his desk, not looking at Owen. "I find out you kept one token out of it, and I will ban you from Madame Aerius' for a month." He grinned at the sound of Owen's concerned gasp.

"Every trading token will leave my hands, I swear it," Owen promised.

"I am counting on that. See it done. I don't know when exactly his 'High and Mightiness' will deign to lower himself to step into our trench."

Sordith did not look up till Owen had closed the door. He sat back with a sigh as he tossed down the quill. Luthian might consider him an opportunistic rogue, but he had not planned to move up to this position any time soon. He had rather liked being the second behind Aorun: it left him room to maneuver and shift power without being too exposed. As word spread that he was the Trench Lord, he found he could go nowhere without 'My Lord' this and that, and besides, the complaints were endless. He put his head down into his hands for a long moment, letting the tension and wariness slowly ebb. No wonder Aorun drank so much.

He ran his hand through his hair and he considered how things had turned out. Sordith had been into every household at some point in his life. He knew which sewers led to the best scores, he knew where he could listen and not be heard. Many had thought his forays into the sewers had been to steal from the upper tiers, a fact he had managed to confirm when he brought back unusual items to sell to the merchants that lined the trenches. His true purpose had been to find his birth father. He had never considered Henrick before he had been assigned to follow Alador. As he had listened to conversations and followed both men, he had soon realized that all the pieces fit.

He was fairly certain Henrick was his father. This made Alador his half-brother. When Aorun had set out to kill Alador, Sordith had realized he could not let it happen. He sighed, further releasing the stress of the afternoon. He had now come a full circle from his beginning thought: if not for Aorun's fascination with Alador, Sordith would not now be the Trench Lord.

He got up from his desk, and headed out into the hall and made his way to what had once been his own rooms. He slipped in the door and looked about. The bed was empty. Had Alador finally risen from his stupor? "Keelee?" he called, worry evident on his face. He sighed with relief when the beautiful woman stepped in from the balcony.

"I thought the fresh air would do him good." Her soft answer drew Sordith to her side.

He gently touched her arm. "And what of you? You were hurt too," he reminded her with tender concern.

"You don't become a bed servant and not get a rough handling now and then," she muttered. "It is the vision of Flame that I cannot get out of my head. The way..." her words muted as she closed her eyes.

"I saw the end. I imagine it is a hard sight to let go of, if you witnessed his full demise." Sordith's tone was tender. He had found he liked Keelee a great deal. He loved her resilience and gentle manner. A man could gaze into her eyes, and in a moment be lost, in those emerald pools. The abuse she had suffered from Aorun's hand made any advance in the near future inconsiderate, and though he intended to make that advance, he was content to wait.

He realized he was staring into their depths again and changed the subject. "How is Alador?"

"He is unchanged. He will open his mouth so that I can feed him, or let me guide him where I wish. It is unnerving, though; his eyes stare through me as if I'm not there. He doesn't show any response other than when bidden." Keelee bit her lip and twisted her long hair between her fingers.

Sordith moved past her on to the balcony. Alador sat there, looking out into the harbor. He was dressed and clean, and Keelee had thought to lay a blanket across his lap. Sighing, Sordith grabbed a chair and pulled it up close beside him. Keelee had moved to the doorway behind them, watching worriedly.

"Alador, brother, it is safe now. You can come back from wherever you have gone." Sordith touched Alador's hand. It was cold and flaccid. Sordith pulled the blanket up a bit when he got no response.

He looked at Keelee. "He is biddable, you say, and yet does not respond to anything but commands?"

"Not a word or even a turning of the head," Keelee replied.

"It is odd. It is like he has just shut a piece of himself off." Sordith looked frustrated. The healer, Lady Aldemar, had been unable to suggest any helpful ways they might be able to snap Alador out of this state. "We will have to wait for his father and hope he knows of some solution."

Keelee's stared at Alador, her eyes filling with tears. She could not hide the misery that she felt at Alador's condition; it was written clearly on her face.

He got up and moved to her, searching her face. "You love him?" Sordith asked. He tried unsuccessfully to hide his concern.

Keelee blinked a few times at the suddenness and directness of the question. "I don't know. I feel like he's this way because of me. I feel so much guilt that I don't know if I have the room to feel anything else." She winced as she twisted the lock of hair too tightly and released it.

"Don't feel guilty." Sordith took her hand, his thumb caressing the back tenderly. "Once Aorun decided he wanted something, he would pursue it with dogged determination. He would have removed anything in his way. It was not your doing."

"Yet, because of me, here sits the only other man who has been kind to me, and my father is dead." Her voice choked as the threatening tears succeeded in spilling over onto her cheeks.

"You cannot blame yourself," he consoled, reaching

up and wiping a tear from her face.

"I… I kept something from Alador. I am afraid that it might have been important. What if it would have stopped all of this?" She attempted to turn from him, her hair moving to shield her face.

Sordith gently pulled her back to him and tipped her chin up. "What did you withhold, and more importantly, why did you withhold it?" his voice took on an edge of authority.

"I don't know what it was. He had this silver tube he was always looking for. One day, I found it under his pillow. The High Minister had been giving me slips to bring him information of use. I took it, intending to hand it over. I just never could bring myself to give it to Luthian." She took a ragged breath, her eyes closing to avoid looking at him.

"Keelee, what was in the tube?" Sordith asked. He let go of her chin, but not her hand.

"I don't know. I opened it, but it was just a piece of paper with words in no particular order. It could have been some secret way of passing a message or nothing. I don't know." She looked up at Sordith. "I just felt, deep inside, that it would be a bad thing for the High Minister to have it."

Sordith pulled her to him and hugged her gently. "You were probably right."

Keelee murmured against his chest softly. "What if it would have changed how things happened?"

"Man has questioned his choices after the fact for centuries. It doesn't change the outcome. You will drive yourself mad trying to find that answer, but you'll never have it," Sordith cautioned gently. He stroked her hair gentlybefore pushing her her back to arm's length. "Have you left these rooms at all?"

Keelee shook her head no. "I didn't want to leave him alone."

"I'll have someone else sit with him for a while. I am taking you to eat, and there are matters that need further discussion." He pushed loose hair out of her eyes and tucked it behind her ear. "I will give you an hourglass, will that be enough time to refresh yourself?"

"Yes, but…" she began.

"You are my guest, Keelee." He looked inside the doorway to his old rooms. "You will have your own room, and I will have a bath drawn for you."

"Oh, please don't trouble yourself. I can stay here with Alador," she insisted hurriedly.

"You could," he admitted. "However, a sick room is depressing, and you have been through a great deal. I will hire a woman in need of slips to sit with him."

Sordith ushered her through the room and back into the main hall despite the woman's protests that he was leaving Alador alone. "I do not think he will be getting up anytime soon, and it won't hurt him to have fresh air for a short time. I assure you that, while you ready yourself, I'll see that all is taken care of."

Keelee stopped for a moment. She turned to him, grabbing for his hand and clutching it in both of her own as she looked up into his eyes. "You promise?"

Sordith rarely made promises, but when those big, luminous eyes blinked up at him, he found the words spilling from his mouth, "I promise."

As she let go of his hand, he placed it in the small of her back to gently guide her to the room he had chosen for her. Sordith had insisted that the housekeeper ensure that it was feminine and warm. The woman was efficient, so he had no doubt that it was ready for Keelee.

He had also had her clothes brought in from the

Blackguard caverns. The death mage, Jon, had helped him gain access to Alador's room. Even so, Sordith was still unsure of who he could trust enough to get close to Alador, so despite the mage's flat insistence that he be allowed to visit, Sordith had denied him.

"Your clothes have been hung here. I sent for anything that you or Alador might need." Sordith smiled down at her before opening the door, and felt a rush of pleasure at the smile on her face.

"Thank you. How did you manage to have this all arranged so quickly?" she asked. She moved about in wonder, touching the soft linens and smelling the flowers beside the bed.

Sordith leaned on the door frame with his arms crossed, content to just watch her explore the room. "There are advantages to being the Trench Lord," he pointed out with a mischievous grin. He watched as she looked out the window, enjoying her obvious pleasure at his choice; but then he remembered his promise and stood abruptly. "I will go see to that bath, and a caregiver for Alador. I will meet you in the main foyer in one hourglass," he reminded her.

Her soft smile and large eyes focused on Sordith."I'm sure I can manage in that time."

Sordith swallowed hard; he just nodded and shut the door before he could say something too forward or stupid. He called out for a servant, and one stepped forward immediately as though he'd been hovering just out of sight. "See that the lady gets a hot bath drawn immediately, and send someone to fetch Madame Aerius," he commanded.

The servant bowed and set off swiftly for the kitchens.

An hour later, Sordith waited in the main hall. He was smartly dressed in a green tunic and black leather pants. He wore his swords and his leather vest, knowing that, even in the company of a lady, he had to be cautious.

He had met briefly with Madame Auries, as she knew most of the women in the trench. The Madame had been able to send someone up to relieve him from Alador's side before the hour glass was two-thirds spent. He had been forced to hurry to be ready before Keelee, but had managed to keep his promise. The man smiled briefly at the thought of such a small thing, and the pleasure it would give to the beautiful woman.

He frowned briefly, clasping his arms behind him and he began pacing. He wondered if he should really be pursuing his brother's bed servant. In fairness, she was of no use to Alador, except as a nurse, at this time. He hoped Alador did not have feelings for her. Sordith briefly considered whether his fascination with Keelee was any worse or better than Aorun's, then shrugged the thought away. He was just taking her to dinner to gain information. '*No harm in that*', he thought.

Hearing a light footstep, he turned and froze. Keelee had braided her hair down her left shoulder. Her emerald eyes were lined with kohl and seemed even more mesmerizing. Her deep blue dress clung tightly to every curve. The bodice of it plunged low, leaving very little left for his imagination. Sordith found himself moving to her before he could formulate a real thought. He took her hand and lifted it to his lips, his eyes locked with hers as he caressed her knuckles with a gentle kiss. "You look very beautiful." he murmured, gazing over her knuckles with genuine admiration. He realized that he had not let go of her hand and dropped his grip.

Keelee colored slightly. "I doubt you have lacked beautiful women in this hall," she teased with the merest hint of a husky whisper.

"Oh, there you would be correct. I, however, tend to be more discerning than my comrades as to my choices of companions," he reassured her with a wink. "Shall we...?" He indicated the door.

"We are not eating here?" Keelee asked, her curiosity clearly piqued as she spoke.

Sordith's answer was casual and smooth. "I thought we would take a walk along the pier. I have a friend with a lovely boat that doesn't sail until tomorrow; he offered to let me have the deck for the evening. I have requested a table be set out for us while the winds are still down. We can speak privately and watch the sunset as we dine."

"Oh. I should have worn something warmer." She looked down with concern.

"I have a cloak that will keep you more than comfortable, and if the wind picks up, we can always return," he promised. He walked her to the door where a servant waited with two cloaks. Sordith helped Keelee into hers, then swung on his own. He had a roguish smile as he escorted her out the door. There were definite benefits to being the Trench Lord.

Chapter Three

Luthian eyed himself in the mirror. Although he still maintained the regal looks of his youth, the pale color of his hair still aged him. The white silken strands were soft and easily cared for, but they could have passed for mountain snow, bleached as they were by magic. He frowned, not liking the pale look of his face. Like most mages, it was gaunt and sallow, the mark of one who used heavy spells.

He smoothed down the red robes of his sphere, having decided to proclaim his penchant for fire during his foray into the trench. Had Sordith not made Alador's situation sound so dire, he would have continued to insist the boy be moved to his manor house. His last visit to the trenches had been satisfying, but also devastating. The ungrateful wretches who lived there had seen fit to rise up against him. He had lost three guardsmen that day and had been forced to defend himself. The stench of burned flesh and waste had wafted to his balcony for a week.

Luthian was unwilling to make any additional demands until he could assess the boy for himself. He had not sent for Henrick yet against the hope that his help would not be needed. The longer he kept his brother out of Silverport, the more time he had to ascertain how to use this situation to his best advantage. Henrick had a way of showing up at the worst possible moments. Luthian shook away the annoyance that the thought had produced. He frowned at his appearance one last time, still feeling he was not quite intimidating enough. He plucked at the sleeves and nodded to himself: still a striking figure nonetheless.

His hair was left loose to blow wildly in the brisk cold wind. The mid-calf robe was decorated with draconic symbols in black woven patterns. His boots were shined so well that when he looked down, he could see his own reflection. It was not as elaborate as he would have worn to a council dinner, but the figure he cut would draw the people's eyes. He wanted to ensure that all who saw him were aware of his status.

He made his way through the hall, out to where four of the Blackguard waited for him. He would have preferred taking more men with him and cleansing the trench while he was about it; but that was not his purpose today. Four would be a sufficient show of strength, and more importantly, enough to protect him for the time required to cast any spell he might need. The four moved around him as he set off for the stairs to the fifth tier.

The High Minister loved walking through the upper tiers of Silverport. According to his decree, the streets were white and glistened in the morning sun. There was no sign of garbage, no guttersnipes seeking wallets, or beggars. It was a peaceful walk, where neighbors often greeted each other. All those who resided in the upper tiers were either magi or in service to a mage's household. It was easy to forget the world he now deigned to visit down below.

It was a pleasant walk that led from gate to opposite gate, through the length of each tier. The design was not convenient, but served as a defense for the city. If attackers managed to breach the city's outer defenses, then they would be forced to fight their way down to the opposite end of the street to gain access to the next level.

With each staircase down, the streets became busier. The third tier was the main tier of commerce. It was bustling with business from those on the two upper tiers as well as those delivering from below, all creating a great deal more noise and congestion than elsewhere. Wagons moved freely on the streets during the day, and call-boys made their way singing out the sales of their masters' wares. Luthian had always loved the third tier. It had music and personality all its own. The streets still were still pristine as the city thrived in the commerce of the day.

It was the second tier where the differences really started to become noticeable. The second tier mages had only simple magical skills, such as enchantment, cantrips, or the moulding of stone. The tier also housed those that crafted items to be sold in the tiers above them. Jewelry settings or pottery were regularly created here and sold to merchants and craftsmen above.

There was another distinct difference, though: despite the decree that the streets be clean and well kept, there was a stench to the air created by the work done on the tier. Human waste, spoiled food, and forge fires mingled into a smell that clung to one's very robes. The looks from the populace here suddenly seemed less inviting, looks that made the High Minister uncomfortable as he made his way through the street. There was no gratitude on this tier, despite the well-kept road and the assurance of housing and food. People paused to watch him pass, and the looks flashed to him were guarded and distrustful. While Luthian had no doubt that he could protect himself from any here, they were outnumbered. Mobs were notoriously hard to control, and even the most skilled mage could be overrun.

He continued his descent towards the trench. As they made their way down the wagon ramp to the first tier, Luthian eyed his surroundings. Poverty was more open here. The streets were anything but pristine, and children ran about untended. The overwhelming smell of garbage and human waste forced Luthian to put a scented kerchief to his nose. The crowds parted to let him and his party pass, and a wary silence preceded them across the tier. The Trench Lord's manor was close to the port entrance to the tier, and Luthian was reluctant to be on the first tier itself any longer than he had to be.

Called the trench due to its below-city depth, it was a dark place that only got true sunlight when the sun was directly overhead. The city sewers emptied into a canal in the center of the trench and the denizens found or made shelter as they could manage on either side. Luthian stood at the stairs for a moment, looking into the dark depths lit by torches and the dregs of filtered sunlight. The smell alone would have driven him away, and yet people stayed. Not only did the canal reek, but the press of unwashed bodies forced the mingling scents up the stairs to his delicate nostrils.

The first ministers of the tiered cities had declared the trenches home to those with no magic. A few would find masters in upper tiers that would allow them to live above in exchange for their service, but most that lived here worked in the trenches as well. He could pause no longer, for he could feel the tension in his guardsmen. With great reluctance, Luthian, High Minister of Silverport, descended into the one place he had often tried to pretend did not exist.

Much to Luthian's surprise, the inhabitants seemed to pay him no mind. Luthian did not know how they could stand the smell. Even with the scented kerchief, his eyes were watering. He carefully picked his way through the garbage strewn openly about. He eyed the shallow wall areas where people had carved a bit of space for protection from the weather. Others had managed cloth dwellings from scraps of discarded material. The people he passed were dirty and thin. He passed one small child and stopped for a moment frowning. The girl child could not be much more than four, and she was barely dressed. Her large eyes stared up at him in adoration. He gave a trading token to the nearest guardsman. "Give it to the child," he murmured. He found that the look she gave him was compelling. It was like a small puppy begging for a bit of love.

"I would advise against that, Minister. If you give a token to one, then you will find every little body in the entire trench suddenly at your side." The guard looked at him evenly, with no disrespect in tone or manner.

Luthian frowned. He nodded for them to move on, but his eyes followed the small child as he passed. She would be a beauty one day, if she lived that long. He sighed, not at the plight of the despondent, but rather that such beauty would be wasted. He shook his head and continued to make his way carefully to the steps of the Trench Hall. When he reached the steps, he eyed them with genuine assessment. Aorun had increased the number of statues that showed the harsh ruthlessness of a trench lord. He imagined that few climbed these stairs willingly. He nodded to his guardsman to continue and began the climb to the trench hall threshold. The steps were well tended, and the garbage evident elsewhere was absent here. Sporadic puffs of sea air from the harbor gave some small relief to the stench.

Luthian did not bother to knock. His guard opened the door and Luthian strode through as if he, himself, lived there. The guard in the hall had his sword out and up before Luthian had finished crossing the doorway. Two of his guards were between him and the Trench Lord's man in seconds. "Put your swords down, ALL of you. I am the High Minister and welcome in this hall." His curt, hard tones cut through the air.

Having recognized this well-dressed intruder, the large oaf of a man slid his sword back home. "E's been expectin' you. Right this way." The big man turned and sauntered down the hall.

Luthian smiled at this immediate consideration. He usually expected such treatment, but Sordith had been dancing on the edge of impertinence during their meeting. He had been unsure of exactly what reception he could expect from the new Trench Lord.

When they reached the end of the hall, the large man opened a door and announced loudly. "'Is Mightiness is 'ere to see you." The sarcasm was dripping from the oaf's mouth, and, without fear, he flashed a grin at Luthian.

"Send him in," Sordith's voice called.

Luthian moved past the man with a slight frown. Sordith needed to give that man a proper lesson on respect and etiquette, he thought coldly. He entered the Trench Lord's office and looked around. It was a room meant to intimidate. Luthian recognized the setup, as he also had a similar parlor when he wanted to make a guest uncomfortable. Just as in Luthian's own office, Sordith sat behind an impressive desk of a red hue. It was an unusual wood color that Luthian did not see often. There was no other chair in the room so Luthian moved to the desk where Sordith sat head bent down as his quill moved over parchment.

"I apologize for not rising, High Minister, but if I don't get my thoughts down on this order, I will quite lose what I was about." Sordith did not look up.

Luthian's eyes narrowed as he scrutinized the man before him. He was not used to waiting for anyone. He took the opportunity to scan the room.

There were major differences from his own office. One wall held nothing but an array of different weapons. The edges gleamed in the flickering light, and Luthian was certain that all were razor sharp. Two of the other walls had shelves carved into them with a display of unusual items. Some he had seen before and some he had not. The last wall held a double door, which, judging from what he could see from the windows, led to a terrace facing the harbor.

His attention was drawn back to Sordith as the man tossed down his quill and rose to his feet. "Right, you are here to see your nephew. I will be more than happy to take you, but I fear your guardsmen must remain here." Sordith's words held firm command.

As Sordith spoke, the four men tensed and almost as one, their hands drifted to their sides. Luthian looked over at them and shook his head. He gave a soft chuckle before looking back to Sordith. He put his hands out in an apologetic gesture. "As you can see, leaving me unprotected does not sit well with my guards."

"I entered your office unarmed, My Lord. I can hardly say the same of you, even without your men. I hold no magic to burn a man where he stands. However, I am quite certain such men would be upsetting to your nephew's state of mind." Sordith's tone was matter-of-fact.

Luthian considered this for a long moment then nodded. "Two of you will wait here, two will stand guard outside whatever room my nephew rests in." He looked at Sordith. "Agreeable?"

Sordith nodded. "Let's get this done, as I have work to do. I'm sure you have as well." Sordith turned and led Luthian back out the door. "Is Alador's father on his way?"

Luthian smiled as he walked beside the man. "Of course, I sent for him immediately. However, he has yet to respond, so I cannot tell you when he will arrive." Luthian let the lie roll of his tongue with ease.

"Good. I am hopeful that he can prompt some sort of reaction from Alador." Sordith turned a corner then nodded to the second door. "Your men can post here."

Luthian nodded his agreement to the two men who had followed them, then followed Sordith as he opened a door and stepped into the room. The room was simple but elegantly furnished. He looked about for his nephew and spotted him sitting at a table. A plump matron was spoon feeding him. He noted immediately that at each step she had to instruct the boy. He watched as Alador obediently opened his mouth and swallowed on her gentle prompt.

"Leave us, Millie. You can finish feeding him later." Sordith's order was firm.

Luthian moved to where he could be in front of Alador and eyed him carefully. The boy was pale and gaunt. What drew Luthian's eye the most, however, was the great streak of white hair that started at the temple and was pristine to the very ends of the boy's hair. The rest of it was lighter in color as well. Alador was looking right at Luthian, but from the empty look in the lad's eyes the mage was fairly certain his nephew was not really seeing him.

"Do you know if Alador was able to cast any spells?" Luthian had only seen such drastic whitening of hair when a mage pulled beyond his strength. It could also account for why the boy was seemingly unaware of his surroundings.

"I don't think so. He was strung up with special gloves to stop casting. Aorun had them made specifically for low mages who had offended him," Sordith answered, leaning against a nearby wall, arms crossed.

"Yes, well, this boy is hardly a low mage," Luthian murmured, considering the situation before him. He sat down in the chair that the matron had left to get a better look at Alador. He reached out and carefully touched the boy's face. It was cold and clammy to the touch. Instantly he collated what he saw with what he knew.

Whatever had happened between Alador and Aorun, Luthian was certain that an intense pull of magic had occurred. The boy was a water mage, so most of the spells he could have cast with that kind of power would have been noted by others. Luthian paused as he mentally replayed Sordith's report two days earlier.

"You said Aorun drowned?" Luthian queried.

"I said either the blade killed him or the water did, yes," Sordith answered.

"You also said that you found Alador strung up and that Aorun had been at him awhile. Tell me, Sordith…," - Luthian's words were pondering - "…where did the water come from that would have drowned Aorun?" Receiving no answer, the High Minister transferred his penetrating gaze from Alador to the Trench Lord.

Sordith was staring at him with an intense, considering look. Luthian's lips twitched up as he pressed, knowing he was on the right track. "The room you found them in was filling with water, wasn't it?"

"Yes," came the curt answer.

"You should avoid lying to me, Trench Lord." Luthian's tone was cold and hard. "You said no spell was cast. Just how far did he fill the room before he realized that he wasn't in danger any more?" Luthian looked back at Alador. He had seriously underestimated his nephew. That error may have cost him the storm mage that he needed to take the isle with minimal resistance.

Sordith kicked off the wall. "What does it matter? Such questions won't heal him."

"It matters because it may determine if he can be healed," Luthian pressed.

Sordith eyed Luthian for a long moment. "He didn't stop until I knocked him out."

Luthian blinked in surprise. "How full was the room?"

"He had filled it to his chin when I finally rendered him senseless." Sordith eyed the vacant gaze of his charge.

"I see," Luthian drawled out. Yes, he had seriously under-estimated the amount of power that his nephew had harvested from that stone.

"Can he be saved, or will he be like this forever? I will put him out of his misery if there is no hope," Sordith stated flatly.

"I will do some research. We will heed the healer's advice for now, and I will send Henrick to you immediately upon his arrival. I have never seen a mage in such a state, so I have little to offer in wisdom or in hope. However, my library is extensive and I will put mages on this immediately. The boy is important to my plans, and if he can be saved, then he must be." Luthian rose, smoothing his robes.

"Important how?" Sordith eyes moved to Luthian as he spoke.

The man's astuteness made Luthian smile. "You are not the only man who has ways of finding out things. I fear that is for my knowledge only. But I assure you, I would prefer my nephew very much alive and cognizant of what occurs around him."

Sordith's eyes narrowed, but he did not press the

matter. He turned and headed to the door. Luthian took one last look at Alador and followed him back to the office where his other two men waited. Neither man said anything during the short walk to the office nor in the entryway. For Luthian's part, he was calculating how he could manipulate Henrick into seeing that Alador should be moved to the High Minister's manor. Luthian only nodded as Sordith bid him an appropriate farewell.

The guards led Luthian back through the trenches, but this time he was not as aware of his surroundings. When they reached the stairs to the first tier, a small child peering from the shadows caught his eye; it was the same girl he had noticed entering the trench. Halfway up the stairs, he turned and tossed the child a trading token. Immediately after doing so, he looked down at the bottom of the stairs then poured the tokens from his belt pouch into his hands. He stepped back through the two rear guards and tossed the tokens to the bottom of the stairs. Chaos immediately erupted below him as people seemed to materialize from nowhere, and fights swiftly broke out.

Luthian smiled slowly. He turned and met the smiling girl's gaze. He put a finger to his lips, and she swiftly nodded.

"Minister, you have started a full-blown riot. We had best depart before it moves up the stairs." As if to emphasize the man's point, the injured scream of a woman pierced the air from below.

Luthian just nodded and let them hurry him away. The mage smiled as he walked. He judged from the memory of her adoring gaze that she would not forget him or his act of charity. She would come to him when the time was right. In addition, he had left a mess for the arrogant Trench Lord to clean up.

The High Minister made his way back through the city, wrapped up in his thoughts. The most prevailing one concerned his nephew. Alador had to be cured of whatever ailment held his mind in thrall: because Luthian was unlikely to ever find a storm mage with such power again.

Chapter Four

Luthian had sent a magic weave to inform Henrick to come home immediately. It had been three days, and still there was no sign of the man. His brother had always been irritating, but for the last five turnss he had been more so. Luthian knew damn well he knew how to cast a travel spell. Henrick's disrespect in not responding immediately bordered on insolence.

Luthian missed the days when his brother resided on a lower tier and groveled to do whatever task Luthian set before him. Henrick was still biddable, but the groveling had ceased after one long trip to the Daezun lands. He was fairly certain that Henrick had found a substantial bloodstone; if he had, then Henrick was somehow blocking Luthian's attempts to discern his level of power. His brother's lack of respect for him - or deference to the post he held - was high on Luthian's list of major irritations.

The door to his office slammed open with a sudden force. Both Blackguards stationed in his office drew their swords immediately. It was such a sudden interruption that even Luthian was startled. There in the doorway was his brother, looking quite irritated. The guards looked to Luthian for orders once they realized that it was the High Minister's brother. Luthian nodded for them to step out, then glanced down to the draft of a speech he had been writing before his thoughts had wandered.

"Have you become so barbaric in your ventures to Daezun lands that you forgot to knock, brother?" Luthian drawled out, not rising from his desk. He glanced up casually, then picked up his quill to continue working on the speech.

"I gathered from your message that there was some matter of urgency." Henrick strode forward as the departing guards shut the door behind him.

"And yet you took three days to arrive," Luthian pointed out as he crossed out a line that did not quite deliver the tone that he wanted to sway the council.

"I was not able to disappear without losing my cover as the carefree enchanter. I had to leave the village properly, and leave my wagon hidden." Henrick moved to the wine decanter without asking for permission. He poured himself a glass and drank it all down.

Luthian was scowling at Henrick's continued lack of proper decorum. "If you were not my brother…" he began as he laid down his quill.

"Yes, yes. I would burn where I stand." Henrick waved a hand dismissively then refilled his glass. "You know how draining travel spells are. Surely you would not deny me a bit of respite." He smiled charmingly at Luthian and took a slow draw from the glass. "Now, what is so urgent that you demanded my immediate return? Are we under attack?" Henrick sounded almost hopeful.

"It is Alador." Luthian's arms crossed as he watched his brother carefully.

Henrick immediately sobered his banter. "What happened?" he asked with genuine concern.

Luthian noted the change. Perhaps he could manage his brother through Henrick's care of his bastard son. "Aorun chose to eliminate Alador, despite his relationship to me." Luthian's announcement was purposefully misleading. He wondered if Henrick knew the level of power his son would possess once it reached its full potential.

"Alador is dead?" Henrick's face had paled as he lowered himself into a nearby chair.

Luthian watched closely, noting the changes in his brother's tone and manner. "Aorun is the one that is dead. Alador is barely better off. Before you ask, it is not a matter of healing, but rather one of magical drain."

"So Alador is Trench Lord?" Henrick asked. He slowly took a sip of wine as his eyes searched Luthian's.

"No. Aorun's second, Sordith, intervened, and was the one to actually overcome the Trench Lord. That whelp reigns as Trench Lord now." Luthian's tone caressed "whelp" with the level of aggravation that Sordith had inspired. "He has claimed protection of your son and will not release him to me. While I could have pressed the issue, I was not sure that it was in Alador's best interest."

Henrick did not respond at first, and the silence was filled with the crackle of the fireplace and the coastal wind howling outside. Henrick set the glass down on the small table beside him and leaned forward, resting his hands on his knees. "You have seen him?" he asked in a lowered tone.

There was definitely a connection between Henrick and his son that Luthian might be able to use. "Yes. I went to the Trench myself to ascertain the level of damage," Luthian admitted.

Henrick raised an eyebrow at this. "I see. What did you discover?"

Luthian nodded and continued. "His hair is significantly lightened with a substantial strip of drainage from root to tip. He stares mindlessly into nothing, and can respond to commands in body, but there seemed to be no response from the man himself. The healer reported that this is not a matter of healing, but one of will and magic." Luthian response was businesslike.

"So he is lost to us, then." Henrick sat back seemingly defeated. "I know our plans rested on his strengths as a Guldalian and a storm mage."

Luthian cocked his head curiously at Henrick's use of the term 'our plans.' He had never heard Henrick speak of it as a joint matter before this. He quickly checked his own thoughts to avoid revealing his curiosity. "Not necessarily. He does not trust me due to a rather…" - Luthian paused to decide how much he should share - "...unfortunate disagreement. I found out he had been faltering his abilities around me . The healer says that he might respond to one he trusts. My research has found that there have been some instances where a strong mage under distress and weakening can withdraw into his own mind for protection. I did not seek to see if this is true, for I think my touch would drive him deeper." Luthian rose and went to refill his own wine glass.

"Where is he being held?" Henrick asked as he picked up his own glass, swirling the wine as he absently stared into its depths.

"In the Trench Hall itself. Sordith…" - Luthian growled out the name - "has taken a liking to him, which is to our advantage. He will have more protection than just you or me. We cannot keep the eyes on him that a Trench Lord can and still let him train in the guard." Luthian had learned a long time ago that if one path to his plans did not seem to be working, it paid to adjust them quickly and take a different path. His ability to analyze situations on the hoof and adjust his plan of action accordingly had been instrumental in his rise to the rank of High Minister.

Henrick drained the remaining contents of his glass and rose. "I will go to see him immediately." He started to turn away, but looked back with a smirk. "With your permission, of course, High Minister."

Luthian rolled his eyes. "Just see to it that we get him back, Henrick, and you might live another turn." Luthian's words held an edge of truth.

"Your repeated threats are becoming tiring Luthian." Henrick turned to face Luthian fully. "I am ready for that day any time you dare, brother." Henrick's resolute response lingered on the air between them.

Luthian realized that his brother spoke the truth. He was ready for the battle for power whenever Luthian decided to make his move. Luthian was thankful at the moment that he had already decided to have Henrick assassinated. He did not like not knowing the true strength of his adversary.

"I will keep that in mind," Luthian promised. Luthian held Henrick's gaze till Henrick finally dropped his in deference and turned to stride out the door.

After his brother was gone and the Blackguards retook their posts, Luthian looked up from the wine glass he was holding. "Get me Severent," he ordered. It was time that his Master of Knowledge did his job.

Sordith looked over the damage reports from the recent riot. It was not lost on him that it had occurred at the bottom of the steps that the High Minister had taken out of the trench. He had no doubt that Luthian had tossed those tokens knowing full well what would occur. He made a note on the bottom of the council invoice for the damage. One of the vending stalls had been destroyed, three were dead, and the miners had refused to work for a half-day because of harm that had befallen family members. Sordith doubted he would receive the compensation, but it would send a message to Luthian that he was fully aware of who was responsible.

His mind turned to what had brought Luthian into the trench in the first place. Sordith had been expecting Henrick for days. He was frustrated as neither he nor Keelee had been able to provoke any mental response from Alador. Sordith had even tried pain, but Alador had not even flinched. He had given up hope. If he did not hear word from Luthian or Henrick by the week's end then he would put the boy out of his misery. The life that Alador was living was no life, even if it had been only about a week.

When his door opened, he looked up to see Owen standing there. He sighed with exasperation. Owen had become like a big puppy dog since Sordith had become Trench Lord. "Yes, Owen, what is it?"

"I think that Guldalian man that you been looking for finally bothered to show up." Owen's tone made it clear that he did not approve of mages at all.

"Well, show him in then." Sordith shoved his annoyance aside and waved Owen out the door. He was finally going to introduce himself to the man he believed to be his father. More importantly, he hoped that Henrick could find some way to help Alador.

His mind was racing as to how to present himself to Henrick. How to present the whole situation? How much did he dare share? Could Henrick really be trusted? He wanted to believe that Henrick was a man of honor, but the truth was that he was related to Luthian. That fact right there made the whole situation murky. He moved around his desk as his door opened. Henrick strode in and straight to Sordith, stopping just short of the Trench Lord. Both men were quiet for a long moment as each assessed the other. The mage was dressed in the robes typical of the mage caste. The black material contrasted with the gold trim. His long black hair was held back by a simple band, much as Sordith's own.

"I understand that you are holding my son." Henrick's tone held no accusation, but there was a tension to his whole presence that Sordith did not miss.

"I would prefer to say that I am protecting your son." Sordith's soft answer was intended to lower the mage's level of intensity.

Henrick paused for a long moment. "Protecting him from whom?" Henrick's eyes were now directly locked with Sordith's.

Sordith looked at him very carefully. "If you have to ask that then you are either one of those I need to protect him from," Sordith crossed his arms and leaned back against his desk, "or you're as blind as a bat."

Henrick wrinkled his nose in annoyance. "I know who the boy needs protection from and why. I wonder why the Trench Lord gives a damn." Henrick had yet to move from his chosen spot, rooted as firmly as a tree.

"Let's just say I have a vested interest in Alador," Sordith drawled out. "After all, without him, I wouldn't be the Trench Lord." Sordith noted Henrick's displeased look and expelled a long sigh. "We could argue and discuss all day why either of us gives a shite, but that's not helping your son," Sordith said, attempting to focus the mage's mid on what mattered most.

"For me to help him, I need to know everything that happened, or at least as much as you know." Henrick clasped his hands behind his back. "Leave no details out. It may make a difference in what my next step should be."

Sordith hesitated. He didn't know if he could trust Henrick, but he did know that Alador was as good as dead in his current situation. "I came through the door of the room that Aorun had Alador in. The man was strung up from the ceiling. It is a set up that Aorun used for torturing those that had failed him. One of Aorun's men was kneeling over Alador's bed servant, clearly intent on ravishing her right there. I watched as that man seemed to crumble into dust." Sordith shuddered at the image of Jayson's hands literally falling off, and the rest of his body collapsing in on itself.

"Once the man was nothing but dust, the room immediately began filling with water. I was a bit busy, after that, dispatching Aorun..." Sordith eyes became vacant as he relived the battle and his own panic at being held beneath the water. He swallowed the lump in his throat before continuing.

"By the time I was sure that Aorun was dead, the water was already to my knees. I got Alador's feet released, but the water just kept rising. I tried to distract him by shaking and calling out to get him to stop." Sordith returned his focus to Henrick who was listening closely. "It was as if he wasn't even there. I finally sapped him, and once he was out, the water stopped rising."

Henrick frowned. "The young fool!" Henrick spat out finally. "I told him… I warned him not to kill in that manner." Henrick put a hand to his eyes and let out a long sigh. "I will need to see him."

"I figured you would." Sordith kicked up off the desk. "Come, I will take you to him right now." Sordith led the way out the door to the inner hallways. As usual, there was no sign of servants, and their footsteps were audible in the stillness.

"He is biddable," Sordith continued. "If you tell him to stand or sit, he will comply. It is like watching a dead man move, such as in tales told to scare children at night."

"Yes, either one of two things has happened, and I am hoping for the first," Henrick broodingly stated as they moved down the hall.

"Care to enlighten me?" Sordith glanced over as Henrick moved up beside him.

"He has either withdrawn into himself for protection from the pain and anguish, or he burned out his mind and he might as well be dead." Henrick's matter of fact words still showed obvious concern. "I had warned him not to kill in such a manner. It twists the mage internally in ways that I cannot heal or help. He will have to find his own way back."

"I believe your son thought he was about to die anyway. A man pressed into a corner will fight back the only way he knows how," Sordith pointed out.

Henrick fell silent, and Sordith did not press him. He could tell that the mage was sorting through what he knew so far. Sordith opened the door. "He is in here."

Keelee stood up from where she sat on Alador' bed, and upon seeing Henrick, she dropped into a deep curtsy. "My lord," she murmured softly.

"Always a skirt," Henrick groaned with a frown. His eyes roved over Keelee. "At least the boy has good taste."

Sordith grinned. "I hear those traits run in the family." He glanced at Henrick, who was also known to be a lady's man. It was one of the things that Sordith's mother had mentioned when he had asked about his father.

Henrick just smiled. "Excuse me, my dear, but could you leave us?" Henrick motioned for Keelee to leave the room.

Keelee looked at Sordith. He nodded once and held

the door for her. "Don't worry, I will let you know what is to happen when we are done," he whispered in consolation as she passed him.

Sordith closed the door and noted that Henrick had sat down beside Alador. He watched as Henrick put a hand on either side of Alador's head. Moving closer to see better, he noted the strange light forming around the two men. It had a red hue to it, and Sordith's hair stood up all over his body. The smell of metal filled the air as the temperature seemed to rise around him. Sordith's hands went to his swords, ready to interrupt if he felt the need.

After what seemed an eternity, Henrick's hands fell away. "He has walled himself off. He is in there, but he seems to be locked away in a world that is pleasant to him. My attempts to push through the barrier his mind has created failed." Sordith saw mystification in the mage's face.

"Alador should not be able to keep me at bay." The obvious concern and confusion only increased as Henrick seemed to contemplate this statement.

"How do we get him out? The healer said someone he trusted. I would think that would be you." Sordith frowned at Henrick. "Wait! Why, may I ask, does your son not trust you?"

"I can think of several reasons at the moment, not discounting the fact that Luthian has been at him." Henrick snarled. He returned his gaze to his son. "But I do know one person that he trusts without reservation. It is possible that she could reach him." Henrick rose off the bed, staring down at Alador.

"Well then, let us fetch this woman. The longer he is like this, the weaker he becomes," Sordith pointed out with no little urgency.

"Yes, well, there is a bit of a dilemma around that." Henrick sighed with frustration.

"What is that?" Sordith moved to Henrick.

"She is about three weeks away over land, and she is unlikely to want to let me use magic to bring her." Henrick rose from the side of the bed.

"Then be convincing," Sordith growled out.

"Have you ever tried to argue with a Daezun woman who is set in her ways?" Henrick asked. His face contorted as if such a memory assailed him. Henrick began to pace at the foot of the bed. .

"Then use that Guldalian charm, because, by your own words, it is the only chance Alador has got," Sordith pointed out.

Henrick nodded. "I may have to resort to a bit of…" - The mage grimaced before continuing - "...forceful persuasion, but I will fetch her."

Sordith watched as Henrick tucked Alador in with all the care of a doting father. A sense of relief washed through him as he did not see the calculation that had emanated from Luthian. No, the one thing that he was sure of now, as he observed Henrick with Alador, was that the man had some genuine concern. "Let me show you out then, for time is wasting."

Henrick nodded and followed Sordith led him back through the hall. The Trench Lord personally walked the mage out his door. "I will keep him safe and fed till you return. I assume you will be able to convince your brother that moving him is unwise?"

Henrick smiled at Sordith. "I do not plan to report to him at all. I will be back as soon as I can."

The two men shook hands, and Sordith watched as the mage hurried down the stairs to the trench floor. He smiled at this first meeting with Henrick. He decided that he rather liked the man. The Trench Lord was so lost in his musing that, for a moment, he did not notice those below looking up at him curiously. Sordith gave them a stern glare and was satisfied with their hurried return to their own tasks. He pivoted and went back into the Trench Hall, considering all that he had heard and observed.

He decided that, when Henrick returned, he would share with him that Luthian had contracted with Sordith to kill him. A man deserved to know when he had a target on his back.

Chapter Five

Following Henrick's departure, Sordith spent two days working on shipping accounts and routing goods to the appropriate tiers. In many ways, he was more of a port manager than anything. Slowly, he was improving things in the trench. He had upped the price for simple things to the upper tiers, such as blankets and base food. He had then routed the equivalent goods to those in the trench, and reduced the price to his cost for the denizens in the dark reaches of Silverport.

This, in turn, had allowed some people to purchase enough supplies to leave the city, and to homestead in the countryside. By reducing the population of the trench, he could already see a shift in the mood of those who remained. Those that had chosen to pioneer outside the city were given a contract for trade should they choose to implement it. Over time, that ought to increase the amount of native food and trade goods coming into the city rather than the dependency on the port that was beginning to develop. Prices were higher for goods shipped from coastal cities and the other lands.

The Trench Lord sat back as he eyed the numbers. He had tried to convince Aorun that this was the way to run the trench, but Aorun had been more interested in lining his own pockets. Sordith saw no need for that, as he was in this position for life, and he had everything he needed. More slips in his own pockets seemed a waste when people outside his door were starving.

He had also started working on a way to improve the lot of those that mined for the city. Sordith had offered bonuses to those that found a rich vein of any noted mineral. He hired additional people to carry fresh water, cheese and bread to those that were working. He had insisted on increased shoring in the shafts, even if it slowed the mining down. Better to lose a day of work than a whole crew of men and a rich vein.

Sordith looked up as his door opened to see Owen with Henrick right behind him. A young woman was draped over Henrick's shoulder, though the mage seemed unconcerned. "I thought you were going to be convincing?" Sordith rose from his chair as he eyed Henrick. The mage was dressed in simple breeches and a tunic. The young woman, or what he could see of her, was dressed in thicker, leather pants and had a fine looking behind.

"This seemed a swifter solution," Henrick pointed out with a mischievous grin. Henrick tried to adjust his load and nearly dropped her. "Daezun females are rather more solid than our fair Lerdenian women. A bed or couch about now would be most welcome."

Sordith nodded thanks to Owen, then led the way to the closest bed. He watched as Henrick gently laid the girl down and smoothed the hair from her face. Sordith had to admit that, for a Daezun woman, she was rather pretty. Most had a sturdy, weathered look, but this girl was striking, and a bit less muscled then some he had met. "So, is this his sister or lover?" he asked when Henrick stood.

"Closer to lover, but in Daezun society, she cannot fully be one until she has been to their circle." Henrick looked at Sordith. "Boy hoped to be her mate before he killed another middlin in his village."

"I see. Do you think she can reach him?" Sordith moved closer and paused to inspect the young woman.

"Alador has been pining over this lass ever since he left Smallbrook. If anyone can, she can." Henrick moved to a nearby chair and sank into it with obvious relief. "I hate to impose, but do you think I could be provided a meal? Magic to travel in such a manner is really quite draining."

"Of course. I will see that food is brought in immediately," Sordith said. He left the two alone and immediately ordered food sent to Henrick. The Trench Lord then set out to find Keelee. He suspected that having these two women in the hall at the same time might prove a bit … complicated.

Keelee was sitting with Alador, as usual. Today she was reading to him. Alador was propped up in his bed staring blankly ahead. Keelee's voice faltered as she saw Sordith. He motioned for her to continue and leaned against the doorframe to watch her.

Sordith smiled at her gentle tone. Her voice had a soothing quality that he admired, and it only added to her beauty. When at last she finished the passage that she had been reading, she stood up, clutching the book to her chest.

Sordith moved across the room to her. "You really need to spend less time in here, Keelee. I think it is time that you got out of the trench for a bit. I could give you some slips to go shopping," he offered. He put his hand in the small of her back as he guided her closer to the door.

"I would rather not. First, the High Minister's spies might see me. Add to that, I would have to pass my father's shop," she said.

Sordith noted the tears that filled her eyes as she mentioned her father. He moved to her and took a hand. He kissed the knuckles tenderly as he gazed up at those deep emerald eyes. "I will respect that. Come, I need to speak to you, and as we are uncertain how aware Alador really is, I would rather it is not here." He took the book and tossed it towards a nearby table before gently guiding her from the room and along the hall.

"I hope I've not displeased you in any way." Keelee was biting her lip when Sordith looked at her.

"No, I doubt you could," he murmured huskily.

Sordith led her out onto a veranda which overlooked the harbor. The late afternoon sun left a bit of warmth in the air. He eyed the shimmering water of the harbor as he considered how to broach the subject of the girl with Henrick and opted for a direct approach.

"Did you know of another woman in Alador's life?"

Keelee's face lost color and she moved away from him to place her hands upon the iron rail that bordered the veranda. "Yes," she answered, not looking at him.

"Is that why you kept the silver tube? You thought it was from her?" he pressed.

"Yes. He was so dedicated to her. I never had a man turn me down because he loved another. Love seemed a convenient term for men to use until another feast crossed their path," she said bitterly. Keelee did not look at Sordith as she spoke.

Sordith took a few steps to her and placed one hand on the small of her back as he leaned against the rail to see her face better. "Keelee, she is here," he said.

Keelee's eyes closed. "She is the one he would trust," she acknowledged.

"The way I see it, Keelee, if this is the woman he has chosen to mate, then you must realize that there is no hope there?" His words were spoken with soft tones. "I want you to know that the Trench Hall is your home as long as you desire to stay here… and in whatever capacity you wish to occupy it. As my guest, employee or… more," he offered.

Keelee's eyes met his, and Sordith smiled at her. "I can't think of anyone I'd rather have on my arm at one of the High Minister's affairs. In fact, it would give me great pleasure to see his disbelief the first time. I might point out as well that he won't touch you once he knows I've claimed you."

Keelee looked back out at the water. "I see. So you hope to have me as your bed servant?" Her voice held a level of hurt. She stared off at into the distance not looking at him.

Sordith blinked in surprise and silence filled the air between them. He realized in that moment that he had not been clear. "I'd rather you consider a proper bonding. It would be more protective for you in regards to Luthian." He pulled her hand away from the rail and turned her to face him. "I did not mean to demean your presence here, Keelee," he swore solemnly. He kissed her knuckles tenderly, never taking his eyes from hers.

As she was turned to look at him, confusion and fear clearly written on her face. "Why would you choose a bed servant to bond with?"

Sordith gave her his best winning smile. "I can't think of a better choice for a bastard-born man than one who is just as looked down upon. I say we show them all that the Trench Lord and his chosen lady can set a far higher standard than any mage in all of Silverport." He squeezed her hand. "I know it is sudden, but I feared that if you saw Alador's own chosen, then you would flee. If I am to be honest, I don't want you to go."

Keelee looked from her hand to his eyes. She stared at him struggling to find words. "I will need to think about this. I … it is sudden and I never expected to be bonded," she whispered up to him.

"I can ask no more. Just promise me, with this

woman here, you will not run." Sordith again pressed his lips to her hand.

"That I can promise." Her tone held a sensual promise. She smiled as their eyes met.

Sordith heart skipped a beat as she looked up at him through her lashes. "Good. Now, I must go see what Henrick is doing. Also, I meant it when I said you are in Alador's room too much. Go walk by the harbor. I can send Owen with you. Or, if you would rather, you may read within my library," Sordith offered.

"I think I will take a walk," she answered. "I need to clear my head, and you have given me a lot to think about." She glanced up at him coyly.

Sordith smiled. "I will have Owen wait for you at the door." He bowed low over her hand and left her on the Veranda. Smiling, he set off to instruct Owen.

Once he had things arranged for Keelee, he headed back to the room that he had put the mage and the woman in. He entered to find Henrick eating the meal with a great deal of gusto. He grinned at Henrick. "You would think you haven't seen food in a month."

"Have to maintain this wonderful, manly figure," Henrick said between mouthfuls.

Sordith laughed and looked over at the girl on the bed. She did not appear to have moved at all. "When will she wake up?" he curiously asked Henrick.

"Whenever I take the spell off of her," Henrick said, not looking up, seeming to be more concerned with the potatoes in the stew than the girl

"Shouldn't we be doing that?" Sordith frowned. "I'd think this is a matter of urgency."

Henrick wiped his hands on his pants as he stood, choking down a piece of bread. "I didn't really want to deal with a hysterical Daezun on an empty stomach."

Sordith rolled his eyes. He moved to the young woman lying on the bed. "I can see why Alador is smitten with her. Do you think you can calm her enough to help?"

"Girl dotes on the boy. She overcame her fear of magic to write to him and to use a transport tube to send her letters. I think, once she is done with the initial shock, you will find her made of strong enough metal." Henrick paused to pop one last sweetmeat into his mouth. "But as you say, time is wasting. Let's get this part over with." He dusted his hands off and wiped his mouth with the back of his hand.

Sordith now had the confirmation that the tube was for this woman, a fact that he knew Keelee had discerned as well. He was sure that, regardless of her reasons for not handing it over to Luthian, it had been a good thing she had not chosen to give it to him. The High Minister was known to use anyone and anything he felt was necessary to achieve his goal. He would not put it over the man to use this Daezun woman against Alador.

He watched as Henrick went and sat on the bed beside the woman. The mage put a hand to her forehead and whispered a few words that Sordith did not understand. They sounded guttural and foreign to his ears. Sordith moved to where he could see both. Slowly, the girl stirred, then her eyes fluttered open.

The moment her surroundings sunk in, she sat up in alarm. "Henrick? What happened? Where am I?" She looked around the stone room and her eyes met with Sordith's.

"Be at ease, Mesiande. You are safe. I need you to look at me," Henrick commanded firmly, putting a hand on her shoulder..

The girl looked at Henrick with a bit of fear and

confusion as Henrick began to explain. "You are in Silverport, the capital of Lerdenia. This is Sordith, and you are his guest," Henrick began.

"You stole me?" she squeaked in alarm, attempting to scramble back from Henrick.

Henrick held her firmly in place. "Well, umm, yes, but with good reason," Henrick stammered.

"What good reason?" Her eyes darted about her. "How did I get here?:

"I brought you. And as for the reason, it is for Alador," Henrick attempted to soothe the panicking middlin.

"Alador?" Her eyes moved back to Henrick, and she stopped attempting to get out from under his grip.

Sordith breathed out his tension with a deep sigh at the obvious change in tone from fear to concern. They needed this young woman to help them, and to do that, she would need to be calm. He suspected that any sense of fear from Mesiande would only drive Alador deeper into whatever place he had gone. He remained silent and did not move; he wanted to give Henrick the space he needed to calm the woman down.

"Yes, Alador has been greatly hurt. He has hidden away in his own mind, and none of us can reach him," Henrick explained. "He needs someone he trusts near him right now, and..." the mage paused and sighed sadly, "he doesn't trust anyone here."

Sordith noted the narrowing of her eyes as they filled with a fire that he had seen in men who defended something passionately. He smiled slightly. If Alador wanted to bond with this Mesiande, he was going to have his hands full.

"Where is he?" she demanded. "Why doesn't he trust you?"

“Not so fast, child. I need you calm and centered before I will take you to see him.” Henrick looked over at Sordith. “Think we can arrange a bath and a dress for the young lady?”

“I’m quite sure I can arrange for both. My housekeeper is rather adept at keeping clothes on hand, after the last Trench Lord. They may need a little alteration, but she can see to that, too. There is still food on the table if you wish to help her settle. I will send in some wine, as well, to help the nerves.” Sordith bowed to them both and turned for the door. He could not help smiling as Mesiande's demanding voice followed him.

"Henrick, how did you get me here?"

Sordith closed the door before he could hear Henrick begin to explain.

Chapter Six

It was a beautiful, sunny day. The soft song of the stream sang a lulling tune as it tumbled over rocks, and the birds overhead sang with a gentle harmony to the stream. Alador was stretched out in only his breeches on a warm, flat rock, warming after swimming in the brisk, glacier-fed water. He watched Mesiande as she fished for their lunch. He had offered, but she had just laughed and said she liked fishing. It had been a perfect day. Every day since they had left Smallbrook, it had been perfect.

A part of him knew they would have to leave this safe place one day. But for now, he was content. He watched the light dance off the highlights in her hair as she tossed the line in. The smile on her face made his heart race, much as when she wrinkled her pert little nose. She had taken to wearing a leather skirt and loose blue tunic top. The increased femininity in her dress and her hair flowing around her only made him want her more. The love between them was pure, untainted by the lies and malice that surrounded the world outside this small copse and pool.

Alador stretched lazily as he sat up. By the looks of the fish that Mesiande had gathered, he thought it best to get a fire started. He dressed and set about starting a cooking fire. It did not take long to get it flickering, and the warmth of it was reassuring. He headed back to where Mesiande was fishing and took up the task of cleaning the fish. Neither spoke; they did not need to, as they seemed to work fluidly together, each knowing what the other needed to do.

Once the fish were cleaned, the two of them moved to the fire, nestled in each other's arms as the fresh catch simmered over the fire. He buried his face in her hair, reveling in the smell of smoke and pine mixed with her own scent. She leaned back against him moving his hands to just beneath her breasts. They contentedly watched the flickering flames.

"Let's never leave here," he whispered into her hair.

"We can't stay here forever, Alador. It will be winter, and we will need a shelter." Her musical matter of fact tones made him sigh with contentment.

"As long as we can, then…?" His begging tone held an edge of panic.

Mesiande was quiet for a long time then finally answered him. His heart had begun to race at her silence. "As long as we can," she finally agreed sadly.

The days that followed were peaceful and content. Alador moved wherever she wanted him to. He let her feed him as they gazed into each other's eyes. There was nothing that her soft wishes could not compel him to do. He watched her every move, afraid that this time with her would end too soon. Mesiande would just smile at him when she caught him watching.

One evening, as they watched the sun set, Alador heard something from deep inside the thick brush surrounding the pool. He tensed, and Mesiande, who had been tight against him, sensed the change and looked up.

"What is it?" she lazily asked, not moving from where she had nestled into the crook of his arm.

"We are not alone." Alador's tone became protective as he slowly pushed her aside. "Get your bow Mesi," his whispered command brooking no argument.

Mesiande moved from his side to fetch her bow as Alador rose to his feet. He scanned the brush worriedly. It was then that he heard his name, a soft call on the wind. Alador furrowed his brow, as it was definitely a female calling him. He moved warily towards the sound, scooping up his sword as he went.

"Alador, come back to me... Please?"

He blinked in confusion, as it had sounded like Mesiande. He looked back to where Mesiande had gone to get her bow. She was loading an arrow, watching him closely.

He looked back into the brush in confusion. What magic was this, now, that someone would use Mesiande to trap him? He touched the center of his magic and was reassured to feel it pulsing stronger than ever.

"Alador… please. It is me, Mesi."

He glanced back at where Mesiande stood, and horror filled him. There stood Flame, the man who had betrayed him to Aorun, with his bow drawn back and the arrow was pointed at him. He dove into the bushes as the arrow narrowly missed his shoulder, tearing through his tunic. The brambles scratched across him as he scrambled deeper into the cover of its foliage.

"Shhh, it is okay. You can come back now." The firm but gentle command was unmistakably Mesiande's voice.

Alador got up and tore through the brush, he could hear Flame close behind. "Run!" he shouted. "Run Mesiande!"

"No, you must come to me. I won't leave without you." Mesiande's voice had a firm command in it. He knew that pert tone so well.

He tore through the brush, cursing at her stubbornness. Alador could not let Flame find her. That thought brought him to a complete stop. He turned and power coursed through him as his anger grew. This place had been their peace and the traitorous Blackguard was stealing it. He waited, crouching down as a ball of crackling light filled his hand. Far off, he heard someone yell, "Get back!" It came from his left. The clear tones of a male commanding. Flame was not alone!

Flame tore into the small opening that Alador had followed, his bow drawn half back as he searched the brush. Alador did not wait and lightning flew from his hand. The crackling ball of energy expanded, and by the time it hit Flame, it was large enough that it engulfed him. Alador did not get to see if Flame survived or was destroyed as an intense pain shot through his head, and everything went black.

As he drifted back into consciousness, an annoying buzz rang through his ears. It began to clear into voices, then words. He tried to open his eyes, but his head was throbbing with pain. Slowly, the words became clearer.

"Did you have to hit him so hard?" Mesiande's disapproval was clear.

"Do you see my wall?" Sordith stated emphatically. "I mean it: Do you SEE my wall?"

"It was not as if he could help it," Mesiande pointed out, attempting to defend Alador. "And... it is just a wall," she added sarcastically.

Groggily Alador wondered what was wrong with the wall. He was confused as to where he was. He remembered being with Mesiande, but mixed in that were images of Flame and Aorun. The images seemed to change with each pounding stroke of pain.

"I will have to get a tapestry to cover that." Sordith sounded totally incensed. "You said nothing in this venture about him waking up and casting spells about."

"It wasn't as if I knew." Henrick sounded amused. His words were followed by a chuckle.

"Shhh, I think he is waking up." That was Mesiande's voice.

Alador's eyes fluttered open, and slowly he was able to focus on Mesiande's anxious face floating above him. "Mesi?" he whispered in confusion. She should not be where Sordith was, or Henrick, for that matter.

Mesiande smiled when he whispered her name. "Welcome back," she said, grinning happily. "I really think you are taking advantage of all this luxury, lying in bed until all hours of the day." Though the teasing was typical of Mesiande, she could not hide the worry in her eyes.

Alador noted that concern. He grabbed her and pulled her into his arms. When she did not resist, he buried his face in her long hair. The smell and feel of her brought his emotions tumbling out. Tears filled his eyes as he realized that she was real. She was really here. Slowly, as he held her, the realization of where 'here' was sank in. He pushed her back so he could look into her eyes. "I am so glad to see you," he whispered, "but it is not safe here. It is a horrible and evil place."

Mesiande reached out and pushed some hair out of his eyes, her touch gentle. "Henrick said if I didn't come then you might die."

Alador's gaze hardened and he looked up to search for Henrick. He pulled Mesiande to the opposite side of the bed from Henrick. "Then he should have let me die." He met Henrick's curious look with his own animosity.

Mesiande nestled into the crook of his arm as she moved against the length of his body. "Don't say that."

"It is true." Alador looked at Mesiande with genuine concern. "You are not safe here." He kissed her forehead and pulled her tightly against him before looking at the two men in the room. "What happened?"

Sordith stepped closer to the bed. "You took on Auron, but you brought one of his men in the Blackguard. When I got word that you had fallen into his hands, you were already being tortured. I killed Aorun and was able to set you free. However, you had already withdrawn into yourself."

"Flame attacked Keelee. I tried to stop him. Did he escape?" Alador was still trying to sort what was real and what had been a dream.

Henrick spoke from where he was with admonition in his tone. "You killed him with the dry cantrip. I told you not to do that, that it changed a man..."

"So does torture and betrayal," Alador snapped. Alador could not hide the loss he felt as he recalled his father's recently revealed treachery. "What of Keelee?" he asked.

"She has recovered from Aorun's assault," Sordith assured him.

Alador frowned. "How long have I been out?"

Mesiande stiffened beside him. "Who is Keelee?" The terse curiosity in her voice drew all three men's attention.

Henrick and Sordith looked at each other then Alador. Alador closed his eyes as he considered how best to answer her question. His head was still pounding, so he took a moment to answer.

"In this city, some women are sold, or sell themselves, to lie in a man's bed. Keelee was a gift from my scheming uncle. She is a very selfish and untrustworthy woman who broke my faith in her." His bitter tones made Sordith noticeably wince.

"There is more to the story than you know, Alador," Sordith stated.

Mesiande bit her lip as she worked to absorb his words. "So your uncle gave you this woman to share your furs?" Mesiande tentatively asked.

Alador had not opened his eyes. He was not going to lie to her. With all the lies he had been forced to utter to stay alive, he was not going to lie to the one pure thing in his life. "Yes," he answered softly.

"Oh…" She did not move away from him but she did not ask anything else either. An awkward silence filled the room.

It hung in the air, no one wanting to touch it before Henrick finally broke the tension and silence. "So, how do you feel?"

Alador considered this question. How did he feel? "Weak… And I have an excruciating headache," he admitted.

"Sorry," Sordith murmured as he looked at the wall, his fingers tracking the new divots that Alador had created.

Alador followed Sordith's fingers. There was a large section of the wall that was blackened, and there were missing chunks at the center. "I don't understand."

Mesiande chimed in to rescue Sordith as he looked back, seeming guilty. As Sordith opened his mouth, she swiftly interjected. "You were coming to and suddenly started throwing lightning about. Sordith knocked you on the head to stop you from hurting me."

Alador's eyes opened in alarm. "I… Oh by the gods, Mesiande, I'm so sorry." He could have killed her, and the realization that he was as much a danger to her as anyone in this city was like a knife being pushed into his heart.

"May I point out that I'm just as tough as you are," she answered saucily. "However, you were not yourself.

It is okay," she assured him. "But that is why your head hurts," she went on drily.

Never had Alador been grateful to someone for hitting him till now. He looked at Sordith. "Thank you."

Sordith slowly grinned. "You're welcome, but…" he drew out, "you owe me a tapestry for that wall."

A soft chuckle emanated from Henrick, drawing Alador's gaze. It hardened again, showing no love for his father. Alador did not want him here. Henrick's own amusement faltered.

"By the gods, what have I done to earn that look?" Henrick asked, his eyes narrowed as he assessed his son.

"Where do I start? How about with the fact you brought Mesiande here, which puts her at risk of Luthian finding out. Let's add to that; you knew about Luthian's breeding program and were an active participant in it." Alador's pain began to fuel his accusations. He pulled Mesiande closer, bringing a gasp of surprise from her.

"Secondly." Alador's scathing sarcasm made even Mesiande wince. "You are out in Daezun lands on Luthian's bidding and are as much a spy as you are a lying, conniving bastard. Lastly, you used magic on my mother to ensure you were chosen in the circle." Alador's last bitter accusation snapped out. "How many siblings do I really have, Father?"

Sordith's gaze snapped to Henrick at the last question, genuine interest written on his face as he stepped sideways - almost as if he feared becoming caught in the crossfire between the two mages.

Henrick's mouth had dropped open and his face had paled as Alador bit out each accusation. When Alador stopped, he stepped forward. "Son…" he began.

"Don't ever call me that again," Alador hissed.

Henrick put both hands out to his side in a placating manner. "You have been listening to Luthian. You know how he twists things."

"Deny one of them. Deny you were sent by your brother. Deny you knew of his breeding program." He counted them out on his fingers, holding them for Henrick to see. "I dare you to deny that you used magic the night I was conceived." He met his father's horrified gaze. Alador's face was red with his anger and it only fueled the pain in his skull.

Henrick's mouth opened and closed like a fish. He searched Alador's face. "There is more to all of this than you know…"

Alador cut him off. "I knew you couldn't deny it." He forced himself to sit up, drawing Mesiande behind him as best he could. "I will ask one last time, how many siblings do I have?"

Henrick's hands fell to his side in defeat. "I don't know," he admitted softly.

"Get out! I don't want to see you ever again." Alador's gaze darkened as he fought back the cold rage that he could feel threatening to consume him.

Henrick stared at him, his frustration hissing out in a long sigh. Finally, he turned on his heel and strode from the room. He slammed the door behind him so hard that some of the soot on the opposite wall drifted to the ground.

Alador closed his eyes and took deep breaths trying to calm the dragon's anger that he could feel just beneath his own. He did not open them again till Sordith spoke.

"Is it safe for me to speak?" Sordith ventured.

Alador opened his eyes and looked at Sordith. "You're my brother, aren't you?" The question was direct and held no accusation. "I never realized how much you and my father looked alike till I saw you standing here in the same room."

Sordith nodded. "I believe so. However, he doesn't know. I haven't wanted to broach the subject, given we all thought you were dying."

Mesiande peered around Alador to look at Sordith. "You're right, you two do look a lot alike, except for the eyes." Her voice trembled as she placed her hand on Alador's arm as if to soothe him.

Alador winced at that tone. He had not meant to scare her. His head hurt horribly, and he was confused. The reality of everything since he had awakened was only making it worse. He could feel the dragon seething inside him more than he ever had. It was no longer just memories; it was as if some part of the dragon was really there.

"Sordith can you leave us alone for a time?" Alador asked politely.

Sordith nodded. "If you need anything, Alador, you just have to ask. You are safe here from the upper tiers until you choose to leave." Sordith grinned. "Thanks to you, I am Trench Lord." He winked at Alador before turning and leaving the room in a much gentler manner than Henrick had.

Alador slowly laid back down. He felt a sense of relief as Mesiande moved back into his arms and laid her head on his chest. "There is so much to tell you," he murmured, burying his face into her hair again.

Mesiande slowly looked up at him. "I think we should just rest awhile. We both heard many things and your head is hurt." She reached out and tentatively touched the lump that Sordith's blow had left. "We have all night to speak."

Alador winced at the light touch. "I've missed you," was his only answer to her suggestion and shut his eyes.

"I have missed you too. Rest now," she stated with greater firmness. "We can talk later." She laid her head back against his chest and splayed her hand to hold him tightly to her.

Alador mused over the things that he had learned since waking up. He reveled in the feel of his love pressed tightly to him. His hand lightly toyed with her hair as he thought. As he lay there, absorbing it all, he realized one thing was certain. Henrick had been right; he had changed.

Chapter Seven

Alador and Mesiande were in no hurry to leave the room that Sordith had assigned to them. A servant saw to what needs they both had. A meal was provided for them after they woke up. They moved the table to the windows facing the veranda; it was raining steadily outside. The sound of the falling rain was soothing as it pattered against the windows; the rhythm reminded Alador of the soft drums at home.

He found himself watching her, memorizing every small detail. The dainty way that she ate and the way her hair fell softly around her face now that it was not in braids. She looked up and when their eyes met they both smiled.

When they finished eating and were again cuddled up on the bed, Alador told her everything. He left nothing out; he even spoke of Keelee and what a bed servant was. It started as a small trickle of explanation, but the more he spoke, the faster all the fear and pain spilled out. A torrent of words and emotions cascaded over them both.

She had looked hurt at first, but as events spilled from his mouth her manner softened. She begged him to leave Silverport, to find somewhere close to the village where she could visit. He had been forced to refuse her, even though this was what he wanted most. Alador knew he had to finish the geas, or he would never have peace. He was so lost in his thoughts that he was startled when she suddenly grabbed his hand with both of her own.

"I have decided I am not going back," Mesiande declared with an emphatic tone.

"Mesi, I have explained why you cannot stay here." His answer was gentle. He reached up and ran his fingers down her cheek.

"Yes, yes, it is dangerous," she mocked. She launched herself against his chest, forcing him down on the bed as she laid across him; she giggled at the look on his face. "I am not afraid of a little danger. Alador, you cannot protect me from everything," she pointed out. "I have survived a dragon attack and worse."

"No, but I can protect you from an obvious threat," he countered.

"What if this uncle of yours decides to come get me from Smallbrook?" she said a bit more seriously.

His eyes closed as his face paled. "I know that is possible, but as far as I know, he isn't aware of you."

"Alador, you don't have to do this alone," she sighed. Her eyes met his with her own fear. "Let others help you." Her voice held an edge of frustration.

"The last time I let someone help me, I was knocked on the head, and woke up in Aorun's…"

"So, what you are saying is that I should be in fear of every man because of what Trelmar did?" she interrupted. Her soft challenge made him wince as if stabbed. Her eyes held his, the determination set in her face as she waited for his response.

Alador did not know how to respond to that. "That is different," he defended weakly.

"No it isn't!" She sat up, her legs on either side of him as she looked down at him. The challenge in her eyes was one he had seen a hundred times when she was determined to get her way.

"Mesi, please, I don't wish to speak about that." His eyes closed as he tried to force away the pain of seeing her sobbing by that river.

"Too bad!" She grabbed both sides of his face. "Look at me." The soft command was whispered so close to his face that he could feel her soft breath across his lips.

Alador opened his eyes to gaze into hers. The love written on her face made his heart race. He reached up and touched her. For a long moment, they just stared into each other's eyes before she finally spoke. His heart raced as she lay across his chest to hold his face still, her hands and body holding him captive.

As she began to speak, she kept her eyes locked with his. "Your father may have done some dishonorable things in the past, but he is trying to make things right now. Sordith has opened his home to you to offer you rest and protection, at risk of making your uncle angry."

She touched his lips with her finger to keep him quiet when he opened his mouth to defend himself. "Shush. You act like you are the only one free of error."

She sat up looking down at him, her manner tender but her tone became firm. "You yourself told me of the men you killed in the name of justice. What of their families? What of their children? How many of those men were just following orders?" There was no accusation in her tone, but the sadness that she felt filled her eyes as she laid the facts out for him.

Alador looked away from her in shame. He had never taken the time to consider the fate of those around the men he had killed. He only knew they protected a vile practice.

Mesiande firmly grabbed hid his chin and searched his gaze. "Sometimes men do what they must when it seems to be for the greater good. But the greater good for whom? I'd imagine that the children of those men would see you as the villain and not the hero." She kissed his forehead before she continued. "Trelmar's mother, still to this day, sees her son as faultless." She sat up, straddling his body in a way that made him very aware of his desire for her.

"What is your point?" he whispered. He did not know how to handle her stark revelations. He felt ashamed that he had not thought of these things himself.

"My point is you won't complete this task of yours alone. Maybe you can't trust anyone right now with an absolute certainty," she sadly admitted. She placed her hands on her chest as she leaned down to whisper in his ear. "Regardless, you need them. Henrick will help you. I've no doubt of this. If his intentions are even just to unseat his brother, he will still help you. I will help you." She leaned down to kiss him tenderly.

"How'd you get so wise?" he whispered huskily when the gentle kiss ended.

"I have always been smarter than you," she teased.

Alador sighed, partly because she was being stubborn and was right; but also because he knew without a doubt that the one person he was not allowing at his side was Mesiande. How was he going to get her to agree to go home?

"Mesi, you have to go home. I won't do what I have to do if I'm worrying about you," he pointed out.

"I can take care of myself," she challenged. She sat up, and the hurt on her face was evident.

"You sure?" His voice became cold and hard.

"I used to shoot better than you, remember?" Her eyes narrowed as she looked down at him. He could see the anger building in her eyes and in the tension in her body as she glared down at him.

Alador moved swiftly, rolling her beneath him. He caught her hands and placed them on either side of her head as he pressed against her, one knee moving between her legs. "What about when they are inside your bow range?" His harshly whispered question brought alarm to her eyes. "Men here will not think twice of taking what they want from a Daezun. Many hold a deep hatred that fuels violence." There was a seething hatred in his tone as he glared down at her, his mind on all the twisted things he had seen since he had come to Silverport.

"Alador... please, let me go." Her fear was written on her face as she tried to squirm out of his grip.

The mage stared down at her, regret schooled behind a cold mask. "Make me. You said you could defend yourself."

Mesiande tried to buck him off, to knee him and even tried to twist her wrists free, but he held her firmly and she could not break his hold. "Alador, please? You're scaring me." Her shrill tone pierced the air between them.

He wanted to apologize; to take back the words he had said. He sat up, now straddling her as he let go of her wrists. Alador regretted the fear he saw in her eyes, but he did not know how else to convince her. "I'd never force you, Mesi," he said, trying to minimize any pain he had just caused her, "but I may be the only man in the city who can say that." She stared up at him, wide-eyed and he could see the tears forming. He knew he had brought her fear to the forefront.

"I'd risk that for you." Her tone held a begging edge. She desperately clutched the front of his shirt.

"I won't let you." He moved to pull her up into his arms, pulling her close despite her slight resistance. "I am sorry I scared you, but you refuse to see the danger you would be in if you stayed here." He buried his face in her hair as she trembled against him. "Go home, Mesi. I can do this, but only if I know you are safe."

"I can't without Henrick, and you sent him away," she pointed out petulantly against his shirt, hiding her face against him.

Alador swore as he realized she was right; there was no way for him to get her to safety. He did not know the spell that Henrick used to travel. Alador inwardly cursed his temper. He was going to have to eat his words to some extent with Henrick. "Mesi, I'm going to have the housekeeper bring you a bath. I need to see Sordith."

Mesiande flashed him a look of triumph despite her wide-eyed and pale state, knowing, for the moment, that she had won. Alador did not miss that look. He had pushed her fear forward only to lose in the end, and felt like he had been a total ass to her for nothing. She scooted to sit on the edge of the bed.

"Don't think this changes anything, my love. You are going home." His words were emphatic as he tapped her nose with his finger.

"How do you suggest I explain my sudden disappearance to my mother and the village?" she challenged. Her question was clearly pointing to another reason to stay.

He paused for a moment, not sure what she could say to explain her sudden absence. "Tell her you were lost," he offered.

Mesiande laughed, slowly recovering from the shock he had given her. "Alador, you know no one will believe that."

Alador sighed. "I will think of something." Realizing that, while he was covered, he would need something a bit more formal and protective, he called on his magic to dress in more than bedclothes. Alador caught her wide-eyed shock in the mirror and smiled. “Mage, remember?”

“Yes, I remember.” Her words were low and stumbling. “It is… it is just odd to see it happen with so little effort.” She was obviously biting back turns of Daezun training that magic was evil.

“A weapon is just that, a weapon. It is how one uses it that matters.” He found himself repeating his own lessons.

“Tell that to the family of the men you killed...” she argued, her voice trailing off.

Alador sighed. “I will try to keep that in mind. Remember, Mesi, every man that falls in battle to a sword also has a family. It is no different.”

She nodded, but said nothing more. She pulled her knees up to her chest and wrapped her arms around her legs. He could feel her eyes following him as he turned and left her in the rooms.

He was not immediately able to find Sordith. A servant told him that the Trench Lord was out, but that Alador could wait for him in his office. He was able to arrange for a bath to be sent in to Mesiande before he was left alone in the office of the rogue he had just discovered was his half brother.

He wandered down the shelves eyeing the exotic items from other lands. It was rather an impressive room. For its size, there was little in the way of furniture. It could have easily been split into two rooms, yet there was nothing but the desk and chairs surrounding it. It had an oppressive feel, even without Aorun behind that desk.

Moving to the wall of weapons, he examined a few he had never seen before. One of these was a strange, spiked device. Several of the sharp protrusions covered the head, with one longer one sticking straight out the end. Its wooden handle was reinforced with a band of iron where the ball joined the shaft. He fingered the sharp spikes before moving on to another.

The next weapon was the length of a quarterstaff, but where he would expect it to end, there was something resembling an axe blade. Alador touched the blade, wondering about the thorn-like hook on the back of the blade. By the look of it, it had seen battle before it had retired to Sordith's wall.

"I hope you are just curious and not choosing a weapon to kill me with." Sordith's lazy drawl caught Alador off guard. He had not heard him even open the door.

Alador reflexively drew power to his hands as he spun about. Sordith immediately put his hands out to his sides to show they were empty, answering not only at the obvious pull of power, but also the look in Alador's eyes.

"Don't sneak up on me like that," Alador hissed.

"Yes, noted. I will point out, however, that you are in *my* office, and clearly not paying attention." Sordith lowered his hands as Alador released the power he had pulled.

"You move without any noise," Alador countered.

Sordith smirked. "Yes, takes a bit of practice, but it is now a habit I don't even think about." Sordith shrugged and moved closer.

"It is time we talked," Alador simply stated.

"Is it a family trait to point out the obvious?" Sordith ginned mischievously. "I didn't think it would take too long for you to gather your wits. Come, I've a more comfortable room, and we can share a drink." Sordith gestured to the door that Alador had come through with the servant.

He led the way to a sitting room that was warm and simply furnished. Alador looked around, taking in his surroundings before he chose a chair that seemed less likely to allow someone to sneak up behind him. Sordith brought him a glass and pointedly took a drink before handing it to Alador. "I know you don't trust anyone or anything at the moment, and I know you don't drink, but I think you'll find this to your liking."

Alador took the drink and sipped it carefully. It was sweet, even though it still had that scalding burn to the throat indicative of strong liquor. He coughed a bit before smiling over to where Sordith was sitting down with his own drink. "Bites a bit," he murmured. He cleared his throat.

"Does it? I guess I have been drinking so long, I barely notice." As if to make his point, Sordith downed a third of his glass before he set it down beside him. "Where would you like to start?"

Alador thought about it as he sipped from his own glass. "I have this habit of causing harm to those that I find I actually need," he admitted.

"Henrick?" Sordith did not appear to need an answer, but he sounded sincere.

The mage nodded. "I now realize that I need Henrick."

"For what? I think you made your points rather clear when you sent him on his way," Sordith pointed out.

"To send Mesiande home. I can't let her remain here. If Luthian ever got word that she exists, that she is here, he would use her against me. I know myself well enough to know that it would work," he admitted. He was taking a leap of faith here, but Mesiande had made a good point. He needed help, and Sordith had kept his promises so far, even if he had been a bit late.

"You rather effectively shut that door." Sordith looked rather amused.

"Hence my coming to you for help." Alador sighed in frustration. "Is he still here?"

"Nope," Sordith answered smugly. "He has returned to the fifth tier."

Alador sighed with a mixture of relief and frustration. "Then I'll need to go to speak with him. He is unlikely to return, as angry as I made him." Alador took another swig at the thought of the coming discussion.

Sordith sat back in his chair as he put his hands lazily behind his head. "Alador, has it occurred to you that you make half of your own troubles?"

Alador looked into his glass, swirling the amber liquid. "More than once," he admitted.

"You know, they say it is a sign of madness to repeat the same errors over and over again and learn nothing from them." Sordith's light teasing tone held a serious edge.

Alador was quiet for a long moment as he continued to swirl the liquid in his glass. "I didn't used to be like that. Since I came into my power, this anger seethes in me that just seems to have a mind of its own." He looked up.

Sordith moved his hands back to the desk as he looked at Alador more seriously. "If you don't get control of it, then one day, you will be in a situation where no one is there to rescue you from the path of wreckage you created."

Alador considered this carefully. Sordith was right: there had always been someone there to minimize the damage caused by his willful and angry actions. "I'll try to keep that in mind," he promised. He was, however, sure that there would be other incidents. When he got angry, he often acted without taking the time to think through the possible consequences.

"I will get you some clothing similar to my men, with my insignia. Luthian is looking for you, and it is unlikely he knows you are on your feet." Sordith picked up his glass, eyeing the contents. "I would also suggest you don't go until tonight."

"To use the cover of darkness," Alador nodded his agreement.

"No, to give Henrick more time to calm down." Sordith grinned and toasted him before he took a drink.

Alador grimaced. As he assessed Sordith, he was fairly certain that the man was older than him. He definitely had similarities to Henrick. "Tell me, how are we brothers?"

Sordith took a musing sip before he began to speak. "My mother was a third tier mage. She had high hopes of bonding with a higher level mage, and had the beauty to make it possible. When I was old enough to ask after my father, she wouldn't tell me anything..." Sordith drained his glass and got up to refill it.

"One night, she was drunk and her tongue loosened. She spoke of a fire mage that she had fallen deeply in love with - his mesmerizing eyes, his smooth skill with words." Sordith turned back to look at Alador. "She must have realized that she had said too much because she switched the topic and refused to return to it. It was enough, however, for me to begin looking. I knew it was a fire mage. I knew he was a smooth talker and good-looking."

He returned to his chair, seeming to ponder the depths of his glass before speaking again. "She died about a turn later. I think back, and I am sure it was from a broken heart. She just slowly wasted away." Sordith was still staring into his glass as he spoke. "On her death bed, she made me promise that if I ever found him, not to blame him. She admitted she had thrown herself at him, and that she had never told him she had a child." Sordith took a deep drink.

The fire in the near wall crackled in the silence as Sordith sought for words. "I never thought about looking to the Guldalian brothers. It seemed unlikely that she would cast her hopes so high. But the more I followed the two of you, the more I realized that there were similarities in her words, his looks and myself that I could not ignore," Sordith's soft admission was filled with sadness.

"But you don't have magic?" Alador probed. "The magic in Henrick is very strong."

"But not in my mother. I suspect that I inherited the lack of magic on her side." He smiled as he looked up from his glass. "…Though some say my abilities stem from a different kind of magic." He looked up and winked at Alador. "I definitely have the same charm with the ladies if I choose to use it."

"So you suspect that you are my brother, but you don't have any proof…" Alador considered Sordith's words carefully.

"No. I can't be certain we are brothers. However, I feel sure enough to call you brother." Sordith saluted him with his glass then drained it.

Alador looked down at his only half-empty glass. One thing was certain: Sordith drank like his father. "I am sure enough as well. I would like to feel there was one person I could trust."

"I think you have more allies than that." Sordith pointed at Alador with the empty glass as he frowned.

"I do? Henrick has proven I cannot trust him to be straightforward. Mesiande, well she cannot stay here." Alador could name no others.

"You forget that paranoid death mage," Sordith pointed out. "It has been all I can do to keep him from storming in with poisons at the ready."

"Oh," Alador closed his eyes as he contemplated Sordith's addition of Jon. Alador had forgotten Jon with the sudden jerk back to reality and discovering Mesiande here. He nodded slowly, realizing that he did trust Jon, as much as he could trust anyone right now. "I guess I had best speak to him. He might actually do that. I will send word to Jon that I'm all right and that I'll see him soon," Alador added.

"Well, that is assuming you and Henrick do not come to blows." Sordith grinned at Alador. "I am fairly certain that that would be an encounter of note."

Alador rolled his eyes. "I've no doubt my father could easily best me. I don't plan to be that stupid."

"You never do," Sordith quipped, "do you?"

Chapter Eight

Alador sat on the bench by the door out of the Trench Hall. He was dressed in grays and blacks, as were most of Sordith's men. He had a grey cloak with a large cowl, the back boldly proclaiming the mark of the Trench Lord. Though, he had to admit, having a sword at his side was the most reassuring thing at that moment.

Sordith had sent Owen up with the gear and to give Alador some sword practice. As he sat there thinking, he realized that Owen might have gone easy on him. The mage hurt everywhere that the large man had struck a blow. As big as Owen was, he suspected that had Owen not pulled his own strength, he would bear a broken bone or two. He had to admit that the few days in bed had contributed to a loss of strength and swiftness.

Sordith had arranged for the three of them to go see Henrick. Owen was coming to guard the door, and Sordith was going in with Alador in an attempt to make peace with Henrick. Alador was unsure of how he was going to manage this feat. His feelings about his father had not changed, yet he needed the mage's help. Something told him that he, himself, was going to be more of a problem than his father's reactions.

When the door opened down the hall, Alador stood. Sordith strolled in looking quite formidable. He was not sure how the man did it. He did not seem to be excessively armored and yet, the new Trench Lord was quite intimidating. Sordith had his hair smoothed back to the base of his neck. His leather pants and jerkin were oiled to a sheen, making the black contrast sharply with the deep blue shirt beneath. His waist bore a contrasting blue leather belt, embroidered with white emblems that

Alador did not recognize. Alador's eyes came to rest on his brother's weapons last. The hilts bore matching dragon heads, each with eyes of glistening red stone.

Sordith followed his brother's eyes and pulled the right blade with his left hand with a bit of a flourish. He flipped in his hand and offered the hilt to Alador. "I had them specially made for me, I just received them."

Alador took the blade into his own hands, marveling at the craftsmanship. The blade resembled a flame and the steel had somehow been yellowed, save for three barbs near the hilt at the top side, and they moved from yellow to red at the tip of each barb. "It seems more a weapon for court," Alador commented. Then he touched the barb and realized while it might look ceremonial, it was sharpened with precision. He winced as a bead of blood formed on his finger tip.

"It is supposed to: to deceive my less astute enemies and convince them I am nothing but a glorified dandy: after which, they would soon realize their folly in underestimating me." Sordith's wicked smile gained an answering one from Alador. "You ready?"

Alador sighed heavily, the dread evident in the hissing air. "As I ever will be..." Alador handed Sordith the blade. "I don't like having to eat my words when I meant them."

"Yes, perhaps you should consider stilling that tongue of yours. Seems to get you into a fair amount of trouble," Sordith reminded him, followed by a wink.

Alador could not help but like Sordith, and he sincerely hoped that he was really his older brother. "I have been told that ever since I found that blasted bloodstone. Sometimes, I wonder if the dragon was in it and not just his magic."

"Is that possible?" Sordith asked as he sheathed his

blade.

"I don't honestly know," Alador admitted.

Owen looked between them curiously. "I hope it ain't possible," he grumbled out. "Cause you sent me to beat on him." Owen looked at Sordith with concern. "I don't want any dragon breathing on me."

Alador gave a half-hearted chuckle. "Don't worry Owen, it only seems a problem when I get angry."

"Noted: don't make the little mage angry," Owen said as he looked down at Alador.

Sordith grinned and opened the door. He led the way down from the Trench House, and both Alador and Owen fell into step behind him. It was clear by Sordith's pace that the Trench Lord was on a mission.

Alador marveled, however, at Sordith when they reached the populace that lived within the Trench itself. Sordith stopped and asked a washerwoman about her day. He stopped at a sweetmeat vendor and purchased one for all the little urchins that had gathered about him. He gave some extra slips to the filthy merchant making him promise to give every urchin a sweetmeat for the day. He reminded him to make sure to only give one to each. The people actually smiled as the three passed through.

Alador had kept his cowl up, his face barely visible, and was relieved when he seemed to draw no unwarranted attention. Sordith was putting on quite the show of loving lord, so all eyes were drawn to the flash and smile of the new Trench Lord and his pouch of slips. Sordith could have easily made his living as an entertainer, Alador thought. His easy manner and quick comebacks gained a smile from even the most hardened face they passed.

As they moved up through the tiers, Alador realized that the system was slow and inconvenient. One had to travel to the opposite end of a tier to move up. He also noted that there were no wagon accesses from the second to the third tier. A merchant would be forced to leave the city and go to the ramp to gain access to the upper tiers.

"Sordith, why don't they make an access route straight up to the top tier?" he softly asked from his half step behind the Trench Lord.

"It is a defensive tactic," Sordith answered.

"I don't understand," Alador frowned. "And why is there no wagon access to the third tier?"

Sordith chuckled. "Haven't gotten into classes on defense in the Blackguard yet, I see. Think about it. I am not going to tell you the answer." He stopped halfway up the steps to the third tier and waited for Alador to sort it out.

"Well, there is access to the upper tiers via the bridge to the third tier from the plain," Alador mused. "It seems to me more of a class separation than a defense strategy. I mean, those on the first and second tier seem to hold you in high regard, but I know from my own experience, they don't hold much love for pure mages."

"They see pure mages as a barrier between them and happiness as opposed to mere survival." Sordith pointed out. "Owen, explain to my naive brother the defense strategy." Sordith eyed his right hand, clearly expecting an accurate answer before starting the rest of the climb up the tiers.

"During a battle, there is a section of the ramp to the third tier that is dropped. This leaves an enemy with only one access into the city; through the trench. There is a walkway along the first tier that looks over the trench. Few tread it due to the stench," Owen answered stoically.

Alador realized that any army seeking entry into the trench would largely be helpless targets to archers if there was such a ledge. "I see." He eyed the first tier beneath them, unable to see this ledge because of the shops and houses that lined the street. "So it would be like shooting trapped prang," he mused aloud.

Sordith clapped his brother on the back. "Hence the reason that a Lerdenian city has never fallen to the Daezun."

Alador looked up the walls of Silverport as it towered up above them. "A fair strategy," he murmured. "But I believe one that overlooks one major flaw." He looked at his brother evenly.

"Oh, and what would you say that is? - given that it has worked for centuries?" Sordith looked genuinely curious. He flashed Alador a bemused look and continued up the stairs.

"What of a siege?" Alador turned to follow Sordith up the stairs.

Sordith chuckled, then answered with clear amusement. "One day, I will give you a true tour of the trench. The trench contains entrances to mines. When a vein is exhausted, the excavated space is used for storage. There are hundreds of such spaces below the city, even below your own mined caverns of the Blackguard."

Sordith led them through the streets towards the next set of steps up. Alador fell quiet as he eyed the streets above them. He eyed the bridge that Owen had mentioned as they passed it. Sordith was busy making an obvious presence as he moved down the street, leaving Alador free to muse. He realized, as they moved up the tiers, that the only way he was ever going to get to Luthian in a battle was either by surprise or from above.

The only way he was ever going to have a hope of gaining access from above was to make peace with the dragons. If he could get the dragons to work with the

Daezun, they could win this war that Luthian was planning. He sighed in despair. He had two major problems to overcome before such a battle could take place. He was as good as dead to the Daezun, and he had shot the one dragon he could approach.

Alador was so lost in thought that he tripped on the stairs to the fourth tier. He sprawled out behind Sordith, cursing as pain shot through his knee. Sordith stopped to give him a hand up. He rubbed his knee, chastising himself for not watching where he was going.

"Perhaps you venture out too soon?" Sordith's query held genuine concern.

"I was lost in thought, not weak," Alador grumbled, dusting himself off.

Sordith nodded to his hood that had slipped back as he spoke. "Well then, mind your step. We are almost there." Sordith set off again.

Alador swiftly pulled the hood back down. Now more aware of their surroundings, he noted that while at the lower levels Sordith had been revered, almost doted upon, this was not the case as they moved across the quieter fourth tier. While the mages moved out of his way, there were condescending glances and a clear indication of dislike. Reflexively, Alador moved his hand to his sword hilt, as did Owen; he felt the tension mounting as the air around them seemed to grow discernibly colder.

"Sordith, it seems to me that it wouldn't take too much start a civil war within this city, would it?" He made sure none but the other two could hear him. Maybe turning the Lerdenians inward on themselves would work to weaken Luthian's hold. Alador considered this possibility as he waited for Sordith's answer.

Sordith also checked that no one could hear them

before he answered. “You would think so.” He shrugged. “But the magic in the fourth and fifth tiers, combined with the power of The Council, keeps the city in balance.” He waited for a mage to pass before continuing.

“Occasionally there have been riots, but to be honest, it’s the lower tiers that suffer. That’s the reason for my position; not only am I a warden of the goods provided to the city, but I also keep the peace amongst those that live in the lower tiers. It is the lower tiers that pay with their lives, not the upper tiers.” Sordith’s answer was hard with clear resentment. He eyed a woman in a window who responded by slamming her shutters closed.

Alador thought about this as they walked through the quiet streets of the fourth tier. “...because they cannot access the upper tiers without great cost, because of limited entries?”

“And now you understand the layout of Silverport,” came the sarcastic answer.

“So it is a method of separating classes as well as of defense,” Alador mused aloud.

“Lerdenians are a proud and elite race,” Sordith answered as he led the way to the stairs up to the fifth tier.

Owen grinned from ear to ear. “Because we ARE elite. We hold the power of dragons and the swords of the Gods themselves.”

His boast brought a growl of anger from Alador that stopped Sordith in his tracks. Sordith spun and stepped between the two, catching the eyes of his suddenly furious brother. “Easy Al, Owen’s just saying what he’s been taught.” He put a hand on the mage’s chest and pushed Alador backwards to further draw his attention.

“He has been taught wrong,” Alador snarled as Sordith caught his hand preemptively.

Sordith winced as the build up of power sent a surge of current through him. “Control yourself before you draw the eyes of Luthian’s men,” he whispered behind gritted teeth, his tone firm and commanding.

Alador glanced up to see that indeed, the two blackguards at the top of the stairs were definitely watching them. He forced the surge of feral anger away, and the power slowly subsided. Sordith let go of his hand, tossing his arm away angrily.

Owen’s eyes were large and held confusion. “What’d I say?”

Sordith spun to Owen, and Alador noted his eyes were cold and hard as he snarled at the henchman: “I will explain later. This is neither the time nor place.” He strode on up the stairs, forcing both men to follow him.

Alador made a point of ignoring Owen. The oaf honestly believed that he belonged to some superior race because they raped and pillaged the very blood of dragons, harvesting them like a crop in a field. If this was what Lerdenian small ones were taught, no wonder they were arrogant.

If there was a superior race, it was the dragons who had not sought to destroy every Lerdenian city. Alador did not understand why the huge beasts did not rain fire and acid down upon the arrogant Lerdenian people. If he were in charge of the dragons, he would destroy every last glistening stone in the Lerdenian crafted piles.

“Then we would be no better than those that attack us.”

The thought — voice — brought Alador to a halt. He glanced around to discover who had said it. He realized that it was the same tone and feeling he had experienced right before he had shot the red dragon, Keensight.

'Are you in me?' he thought to himself. Sordith’s

question – was such a thing possible? - had made him wonder. There was no answer, and he felt suddenly stupid. He realized he was lagging behind and hurried to catch up.

He stared at Sordith's boots as they moved onto the fifth tier. If any were to recognize him, it would be here. So watching Sordith's boots let him stay somewhat indiscernible, but also allowed him to think. Was it true? If the dragons retaliated, would it make them no better? He did not think so. At some point, one had rise up and defend against the tyranny of others. He was so lost in these thoughts that he almost walked into Sordith when he came to a halt.

Alador looked up to see his father's door. He took a deep breath to brace himself and let it out slowly. Henrick had lied to him at every turn, and yet he could not get Mesiande home or speak to Keensight without the mage's help. He saw no alternative.

"Owen, stand guard here. Noone is to enter till I return, and I mean no one." Sordith glanced over at his second and his firm command brooked no argument.

Owen merely nodded and saluted across his chest before turning to face the path from the doorway. He stood feet planted and arms crossed. Alador grinned. He would not want to take Owen on in a sword fight, but even more so, he would not want to take him on in a battle of fisticuffs. He was fairly sure Owen could put him out with a single punch.

Alador inwardly braced himself and opened the door. He knew it was unlikely that Henrick had barred him access. The servants were mysteriously nowhere to be seen as the two men made their way into the hall, their footsteps echoing loudly off the pristine floors.

Alador led the way to Henrick's favorite room, the

only one in the house with any true warmth. As he opened the door to the library, the familiar heat met the cold of the hallway. Alador had not knocked and stepped into the room as if it was his own, more out of habit than intent. Sordith followed and Alador heard him shut the door behind him.

Alador spotted Henrick sprawled out before the fire. He had one booted leg over a chair arm and he was crooked in the opposite corner of the chair. His other leg was outstretched towards the fire. The mage was staring into the fire, drink in his hand.

"Hello Henrick," Alador firmly called out.

Henrick looked over then staggered to his feet nearly spilling his drink in the process. "Ahhh look, the angry son returns." The mage was dressed in a simple dressing gown. Henrick's hair was unkempt, and as he staggered to his feet to speak. Alador realized that the man was deeply in his cups. He had never seen Henrick out of control before and stood staring at him. Now he had no idea what to say, as he had never dealt with Henrick in such a state.

Sordith stepped beside Alador and with a great deal of amusement, stated aloud for both. "Ah, the gauntlets are already tossed, and Henrick has a head start on the wine." Sordith eyed the table at the side of Henrick's chair. The wine decanter held only a third of the liquid that had once filled its confines.

"I will have you know I am quite reasonable." He gave an exaggerated bow and stumbled as he came up. Somehow, he did not spill the contents of his cup. "Come, have some drinksh." Henrick indicated the bottle to his left, though it took a second or two for him to hone in on it.

Alador sighed softly. "I need him sober." He turned

and moved to the bell pull.

A servant swiftly opened the door in response. "Yes, Lord Guldalian?" The servant bowed low.

"Yesh, bring more wine. A lot more wine." Henrick shouted out his command.

Alador moved closer to the servant, murmuring in low tones. "Bring tea, lots of it, and food," Alador commanded. "Don't bring more wine." He looked at the servant then to Henrick. The servant followed his gaze and nodded indicating he understood. He repeated the bow and left.

Meanwhile, Henrick had staggered over to Sordith and put an arm around his shoulder. "That boy ish really depressing to be around." He took another drink of his wine.

Sordith laughed and helped Henrick towards his chair. "Yes, he does have a rather serious manner. Didn't you ever teach the boy to have a bit of fun?"

Henrick just shrugged and downed his glass before he spoke. "Tried... Boy doeshn't have a nounce of joviality in him." He moved unsteadily back to his chair and flopped haphazardly into it.

"That's not true," Alador defended with a frown as he moved back to the two men.

Sordith eyed them both and sat down in a nearby chair. "I would have to agree with your father. When did you last do something just for fun?"

Alador blushed and stammered, "Well… There … Um."

Both Henrick and Sordith laughed heartily. "Besides that Alador... No man would deny that pleasure," Sordith pointed out.

Alador realized that he could not think of anything since he had left Smallbrook. Well, nothing apart from being in Keelee's arms. With a deep red hue and a clear tone of embarrassment, he crossed his arms. "Whether I do anything 'just for fun' is not the point," he snapped.

Henrick's eyes appeared to sober for a brief moment as his soft-spoken answer seemed to shout across the room. "I would shay that's exactly the point." His eyes held Alador's for a long moment. He tried to take a drink and realized his cup was empty. "I need more wine."

Chapter Nine

It took three pots of tea, Sordith telling stories, and a couple of walks on the terrace before Henrick had sobered up enough to hold a rational conversation. Fortunately, Sordith was quite adept at making Henrick laugh with tales of the nobility, as well as some of the things he had secretly observed. Alador watched and waited. He had removed himself from the conversation, having only one purpose for being here.

He used the time to consider his situation. Mostly, he dwelled on Henrick's statement about not having any fun being the point. Now that he had thought about it, there had been moments of enjoyment. His favorite was the day he had upset Luthian at the pool in the High Minister's garden. However, despite these brief moments of amusement, he wanted to go to a home he no longer had. How could he find happiness for himself and Mesiande within his current reality? A part of him longed to go back to the small glade he had dreamed about when he had been ill. When he thought about it even now, it had seemed so real.

He continued his internal review as Sordith and Henrick bantered about which dragon was truly the deadliest. Reality…? What was truly his reality? He was a mage who did not want to be one. Worse, he was in love with a woman he could not bring here. He lived in a city where he could not really trust anyone. Well, that was not quite true, because he trusted Sordith and Jon. He really needed to speak to Jon soon.

However, the truth was that reality was not leading to any happiness. Yet, he thought, railing against his own reality was doing nothing to improve it. If he did not learn to accept his situation, then both Henrick and Sordith were right: he would never be truly happy.

He groaned and placed his head in his hands as if trying to rub away the thoughts that plagued him. This drew the attention of the other two men. He looked up to find them both looking at him. "What?"

Henrick must have sobered enough, because, rather than the easy banter of the last hour, he turned his attention to Alador with more seriousness. "Why are you here?" he gently queried. "You made your position quite clear in our last conversation."

Alador sighed. "I was angry and confused. I spoke rashly," he admitted.

"So you didn't mean the things you uttered?" Henrick pressed, a hopeful look on his face as he leaned towards Alador.

Alador met his gaze evenly, his eyes hard as the anger surged within him. "Oh, I meant them. I just shouldn't have said them."

"That is hardly an apology," Henrick pointed out.

"I'm not apologizing," Alador rebutted.

Sordith shook his head at Alador and spoke softly. "Sometimes you are too damn honest."

"And you not enough so," Alador snapped as he looked at his brother.

Sordith pointed at himself. "Rogue, thief, Trench Lord… Not in my job description." He winked at Alador.

Henrick looked between the two men. "Am I missing something here?"

"Yes," Alador answered.

"No," Sordith snapped out at the same time. He flashed Alador a warning look.

"If I am going to do this, if I am going to stick this out, I want all truths on the table," Alador stated. He met

Sordith's gaze evenly until Sordith looked away. "Tell him."

Henrick looked at Sordith. "Tell me what?"

"I should have left you to Aorun," Sordith snarled, clearly unhappy as he crossed his arms and set his jaw.

"Yes, well, you didn't." Alador did not move from his tense position in the chair. His feet and shoulders were squared, though he had not stood. His eyes held Sordith's in clear challenge.

Henrick looked between them both curiously. "Someone want to tell me whatever it is that you two are arguing about?" Henrick clearly did not like being in the dark.

"Fine!" Sordith snapped as he glared daggers at Alador. Finally, he looked at Henrick. He stood up and bowed low. "I have already presented myself to you as the Trench Lord of Silverport. It seems I am now to present myself as Sordith Guldalian, your bastard son."

Henrick stared at Sordith open mouthed for a long moment. He finally closed his mouth and shook his head. "By the Gods, surely you must be mistaken?"

"I don't think he is," Alador stated. "When you stand side by side, I can see the resemblance."

Henrick rose up and went to the mirror to look at himself then at Sordith, then back to the mirror. "Why did I not know of you?" He sounded more worried that surprised.

"My mother chose not to tell you, and would not give me your name." Sordith was watching Henrick closely. "I knew only that he was a fire mage of an upper tier and that he was good-looking. My mother's name was Sadira Sammler. She would have been young and overly willing. She had long hair that was the color of a burnished nut." Sordith looked at Henrick. "Does any of that jog your memory?" He sounded hopeful.

"Sadira… Sadira..." Henrick moved into the fire to gaze in to it. "I DO remember her. Lovely girl, and as you said, remarkably compliant. I took a fairly long sea voyage after we… had enjoyed each other's company for a short while, and when I returned, I must admit, I never got round to seeing her again." Henrick turned to look at Sordith.

Alador was relieved that his father had at least acknowledged the probability of paternity, but at the same time he was incensed that his father could use a woman and toss her to the side with so little concern. He did not speak, knowing this was a moment Sordith had been hoping to have. Again, he wondered just how many siblings might be trailing in his father's wake.

"My mother made me promise not to hold it against you. She admitted the fault was hers and that you did not know of my birth." Sordith moved to his father's side. "I have searched for many turns, and were it not for Alador, I would have never considered a Guldalian as a possible parent. I did not think my mother would have aimed so high."

"It was not so high at the time," Henrick admitted as he considered this new turn of events. "I was a fourth tier mage, and Luthian was in the limelight so much in those days that few took note of his quieter, less talented, younger brother." Henrick suddenly brightened. "This is a cause for celebration! Let me have a keg brought up and we shall drink to this revelation."

Both Sordith and Alador hastily shouted "No!" at the same time. Henrick looked at them confused.

"This is not the reason we are here, and we just got you sober enough to reason with," Alador hurriedly pointed out.

"Then why are you here?" Henrick turned to look at Alador. His tone held an edge of hurt.

"I need you to do a couple of things," Alador admitted.

"Not apologizing, meant what you said… and you want me to do a couple of things?" This clearly amused Henrick.

"Yes," Alador stood up. "As much as I hate it, only you can do them."

"Admit you need me," Henrick pressed. His eyes held Alador's in challenge.

Alador bristled and his face began to redden. Sordith stepped forward and put a hand on Henrick's arm. "He has been rather volatile since he woke up. I think that damn dragon lives within him. I wouldn't push it"

Henrick turned towards the rogue. "You are asking me to help this impudent pup – the ingrate whose life I have now saved TWICE?" Henrick looked at Sordith as his rogue of a newly discovered son let go of his arm. Henrick pointed at Alador, not looking at him. "The boy is hard-headed, ungrateful and spoiled."

"Hey now…!" Alador sputtered. He shifted uneasily in the face of that accusation.

"Have I not saved your life twice?" Henrick crossed his arms as he turned and looked at his son.

"Well, yes," Alador admitted.

"If I was really in with Luthian, why would I do that?" Henrick tipped his head to gaze at Alador.

"So I can cast this stupid storm spell he wants." Alador drew himself up, ready to defend his position.

This clearly caught Henrick a bit off guard and he stared with large eyes as his mouth open and shut a couple of times. Finally, he looked away from Alador and sighed heavily. "Is there nothing I can do to repair this vision of myself that you have created?" he gravely asked.

"Yes, you can do the two things I ask; then I will see to the end of the bloodmines, which you do appear genuinely interested in." Alador crossed his arms, feeling empowered now that he had put his father on the defensive. "Personally, I think it is more to spite my uncle than true concern for the dragons." Alador's sarcasm was dripping.

Henrick stepped forward and backhanded his son so suddenly that neither Sordith nor Alador had really had a chance to stop it. "Do not ever question my desire to end the dragons' suffering," he hissed as Alador staggered backwards.

He pursued the younger brother across the room as Alador backpedaled. "You can question my honor..." Henrick snarled. "You can call me a whoremonger and a bastard. You can even continue your tantrums about your mother, but this is never to be questioned." The tone in Henrick's voice was deadly.

Alador's hand had gone to his cheek the moment he had a chance to recover from the sudden blow. As he drew himself back up, he could feel the heat radiating off Henrick. Their eyes met in equal hardness.

"Listen, if you two are going to start casting spells," Sordith said, attempting to ease the tension, "let me leave first? I have no desire to be at the end of a lightning bolt, then set on fire." He edged backwards as the two mages stared at each other, not seeming to have heard him.

Alador could taste blood in his mouth as he held Henrick's gaze. "Understood," he conceded with a whisper.

Henrick was still bristling with anger that was not hidden. "What is it that you need of me?" he snapped.

"I need you to send Mesiande home, in a manner that won't put her into trouble with the elders." Alador looked at Henrick hopefully. He rubbed his cheek absently and moved his jaw around as it already felt as if it were stiffening.

"You have spent months lamenting her absence, and now you want me to send her home after a single evening?" Henrick looked genuinely confused. He slowly turned away from Alador, sighing with disgust. He made his way to the side table, and despite the two other men's protests, poured himself a glass of wine.

"You know what Luthian is capable of doing to get his way. Do you think for a moment she is safe here?" Alador asked, a tremor of fear for the middlin in his voice, despite his attempt to hide it. He followed Henrick to the table.

"Do you think, if he knows of her, that she is safe anywhere?" Henrick poured himself a cup and capped the decanter that held the wine, not looking at Alador.

"There is no indication he is aware of her yet," Sordith offered. "I've been keeping an ear out for any mention of Alador or those around him."

"It is more likely he will find out with her here." Alador sighed. "And I know if he got his hands on her, I would… I would do whatever he wanted to keep her safe," he warned them both.

Henrick eyed Alador over his wine glass. "This skirt is your weakness," he pointed out.

"All women are yours. At least I limit myself to one," Alador gestured to himself, flustered that his father would not just agree.

"Yes, but when all women are mine, none can really be used against me, now, can they?" Henrick grinned. He moved to the fireplace, staring into the flames.

Alador waited, as he was afraid any additional comments from him would lead to his father refusing. He sighed with relief at his father's next words.

"Alright, I will send the girl home. I don't see her willing to go, after the conversation she and I had before we brought you back." Henrick turned back and indicated Alador with his wine glass. "How do you propose to make her go? I can't take an unwilling woman back and explain her absence. She is likely to call me a liar before the elders."

Alador had not yet come up with a solution for this. He had yet to get Mesiande to truly agree to go home. He knew that she was at least as stubborn as he was. He decided that a drink was a wise idea after all and poured his own glass. He glanced over at Sordith and poured him one as well.

"Finally, now we are making progress." Sordith moved over and took the glass and decanter. "I will go get more." Sordith sauntered from the room, taking the nearly empty decanter with him.

"Get food too," Henrick called after him. He looked back to Alador.

"Can't you make her forget she was here?" Alador asked, now the one staring into the fire as he drained the glass.

"You want me to change her memories, and use the type of magic that you have accused me of when I met your mother?" Henrick almost sounded amused. "Seems that your moral lines shift to suit yourself," he accused softly.

Alador stiffened as he realized that Henrick was right. He had just asked him to mess with Mesiande's will and mind, the same thing he held over Henrick's head when he thought of his mother. "You are right. I'll just have to convince her," Alador sadly replied. He threw the glass into the fire in frustration.

"Short of making her hate you, I don't really see you doing that. She's as stubborn as you are, and, short of having nothing to remain here for, I do not seeing her agreeing to go home," Henrick pointed out, raising an eyebrow at the destruction of his glass goblet.

Alador realized Henrick was right. He was going to have to make Mesiande hate him to get her to go home. A sharp pain centered in his heart and his breath caught at the hurt he was going to have to inflict. The pain radiated into the palm of his hand and laid his head against the mantel. "Then I will make her hate me."

Henrick looked at him in surprise and his demeanor softened. "I do not envy you the words that will make that happen, son."

"Don't call me son," Alador answered absently, his tone weak and hurt.

Henrick's snort of frustration was his only answer. They both were quiet. Henrick sipped his wine as Alador stared at the fire in the hearth, his head still against the mantel. They both startled when the door swung back open and Sordith brightly sauntered into the room.

"Keg and food ordered and coming." He looked quite happy as he set the refilled decanter back on the table. "Are you two done discussing the two things?" He looked between the two silent men.

"No! I haven't gotten to the second matter…" Alador's tone was morose as he picked up his head.

"Well, I do suppose asking to go speak to a dragon isn't an easy topic to broach," Sordith offered.

"You still mean for me to seek out Keensight for you?" Henrick's gaze moved from Sordith to look at

Alador. "I think your first task far easier than your second. The dragon is not one fond of visitors and, as you have pointed out, you shot him."

Sordith looked at Alador in surprise. "You shot a dragon you intend to go and speak with?"

"Yes," Alador simply stated, in no mood for teasing banter.

Sordith looked at Henrick. "Does madness run in this family?" His tone held genuine concern.

Henrick chuckled. "It may."

Alador flopped into the nearby chair. "I know it's crazy, but I don't see any way of stopping the blood mining other than by enlisting the help of the dragons themselves." He ran a hand through his hair. "They don't seem intent on stopping the blood mining through violence or war." Alador let out a sigh of frustration. "I don't see a way to fulfill this magically imposed task without them," he repeated. "It's not like we have a list of dragons that one could go out calling upon."

Henrick laughed at that. "I will see if I can persuade him to speak with you. I cannot promise."

"No. I don't want him to know I'm coming. I just want you to take me to him. I don't want Keensight ready for me," Alador insisted.

"S…" Henrick stopped himself at Alador's harsh glance. "Alador, that is certain death," Henrick pointed out worriedly.

"He didn't eat you." Alador countered.

"Okay, there has to be a story there," Sordith said eagerly. He looked genuinely interested.

"Later," answered both mages, not taking eyes from one another.

"There is no doubt that you two are related," Sordith grumbled and filled his own glass from the decanter he had returned to the side table.

"Henrick, listen to me. I know of no other way to get Keensight to help me than to prove I'm a worthy ally. True, I shot him." Alador admitted. "But if he's as intelligent as you've made him out to be, then he should see that if I could do that, I might actually be worth helping." Alador pleaded with the fire mage, "If I am going to finish what the blue dragon pressed upon me, let me do it my way. Your way has not worked out well for me."

Henrick searched Alador's eyes. This time he downed his glass. "May the Gods help us all," were the words that signaled his concession.

Chapter Ten

Alador woke the next morning with a splitting headache and an uneasy stomach. He groaned as he sat up on the bed. He carefully pulled himself up, taking care not to move too suddenly. The room was already spinning, and the light coming through the window was piercing. He had lost track of the many decanters they had emptied. He had not intended to drink that much when he had poured that first glass, but it numbed his fear of what he knew he was going to do today. Meanwhile, the other two had spent the evening getting to know one another.

The door flew open, hitting the wall with a solid bang, and Alador winced in pain. He opened one eye to see his brother standing there. Sordith looked truly alarmed.

"What is so important that you come in here like a herd of stampeding korpen?" Alador groaned out and covered his eyes with his hand to shield some of the light that had only increased the pounding in his head.

"Keelee and Mesiande are taking their breakfast together on the veranda," Sordith stated.

Sheer panic shot through Alador. "Shite!" Alador frantically looked around for clothing. He had just shucked what he was wearing the previous day and had fallen into bed. He grabbed his pants from the floor. "I thought you were keeping them apart," he said as he hopped around trying to get his pants on.

"I thought I was too. Keelee had been told to stay away from her. I don't know how they found each other." Sordith ran a hand through his tousled black hair. "I don't want Keelee bolting."

"Probably Mesi's doing, she has always been curious. Why didn't you send Keelee away, damn it all," Alador cursed as he realized he was trying to put his head in the sleeve of his shirt.

"Where would she go, Al? I mean, Aorun murdered her father, and she has no other family," Sordith pointed out.

"Send her back to Luthian, she deserves whatever he metes out to her." Alador sat down to pull on his boots.

"Would you really send a woman who has earned Luthian's anger to her fate?" Sordith asked softly.

Alador realized that a strange silence had settled on the room. He looked up to see Sordith staring at him, waiting for an answer. Part of him wanted to say yes, for her betrayal, but the look on Sordith's face was telling. "You like her."

"I do. If you still want her, I will step aside. I do favor her, if you do not." Sordith moved over, his manner serious. "However, regardless of what you decide, I won't let you hurt her. She could have given up Mesiande to Luthian, but she did not."

Alador could not help releasing a deep heaving sigh. "So she did not … He does not know?" He pulled on the last boot and grabbed his belt.

"No. You should ask her the reasons she kept the case when you can do so without anger. It is not what you think." Sordith opened the door and looked back at Alador. "Do you...?"

Alador straightened his tunic and looked up at Sordith in confusion. "Do I what?"

"Want her?"

Alador shook his head then grabbed the side of his head as the movement caused pain. "Mesiande is the only woman I truly want. She is more than enough of a handful for me."

Sordith grinned. "Then let us be off to have breakfast with our two lovely ladies and interrupt them before we have a squall on my veranda."

Alador stomach heaved at the thought of food. "I am afraid I drank to much last evening. You have anything for a headache?" he moaned.

Sordith just chuckled and strode over to the small table that held a silver tray with goblet and wine. He poured a half glass and brought it over to Alador. "Drink up. You will feel much better. Afterward, take in a great deal of water. It will pass soon."

Alador bit back bile as he eyed the goblet. "That is the reason I am ill in the first place."

"Exactly, so take a bit more to ease the pain of its absence. Trust me. I have woken more than one morning with an angry stomach and pounding head." Sordith was still holding out the goblet. "Besides, if we don't get out there, you may have more to worry about than a headache."

Alador took the cup and wrinkled his nose at the thought. Then taking a leap of faith, he downed the glass, hoping it would not come right back up. "In the caverns, there is a supply of an elixir to cure such an ailment."

"Yes, well mages depend too much on potions, elixirs and magic. They don't know shite about taking care of themselves without these things. If you truly want to be rounded, then continue to learn as one without magic as well as one with. It might save your life at a time when your power is exhausted." Sordith took the goblet from Alador and set it down, practically dragging Alador out of the room.

Alador swiftly fell into step with Sordith. He used a bit of magic as they walked to put his hair in order at the base of his neck. “What time was Henrick coming by?” He could not quite remember what they had decided.

“We slept late, so he should be here in an hour or two at most.” Sordith led the way through the halls to the veranda where the two women sat eating. Through the glass, they could see that both seemed to be smiling. Alador was not sure if he should be worried or relieved. Sordith opened the door and stepped through. He dropped into a gallant bow just past the door. “Good morning ladies. A fine winter’s day to have a breakfast outside.”

Alador stopped in the doorway, his mouth dropping open as Mesiande turned her head to look at him. Her face was flushed from the cool morning air, and as she looked at him, her eyes held admiration and loving concern. Matching ribbons were braided into her hair and the braids were drawn up behind her head to keep her long hair out of her face. The color brought out her eyes and the burnished gold in her hair. She was dressed in a gown of gentle orange. The bodice did little to hide that she was a woman fully grown. A dark brown cloak completed the ensemble and contrasted with the dress. She was breathtaking. He could not remember ever seeing her look as beautiful as she did right now.

Sordith moved to Keelee’s side and took the woman’s hand. He kissed the back of it, lingering over her small fingers as he met her eyes. Alador watched as Keelee flushed with color and looked away.

The mage knew he could not be so gallant. He needed to send Mesiande home, not give her reason to stay. At that moment, he was thankful for a bit of discomfort from the night before. It would make it easier to play the cad, rather than the lover. He moved around the table and plopped down in the chair next to Mesiande as if he was dropping down beside one of his brothers.

"Morning Mesi. I hope you slept well." He reached across her and rudely grabbed a biscuit.

Mesiande looked from where Sordith was just letting go of Keelee's hand and flashed Alador a disappointed look "I did. I waited up, but you did not come back." She searched Alador's face worriedly. "Is everything alright?"

"Of course. We met with Henrick to arrange to send you home, then we went out drinking." He stated it with a manner that seemed to indicate he had not cared she was waiting back at the Trench Hall. Alador shoved the whole biscuit into his mouth. The last thing he wanted to do at that moment was to eat, but he did want to be as brash and callous as he could.

"Oh." Mesiande bit her lip and looked down at her plate for a moment. Suddenly, she kicked Alador under the table.

"Ow!" Alador rubbed his knee.

She looked up at him ever so sweetly. "Oh sorry, I didn't' realize you were so close."

Sordith sat down beside Keelee. "So, what have you two lovely ladies been speaking about this morning?"

Keelee smiled. "Alador's lack of charm and big heart," - she smiled at Alador sweetly - "...along with his total lack of awareness when it comes to feminine moods."

Alador chuckled and winked at her. "I never heard you complain in my bed." He did not look at Mesiande when he heard the sharp intake of breath. He knew that had hurt, but this was the route he had to take to get her to go back to Smallbrook.

Keelee met Alador's gaze in confusion as she said, "I was sharing with Mesiande that you never stopped going on about her, and how you denied my presence many times because of your love for her." She looked from Alador to Mesiande and back.

Sordith was also frowning at Alador. "I think a little more tact is warranted here, brother." Sordith flashed Alador a warning look as he hissed this through his teeth.

Alador realized he was not going to pull this off with Sordith criticizing every step. Then there was Keelee, who was obviously trying to reassure Mesiande that she was no threat. "You are right. If you will excuse us, I would like to speak to Mesiande alone. Would you like to see the docks Mesi?" He stood up too quickly and had to bite down the bile that rose in his throat. He swallowed it down and offered her his hand.

"I ... Yes," came the confused answer.

The weather was brisk that morning, Mesiande already had a cloak on, so as Alador pulled her up and led her from Trench Hall, he stopped at the door to retrieve the cloak he had worn the night before. Protected from casual identification by the cowl, he felt a bit more comfortable taking her down to the docks. He held her hand as he led her down the long stairs to the Trench. Her eyes were wide as the stench of the sewage canal assailed her.

"It will be better down on the docks," he promised.

It took a while to reach the end of the pier, leaving Alador more time to consider how he was going to make her want to go home. Mesiande was fascinated by the big, three-masted vessels and stopped often to ask questions and point out things she had never seen. Alador took the time to answer her questions as he knew that soon she would not want to speak to him again.

He took her hands and looked deeply into her eyes. Every part of his heart was screaming out to find another way. He swallowed hard and finally spoke. "You look quite beautiful in that dress, Mesiande. You would fit in with the finest halls if you were not Daezun," he offered. He tipped her face up to look at him and kissed her lips gently. A large lump formed in his throat, and he forced the threatening tears down.

"I...thank you." She looked up at him. "What has changed?"

"Changed?"

"You ... seem different this morning," she said with a frown.

"Ah yes, the change." He smiled and chucked her under the chin. "I have decided you can stay. Of course, the only way you can be close to me in the Blackguard is as a bed servant." He turned to look out at the breakwater. He could not look her in the eye and do this. "But if you are determined, then you may take your place in my rooms." He clasped both hands behind him, mimicking Luthian's arrogant and heartless air as best he could. It also hid the trembling of his hands.

"A BED servant?" Her voice held both surprise and small amount of shock. "Isn't that how Keelee came to you?"

He took a deep breath and turned back to her. "Yes. A bed servant warms their master's bed, sees to his clothes and room. Of course, there is the pleasure in the night." He reached out and pulled her close to him as he gazed down into her eyes. "I assure you that will be my most urgent need." He kissed her passionately before she could speak.

Mesiande stared up at him until she caught her breath. "I thought… it would be more as housemates?" Her question held her confusion and disbelief.

"Well, you see, as a housemate, I would have to

worry about Luthian using you against me. This way, he will see you as beneath his notice. Of course, to cement that illusion, I will have to loan you to a few other men for their use in the night." The words seemed to stick in his mouth, but he still managed to spit them out. He turned away from her again staring out at the water, internally bracing himself. "However, if you are determined to stay, then this is the way it will need to be done."

"You could do that?" There was an edge to her voice that he did not recognize. "Keelee said you never gifted her."

Alador inwardly cursed; the two women had talked more than he had anticipated. It was all Alador could do to hold that mask. Every instinct within him was begging him to explain his coldness, to keep her close and happy. He could not do it here in Silverport, not as long a Luthian drew breath. "Do what?" he asked casually, knowing full well the question.

"You could send me to another's bed?" She bit out the words with a terse tone.

"Of course, just think of it like circle. Women often choose men different from their housemates during circle." He continued to stare at the water rather than look at her. "I am sure if we had stayed in Daezun lands, you would have taken someone other than me to your furs. Gregor, for example."

There was a long silence. He took a breath as he prepared himself to turn and look at her when suddenly there was a firm kick to his behind. Unprepared for such an assault, he hit the cold water face first. When he managed to flail his way to the top, she was standing there with her hands on her hips, glaring down at him.

It was all that he could do with boots and cloak to

get a hold on the dock. He looked up at her with a harsh glare. "What, by the Gods, was that for?" He worked the cloak loose to pull it off and heaved it onto the dock. He was not going to be able to pull himself up, weighed down as he was.

"I figured you were so full of yourself that I thought I would see if mages really could walk on water," she growled down at him. "If that is the man you are becoming, then I don't want anything to do with you." Her hands were still on her hips as she glared at him. She stomped on his fingers, sending him under water again.

Mesiande knelt down as he came up sputtering. "I didn't want anyone else to ever be in my furs but you," Mesiande snapped. "I see Silverport has truly influenced you. If this is who you want to be then I never want you in them," she hissed. She stood up. "If you decide to be the man I love, come find me." She picked up her skirt and stomped up the dock angrily.

Alador watched her go with wide eyes. He had wanted her to go home. He had wanted her to be hurt or angry enough to go. Now that he had achieved it, he wished he could take everything back.

It took a great deal of effort, given the height of the dock and the fact that his boots were full of water, to pull himself back up on the boards. A sailor stood nearby watching. "You sure pissed that one off." He chuckled and shook his head. He strolled off, not even offering Alador a hand up.

Alador did not move, his breath coming in ragged gasps. He had never felt so dirty in all of his life, as if Luthian's very presence clung to his skin. Alador knew that he had hurt her in a way that he likely could never repair. But now she would go home, and she would be safe from this evil place, as well as the plotting and conniving of his uncle's imperialistic ambitions.

When he had managed to compose himself, he struggled back up to his feet. He cast a drying cantrip, as the wind was cutting through his wet clothes. Slowly making his way up the docks, the bedraggled mage headed for the Trench Hall. He hoped that Sordith and Henrick would have her away before he got there. Alador did not know if he could look her in the eyes at this point. Lost in his thoughts, he started up the lengthy staircase to the hall. He startled when he heard his brother's voice.

"You bastard! How could you?" Sordith snarled.

Alador looked up just in time to see the fist that connected with his jaw. Alador tumbled back down the few steps he had climbed. He managed to get up to his hands and knees when Sordith's boot connected with his stomach. He lay there gasping as the angry man towered above him. "Let… me… explain," he gasped, holding his stomach.

"You better be quick, or I am going to beat you senseless," Sordith hissed down at him.

"I had to get her to go home. She wasn't budging so...I tried to make her hate me," Alador gasped again.

"Congratulations, it worked." Sordith clapped his hands together in a slow and sarcastic manner. He did not bother to help Alador as his younger brother made it to his knees.

"I had to, Sordith. There was no other way to get her to go and not put Henrick in danger." Alador was sure something had broken inside besides his heart. Blood filled his mouth. The pain of the kick combined with the taste of blood, a hangover, and the salt water swirled together, and he vomited onto the steps.

"There were other ways, you idiot! You did not have to destroy her like that." Sordith moved back and forth like an angry feline. "Find your room and stay there until Henrick and I can get her calm and off to her home," Sordith finally snarled. The command spat at Alador left no room for argument.

Alador nodded. "I understand," he miserably answered.

Sordith spit just short where Alador had his hands on the ground. "In fact, just stay there till I calm down. I'm not sure I still won't beat you senseless." Sordith turned on his heel and stomped back up the stairs leaving Alador kneeling and bleeding on the bottom of the steps.

Sordith stopped after about four steps and turned to look at Alador. "I don't ever want to hear how people broke your trust again." Sordith's tone was cold and bitter. "What you did today violated that woman's trust and love. Words cut deeper than any physical assault. She said your words hurt her more than Trelmar ever could." Sordith's words were snide, his anger palpable. "You're no better than those you accuse of having misled and hurt you."

Alador's eyes widened as he stared up at him. The truth of his words wrenched the mage's heart harder than the words he had spoken to Mesiande. The realization of what Mesiande had said to Sordith drowned everything else out, even the taste of blood. His eyes followed his brother until he disappeared. Alador struggled to his feet staring up at the large manor house. He had done what he must without considering the cost to Mesiande. He was no better than Henrick or Luthian, and the pain of *that* realization cut through him.

"By the Gods, what have I done?" he whispered as tears slowly fell down his cheeks.

Chapter Eleven

Sordith had not sent for Alador in the last two days, and even Keelee had not been to see him. The one time he had seen Keelee in the hall, she had turned on her heel and gone the other way rather than talk to him. He could not blame them; he knew he had earned their ire.

Despite his fear that he had gone too far, he knew that there was no other way Mesiande would have followed Henrick's guidance when they returned. She was headstrong and forceful when something was in the way of what she wanted. He sighed as he stared out his window at the harbor. He could not stay here any longer. He was bored and restless and Sordith's decree had limited what distractions that he could access. It was time to report to Luthian, he finally decided.

He put together a few items and slowly put on the armor from the Blackguard. His lower ribs were still bruised where Sordith had kicked him, and he felt the pain every time he had to bend or take a deep breath. In addition, he had lost weight, and the fit was too loose no matter how he adjusted the straps. Once he was dressed, he headed for Sordith's office. He knocked on it tentatively, having had no idea what reception he was going to get from Sordith.

"Come." The tone was businesslike and hard.

The brisk call only served to raise the tension Alador was feeling. He stepped into the room and eased the door shut. He met Sordith's gaze. The hard look and narrowed eyes told him clearly that his brother was still angry. "What do you want?" Sordith snarled, throwing down his quill as he sat back in his chair.

"I came to say good-bye. It appears that I've

outstayed my welcome, and I need to face Luthian at some point." Alador drew himself up, his posture more erect and formal, his hands clasped behind him. "I'm very thankful for your help, and though you're angry with me, I'm still proud to call the Trench Lord my brother." He saluted his brother across his chest.

Sordith did not return his salute, letting him stand there uncomfortably. He finally nodded in acknowledgment as he let out a breath of tension.

"Just because I'm angry with you does not mean I don't hold that we're kin." Sordith leaned forward clasping his hands as he laid them on the desk. "However, you need to seek council more often. You're like a wild, cornered prang. You bounce here and bounce there in reaction to what's occurring without a thought to the long term consequences. It's by the sheer grace of the Gods that you're not dead," The Trench Lord rose to move around his desk, clearly not done with his lecture. He planted himself in front of Alador as he leaned back against his desk. "That girl did not deserve to have her heart ripped out and ground under your heel."

Alador started to speak, but Sordith put up his hand. "I'm not done yet." He leaned back on his desk arms crossed. Alador felt like a young middlin standing before the elders. He shut his mouth and remained quiet. "What you're facing, what you're trying to do, you cannot do on your own. You need people to help supplement your efforts. You need family, friends, and allies whether you can completely trust them or not." Sordith stood up and moved to his brother. He placed his hands on either side of Alador's arms. "You are truly a Guldalian." Sordith shook his head with a concerned frown. "When you see something, you rush at it without a care to the harm you will cause."

Alador stiffened and attempted to pull away, but Sordith gripped him tight. "I know you don't want to hear that.; -his tone lost its hard edge - "...but I can tell you that by watching from the outside, the apple hasn't fallen far from the family tree.

Sordith pinned him with his gaze. "What kind of man do you want to be? You could choose to stumble down the path you're on right now and end up cold, ruthless, and friendless," - he paused - "...a replica of your uncle, which, no offense, you show signs of becoming; or you could choose instead to become your own man, geas or no geas."

Alador dropped his eyes as Sordith let him go. "I don't know how," he admitted.

"Step one, seek counsel when your emotions run high. Step two: learn to ask for help." Sordith was holding up fingers as he counted it off. "Step three: accept your circumstances, because you just keep fighting what you've no power to change. It's a waste of your energy." Sordith dropped his hand. "You'd be better suited to put that energy into areas where you have control and influence."

Alador took a deep breath. Sordith's words were sound and he knew it. He deflated under his brother's wisdom. "You're right," Alador admitted under his breath.

"What did you say?" Sordith grinned at him.

"You heard me." Alador pushed the man back a little in frustrated humiliation. "I react too fast. I can't control my temper." Alador ran a hand across his face as he admitted his faults. "I play my hand too loosely. I have been like a small one doing anything to have a friend. I'm constantly focused on things that are beyond my control."

Sordith nodded. "Still feel it's time to leave?"

Alador contemplated the question. "Yes, I know how I'm going to proceed." Alador ran a hand through his loose - drab hair. Well, drab except for the strange white stripe he now bore.

"Then TELL me! Step one, remember?" Sordith moved back to lean against his desk. "Let's plan, rather than you rushing off into another disaster." Sordith grinned at him, not letting the point fade.

"You'd help me with this geas? Would you really help me thwart Luthian and stop the bloodmining?" Alador searched his face. Could he dare to hope that his new-found brother was truly interested in helping the dragons, despite his Lerdenian roots?

"I've no interest in bloodstones, as I'm not a mage. Also, helping you will not impact my profits unless I'm caught. I've no love for the High Minister, despite how well he runs the city. But...I have a more important reason."

"What is more important than any of that?" Alador asked curiously.

"My brother needs my help," Sordith said evenly with a slight smirk. "That is what family does."

Alador and Sordith had talked for a couple of hours about possible tactics and strategies to accomplish a successful assault on the bloodmines. In most areas, Sordith had agreed with with Alador's plan of action, but he had also offered up a few ideas that Alador would never have considered.

As he left the trench, Alador realized that for the first time since coming to this city that he did not feel frantic. He had confidence in the plan that he and Sordith had created. Sordith had divulged the fact that Luthian had ordered Henrick's death. They planned to use that to move everything forward.

Alador reconsidered his stance on Henrick. He was still angry with his father, but he could now see that at least some of Henrick's actions had been prompted by his own need to survive in the harsh reality that Luthian had created for so many.

The one thing that Alador had not managed to let go of was the manipulation of his mother in order to provide another recruit for Luthian's army. Connected to that was the fact that Henrick had not told Alador of the High Minister's breeding program.

Alador made his way through the city and up the tiers, but this time with a new perspective. He studied the side streets and the winding path to the upper tiers with the eye of a would-be attacker rather than a defender. Silverport was made for defense, but it had its flaws. It was tightly packed, so if a tier could be taken, higher tiers could flood with panicked citizens. This would hamper any higher tier efforts at defense.

In response to this, Alador had no doubt that Luthian would sacrifice however many citizens he thought he had to to hold the city. Any assault on Silverport would either need to be swift or accept a huge loss of those not able to fight, unless – and they had considered this - Sordith could safely offer many of the first through third tier citizens sanctuary in the vast spaces of the mines.

Neither he nor Sordith had any concern for the mages on the fourth and fifth tiers. They deserved any losses they sustained.

When at last he reached the council tier, he was not surprised to be waved straight through. He was dressed in the garb of a mage, as his uncle preferred, and he had been announcing his true identity as a Guldalian at every tier check.

By the time he had reached the High Minister's front door, there were four guards waiting for him. Alador smoothed his deep blue robes as they approached him. "Have I committed some crime that I am greeted at my Uncle's by armed men?" Alador's voice dripped sarcasm as he smiled coldly at them.

Alador knew he made a striking figure; he had dressed for that purpose. His deep blue robes were trimmed in silver. His black cloak held an embroidered blue image of Renamaum and was also trimmed in silver. The black boots were shined to the point he could see his own reflection. The knee length robe was split and his leather pants were also polished so they shined. He casually put both hands out to show he was not armed. Well, at least not by any material weapon.

"Your Uncle feared for your safety and sent us to escort you to him," one of the Blackguard stated curtly.

"Ah, may I point out that this would have been far more helpful in the lower tiers than on my Uncle's own steps?" Alador smirked. "I doubt I'm in danger here unless it is from my Uncle himself. Somehow…" he drawled out, "I don't see you protecting me from him." He grinned at the guardsman and strode into his uncle's manor.

The four guards fell into step as Alador made his way down the long hall towards the ornate door to his uncle's office. The hall was deathly silent, save for the echo of their steps. He eyed the intricate carvings and smiled before opening the door. He did not knock, as he knew he was expected.

Luthian did not rise from his seat as Alador entered the room. Two of the guards stepped in with him and shut the door. Alador noted their posting by the doors. Given the tension he could feel, he decided a subtler approach to his uncle might be appropriate. He crossed the large room and moved to the desk; he placed one hand on his heart as he bowed low.

"Good day, Uncle."

Luthian looked him over very slowly while laying down his quill. He was clearly assessing his nephew's current capabilities. Alador knew that, other than being thinner and a bit pale, he had recovered much of his strength. Luthian must have come to the similar conclusion as he sat back in his chair.

"How are you healing?" Luthian's question sounded genuinely caring, his voice sending a soft compulsion to answer that Alador did not miss.

"Physically, the wounds are healed. I've lost a bit of tone from my time in bed." Alador straightened up and clasped his hands behind him, letting them rest beneath his cloak. He stood before Luthian's desk as if he stood before the Blackguard's High Master.

"And mentally…? I understand that Aorun resorted to torture." The distaste in Luthian's measured tone was evident. The High Minister was watching Alador closely.

"He did. I fear that I may suffer yet awhile with bad dreams and feelings of apprehension." Alador nodded thoughtfully.

"You are stronger than I have given you credit for, and you obviously have a great deal of power at your disposal." Luthian leaned forward and the chair creaked in the tense silence that followed. He held Alador's gaze for a long moment. "Power you hid quite well, I must admit." Luthian's words were soft but their cold edge showed his displeasure.

"I did hide some of my capabilities from you," Alador admitted finally looking down at his boots as if in shame. "However, I don't think even I knew what I was capable of doing." Alador slowly looked up, his face schooled carefully in a mask of pain. "A man in desperation will sometimes overreach. I understand that the spells I cast to save my life could have killed me or just as easily left me mindless."

Alador had decided that the best tactic was to offer as much truth as he could. His uncle expected lies, so the truth might catch him off-guard. "In fact, it nearly did." He dropped his gaze again, as if this fact was weighing heavily.

Luthian nodded. "You left angrily the last time we spoke. I would ask where you stand today? After all, we did swear there would be… "truth" between us."

Luthian's reminder struck Alador as patronising and two-faced. He wanted to scoff that he very much doubted that Luthian ever told the whole truth to anyone; but instead, he appeared to consider the question very carefully.

"You're the High Minister, my elder, and my uncle," Alador stated curtly. "As a member of the Blackguard, I am pledged to carry out your commands." He raised his eyes to meet his uncle's. "Personally, I dislike you. You use people as if they are objects. However, I don't have to like my commander to serve him." He kept his hands tightly clasped behind him in an attempt to maintain his composure.

"Interesting… May I ask what has brought this change about?" Luthian was eyeing him with a penetrating gaze. He stood slowly and leaned forward against his desk. Alador felt a gentle pressure of magic, and he let Luthian in. He had nothing to hide but

Mesiande, and she was secure behind walls of magic. Luthian could not breach them unless he knew specifically what to look for, a defense his father had taught him during their half days.

"I find that I've nothing left to live for besides my service in the Blackguard. Aorun took Keelee and killed her father. He took what pride I had in my heritage and used it as a reason to torture me. It seems to me, moving forward, you are the only one who has ever had some measure of honesty."

Alador took a measured breath and continued to speak slowly. "I'm as much Lerdenian as I am Daezun." He drew himself up as if proud of his next words. "AND... I am a Guldalian. I cannot trust my father and wish no further association with him other than when absolutely necessary. It's time that I accepted my circumstances."

Alador took a deep breath and spoke through gritted teeth. "If you don't mind, please get out of my head. It's taking everything I have not to lash back at the intrusion." He had been careful to make sure every word was truth.

Luthian looked a bit taken aback. He released the spell of seeking he had subtly cast, sat back and eyed his nephew. "And if I asked you to cast the storm spell in Daezun lands…?" His words held scheming calculation.

Alador knew that this was what Luthian wanted most and chose his answer carefully. "If I felt it was for the greater good... of the people, in the long run," -Alador paused - "I would cast your spell." His soft answer held just an edge of conditions attached.

"Are you sure?" Luthian pressed. He stood up and moved around the desk to look down at Alador. Though

Luthian was now beside him, Alador did not shift his position.

"I'd only have one request," he replied. "I would make it as your nephew and not as a soldier under your command." Alador's eyes dropped in deference.

"Curious. What would that be?" Luthian sounded genuinely surprised.

"I would ask that you do not make me cast it in a way that would harm Smallbrook. Despite my casting out by the elder council, my siblings and my mother still reside there. They did not reject me, and I wish no harm to them."

Alador knew he was daring to show weakness, but he calculated that Luthian would latch on to it as a way to manipulate and manage his nephew. He knew that Luthian looked for an edge and rather than let him find a real one, he hoped this would suffice, leaving him some room to maneuver.

"And if I agree to this - that I will never ask you to harm the family you were raised with - then what?" Luthian's tone held the triumphant edge of one close to a personal victory.

Alador turned and bowed low as he spoke, both arms out wide, palms towards Luthian. "Then I am ever your servant to command."

Chapter Twelve

Luthian took in Alador's newly subservient attitude, his eyes following him as he straightened up out of his bow. This submissiveness from his nephew was welcome and seemed sincere. He did know that such traumatic situations combined with the heavy use of magic could change a man, even twist the soul and character. However, he also knew that Alador had swiftly learned to play the game.

"You will work with me as I desire? You will do as you are requested? All I have to do is save this Smallbrook and its people from direct harm of life or limb?" Luthian was pressing the issue. It was a small price, one village for all that he needed to unite the island under one rule. If necessary, there were other ways to apply pressure to those in Smallbrook without resorting to direct harm.

"All that you request of me, I shall honor in exchange for this one small boon," Alador agreed. He eyed his uncle with hopeful expectation and let it show in his eyes and face.

Luthian stroked his chin, apparently considering but more to have time to observe the boy and assess his sincerity. He had to admit, he liked this change in the mageling; but at the same time, the High Minister had not risen to the top of the tiers by accepting people's words at face value. "I agree to your terms, but know this: if you are playing me false, I can assure you that my vengeance will start with Smallbrook."

"I would expect no less," Alador admitted. "I know firsthand the anger one can feel when those you trust break faith." Alador's response was filled with heartfelt pain and seemed genuine to his uncle.

Luthian considered this carefully. "What of Keelee?"

"The greatest betrayal of all.... I found her with Aorun, no doubt sharing my every move," Alador snarled.

'*So the girl had been playing both ends; interesting*,' he thought. Luthian had known she was quick and intelligent, but he had not expected her to align with Aorun.

"I see." Luthian nodded. "Are you well enough to return to the service of the Blackguard?" He knew that Alador still had things to learn if he was truly going to realise his maximum potential by Luthian's side as his personal weapon of mass destruction.

"Before I return to the duties of the Blackguard, I ask permission to travel into an unoccupied area with Henrick to practise this spell where I can do no harm." Alador gravely met Luthian's gaze. "It would be most unfortunate if I lost control of such a storm here in Silverport."

"Yes... Quite..." Luthian considered this carefully. "You would travel with Henrick despite your distaste for him?" He gave a small snort of disgust at the thought of Henrick. He did not trust his brother, and he was definitely wary of this sudden change in his nephew.

"He lies," Alador snapped. "At least you don't hide your intentions or desires from me. However, he's good at teaching me my limits, and how to overcome them. I need to learn how to create a storm to the point that it doesn't suddenly take a life of its own. He can do that, despite being a fire mage." Alador's voice was cold and there was a trace of derision when he stated the word 'fire'.

As he watched his nephew, there was one thing that was certain: the disdain for Henrick was not feigned. However, the rest seemed somewhat rehearsed to Luthian. He was pleased to have successfully driven a wedge between the father and son. It would make the death of his brother easier for the boy to take. He also hoped to have this boy at his right hand one day in his quest to unify the island.

"I will write the order now. You can deliver it to the High Master, and then make your arrangements to travel. I want you back in full service in a fortnight. Understood?" Luthian would not move until he had that clear understanding with his nephew. He watched the boy closely.

"Understood," Alador said and nodded. "A fortnight should be plenty of time to figure out what I can do and where additional study is needed." Alador's slight smile softened the hardness in his face. Luthian realized that this hardness was also new. Perhaps Aorun's assault had turned things in his favor. He smiled grimly: he might even have thanked the Trench Lord, had he not gone and gotten himself killed in the process.

Luthian moved back around his desk and slipped into his chair. He pulled the fine parchment from his drawer and swiftly wrote out the order. He could feel Alador's steady gaze. He rolled the order and lit the candle to seal it, absently watching the red wax dripping like blood onto the page. He pressed his ring into the wax and looked up. Alador had not spoken the entire time, and still stood as he had since entering, hands clasped behind his back.

He paused when he looked up at Alador. Perhaps now was the time to ease the tension between them, he thought. "I know, Alador, that our last meeting was a rude awakening, and that I delivered it unkindly. I do, however, hope that we can mend that meeting and return once more to the close association we had before I discovered you were playing me for a fool regarding your strengths." His voice was silky smooth as he held the scroll out for the boy to take.

Alador moved forward and took the scroll slowly from Luthian's hand. His eyes met Luthian's with regret. "I should not have done that, Uncle. I trusted Henrick. He's my father, and has guided me throughout my life, and more closely since my powers manifested." Alador tucked the scroll into his belt. "I played you false at his advisement. I assure you, it won't happen again. I hope that you can find it within you to forgive my naive trust." Alador looked up at Luthian hopefully.

"You are young… and he IS your father." Luthian sighed and waved in dismissal. "We all must learn the lesson at some point that most people can only be trusted if their goals are the same as yours. The moment those goals are at cross-purposes, they will betray you." Luthian's tone was matter-of-fact. "Live for the moment, Alador. Find pleasure in soft flesh, a good drink, and - most importantly - the feeling of the power flowing through you." He smiled at the mage, knowing that many of the perfect world ideals that Alador had come to Silverport with were just illusions that could never come to pass.

"Surely, Uncle, you want more than this from life. What goal motivates you to do more than sit in luxury feasting yourself into slothfulness?" Alador eyed his uncle intently. "You are always on task; I know there is more to your goals than a pretty woman in your bed."

Luthian examined Alador but could not hear any intended insult in the question. "I suppose that a larger task does prevent indolence." Luthian smiled and rubbed his hands together in anticipation. "Come, I will show you." He rose from the desk and led the way across to a small door in the office that he had never opened for his nephew. He was taking a risk, given his wariness of this change in Alador, but the boy was a major factor in achieving many of his goals.

Luthian unlocked the door and eyed the torches that immediately flamed up in response. The room was a simple one. It held a large square table on which a topographical map had been built. He had paid a great deal of medure for an especially adept artist to render the entire island for him in raised detail. The man had been given unlimited access to his stable of lexital to make an aerial view of the lands. Luthian had been quite pleased with the results.

Alador moved to the table as Luthian moved around it. He reached out and touched a rising mountain top with amazement. "This is our lands from the air?"

Luthian smiled with pleasure. It was good to see someone admire his efforts. "It is. Paid handsomely for it, I can assure you. Took the man a full two turns to add every detail." He ran a finger lovingly along the edge in front of him.

Alador examined the map with a scrutiny that Luthian admired. He could see the intelligence behind the youth's eyes as he took in the connections between Lerdenia and the Daezun lands. "Now, so I make no error, where is this Smallbrook of yours?" He asked casually; he already knew where it was but did not want Alador to be alarmed that he was so familiar with his home of origin.

Alador surveyed the map running his fingers across the uneven surfaces and tracing known landmarks.

Finally, he pointed to a dot along a small river about midway down the east side of the map. Luthian then traced the river into the mountains to be certain what peaks fed it. He moved slightly north. He ran his finger in circle around the east side of the mountains, and everything north of where his other finger had stopped.

"When you are ready, I wish you to place everything in this area I have circled into a deep winter. I want the snow piled high." Luthian looked up at Alador. "This is your first task to prove your loyalty, and to begin what I have planned."

Alador eyed the map carefully. "Uncle, the Daezun people are well stocked for such a winter." He looked up. "They will just hunker down until the spring thaws."

"Yes, I have accounted for this." Luthian licked his lips in anticipation. "However, even more snow will fill the mountains and you will then bring an early warm spring thaw." He waited to see Alador put the piece together.

"Flooding many of the riverside villages and towns..." Alador frowned. "I fail to see how this will help you achieve your ends."

"But what will come from that? Finish this tale for me nephew," Luthian coaxed.

"Well, some will move south, the other villages will be forced to absorb them. Others will rebuild and with an early thaw, begin planting." He frowned. "Even if you repeat the cycle, they will survive the next winter."

"Unless…" Luthian coaxed softly.

"Unless…" Alador tapped his lips, clearly attempting to follow the plan. "Unless the summer has little rain and the crops fail. They won't be prepared for a repeat of such a winter. They will starve or move south… which will increase the pressure on the villages that take them in.

That would deplete resources in the lower villages." Alador looked up at his uncle to see if he had discerned the plan correctly.

Luthian smiled his approval of Alador's quick mind. "When we are ready, we will flood the south with unending rain." Luthian's tone held an edge of malice as he rubbed his hands together. Their crops will mildew and fail: pushing all the Daezun into a small area and forcing them to reach out to Lerdenia for help.

Alador ran a finger around the area where Smallbrook lay, moving to the opposite side of the table from Luthian. "And this allows you to keep your promise that Smallbrook will not be touched. However, Uncle, they will be impacted." He looked up at the author of this grand scheme to subjugate the land of his birth.

"If you have fears for your family, you are welcome to make a home for them in Lerdenian lands. I am sure the trader who brought that drained stone to me paid you handsomely for it. You undoubtedly have the slips to set them up along the border lands."

Alador nodded. "I do. I will consider that advice." He looked up at his Uncle in admiration. "It is a fine plan with minimal loss of life. I must say, I am impressed."

Luthian smiled at the praise, he enjoyed the admiration in the younger mage's eyes. "Yet impossible without a strong mage who can control storms and weather. My previous attempts could not bring enough weather to bear to make a true impact." Luthian slammed his hand down at the edge of the map, making Alador jump. "But you, you hold almost the entire power of a full-grown blue dragon. You can do this, and it makes me even more proud that it will be a Guldalian hand that wields the power." His tone implied they had already won this battle.

There was a pause as Alador considered the map. "Even if that power is held by a half-Daezun?" Alador questioned quietly. When the boy looked up at him, Luthian could see the uncertainty of a lost youth in his eyes. '*What better emotion to play upon*?' Luthian mused.

"We were all one blood once, long ago, Alador. You are turning into a fine man, a well-skilled politician and a strong mage. I could not be prouder." He heaped on the praise smoothly.

He was satisfied with a flush of color from his nephew's cheeks as the boy dropped his gaze. Yes, Luthian thought, Aorun had indeed done him a favor.

"Now that you know what motivates me, let us see about inspiring you. If you can achieve this for me, what gift do you wish in return?" Luthian asked, curious what would move the boy and how he could use it to keep Alador in line.

"Lift the ban on half-Daezun attempting a higher tier. If you wish to unite the island under one rule, then you have to start finding ways to integrate them. Otherwise, the Daezun will see you as the conqueror and not the benefactor you seek to unite them under." Alador's answer was swift, and Luthian could tell the mageling had thought on this before.

"Points well spoken, but I see a more personal motive here…," Luthian pointed out as he assessed Alador carefully. The boy was quick to move when he wanted something. Now Luthian knew two things he could use to control the boy: a rise to power and family, both of which were easily manipulated.

"Of course, I am not that far removed from the 'pure-blooded' trunk of the family tree. I desire power as much as any mage, and would hope to sit upon your council one day… in an executive position." Alador smiled with a hint of pride, but Luthian saw greed and vanity as well. "I will be able to advise you on the matter of managing an island half-full of Daezun." He circled the table, tapping the half of the map where the Daezun resided.

"You bring the hard winter I seek to the north east and I will lift the ban," Luthian offered. It was unlikely that any half-blood other than his nephew could rise far anyway. He had found that few of the half-Daezun had enough skill to master any fourth tier levels of power. Luthian felt no harm in offering the boon. If the boy betrayed him, he would use him as an example to others who set their ambitions too high.

"Agreed." Alador circled the north east with this finger as he eyed the markers that would keep Smallbrook safe. Luthian was not lost on what the boy was calculating. He was clearly making sure that nothing he did would have an impact on this little village he sought to protect.

Luthian smiled. He would send a spy into Smallbrook and gather up the names of everyone that might be of use to him. "Best head back to the Blackguard. You have travel plans to see to, and only a fortnight's leave to learn what you must." He snapped his fingers in front of the boy's face as he seemed lost in thought. "The first spell will need to be cast by the turn change." Luthian eyed him. "That gives you an additional month to be ready to bring in a winter such as this isle has never seen."

Alador had startled, then nodded at Luthian's final words. He took one last look at the map, gave a respectful bow, and turned to leave the small room. For the first time, Luthian got a full-view of the back of the lad's cloak. The blue dragon formed in silver thread on his back was magnificent, but what caught his gaze was the eye. It held a hatred so embedded that Luthian shivered at its gaze. He had never seen such fine work on a cloak. He followed his nephew to the doorway and called after him.

"Alador. One… one moment." Luthian practically stammered out his words.

"Yes, Uncle…?" Alador turned to look at him.

"Who is the tailor that made your cloak?" Luthian was intent on hiring a man who could bring such feeling into embroidery

"I was. I used magic to form it." Alador pulled the edges of the cloak forward to admire the silver thread work.

"The dragon on the back...: how did you visualize such detail? Have you seen such a dragon?" Luthian pressed, surprised that his nephew had created such a work of art for his own simple use.

"I guess in a book or something." Alador shrugged. "I don't know. I just saw him and pressed the image onto the cloak. I don't remember where I saw it." Alador let go of his cloak and returned his gaze evenly to Luthian. "Anything else, High Minister…?"

"No... no, that is all." He watched Alador as his nephew bowed low again and turned on his heel to depart. His eyes followed the boy out of the room until the guard shut the door. For the first time since Alador had entered the room earlier, Luthian was certain he was lying. That dragon was consumed by hatred for whomever or whatever was trapped in its gaze.

The small room felt suddenly cold and damp and Luthian shivered. He turned and locked the door once more. One thing he was certain of: he never wanted a dragon to look at him with such a vengeful gaze.

Chapter Thirteen

Alador left the Council tier feeling satisfied with what he had just learned and accomplished. He had bought himself enough time to go to the dragon and plead his case. He had enough information to warn Dorien so that the Daezun could prepare. He would have to thank Sordith: using his disdain for his father's choices had indeed warmed Luthian. Alador knew the High Minister did not trust his brother and had been able to use that for his advantage. It had been a risk letting his uncle into his head so easily, but he had been careful to utter no lies.

He moved with a bright step as he headed for Henrick's home. He would need to make sure his father would be ready for the journey to Keensight's cave tomorrow. Today would be a day for preparation and tying off other loose ends.

He entered the grand house and made his way to his father's library. He was not even sure where his father's private rooms were, as every time he had visited his father had been in the library. Today was no different; Henrick was reading before the fire. He looked up as Alador entered.

"How did it go?" Henrick asked offhandedly and looked back to his book. "No, I did not read your mind. Sordith visited a short while ago," Henrick stated.

"Well enough. I now know Luthian's plan and why he needs me. I will have to concede to his wishes until everything is in place. If we are careful, I think I can protect my people and still appear to be furthering Luthian's ambitions, at least for a short time." Alador sat down in a chair opposite his father, watching him closely. He realized that Sordith's words at the bottom of the stairs had changed some of his views on his father. He frowned at the swirling, confused emotions that welled up at that thought.

"What is the overall plan?" Henrick set the rich, leathered tome beside his chair.

"He plans to starve them out and force them to seek aid from the Lerdenian people. That aid will come at a high price." Alador loosened the clasp of his cloak to let it fall behind him. "I will admit, if I had a wish to unify a land, it is a plan with the fewest losses. It is rather brilliant," Alador admitted. "I would probably be excited if it was not a plan against my own people and family."

"You don't seem concerned?" Henrick tipped his head to look at Alador.

"I'm not. He doesn't know the Daezun, and he is not taking into account my own skills at the game he plays." Alador shrugged with more than a trace of youthful arrogance. "As far as lying and deception are concerned, I've had good teachers in him and you." He sat back, still watching his father closely.

Henrick sighed. "I have never deceived you. How many times must I tell you this?"

"I guess till you believe it, because I never will," Alador answered seriously. "However, let us take those lies off the table for the moment. You have taught me well when it comes to my uncle, and you cannot tell me you don't play the game with him, for he doesn't seem to know your true intent."

Henrick slowly nodded. "This is true, I do lie and deceive your uncle." Henrick smiled slowly at the thought. "I fear it has become something of a delight when I can get one past him." Henrick grinned with mischievousness.

Alador smiled slightly. "The problem is knowing how much of what you portray is really accepted by him. For now, I am going to assume I failed, and move accordingly."

"Probably a wise choice," the older mage mused. "So, what is the next step? Sordith told me that you and he have created a basic plan, but would give me none of the details."

Alador nodded growing a bit more serious. "We go to see Keensight tomorrow. I hope you're ready, because I've only a fortnight to be away to learn what I must." He paused and took a deep breath. "In addition, I have to figure out how to bring a snowstorm and hold it." He looked more directly at Henrick. "I told Luthian that you would help me learn to control it. I hope you can do that."

"Oh, is THAT all?" Henrick said with a bemused smirk. "I think Keensight a better choice for that, if you can win him over, but I'll do what I can." He eyed Alador with rather more seriousness. "I cannot convince you how unlikely it is that you'll win this dragon over? Dragons have long memories. He is not going to forgive you that sore throat easily." Henrick sipped his wine and swirled the glass, staring into it.

"He's not so innocent himself." Alador got up and poured himself a glass of wine before continuing. "I plan to remind him that HE planned to make me a pile of cinders when I shot him. I can only hope he sees reason, for I truly shot in self-defense of myself and the small ones hiding in the brush nearby."

Henrick shook his head. "Dragons don't think this way, Alador. You may end up as a pile of ash before you even finish explaining."

"It's a risk I must take," Alador stated firmly. "Your job is just to get me there. If I end up a pile of ash, then I beg you to go to Dorien with everything you know. Luthian will eventually figure out a way to bring a war, or the storms he desires." Alador paused and added softly: "…with or without me."

He returned to his chair and looked directly into Henrick's eyes. His worry was clearly written on his face with the intensity of his gaze and his furrowed brow. "You owe me that much. Promise me, if I fail to win Keensight over, you will go to Smallbrook and warn Dorien."

Henrick held Alador's gaze for a long moment, then looked over into the crackling fire. It was the only sound in the room for a long moment before he gave his answer. "I swear it."

Alador drained his glass, setting it aside as he rose from the chair. "Well then, I must be off." He rose with his cloak and swung it around his body again.

Henrick gasped as the dragon swirled passed him. "You wore that in Luthian's presence?" He stood and moved around Alador to get a better look at the dragon on the back.

"I did." Alador grinned as he turned to face Henrick.

"Why would you do that?" Henrick looked truly puzzled. "The intensity of it betrays the fact that you have seen this dragon. We don't want him guessing it was a geas stone."

"Because, whether Luthian realized it or not, I have declared war on the Lerdenian Empire," Alador coldly stated. "I have declared it on behalf of the Daezun, of Renamaum, and of the dragons." His passion grew as he continued. "This image will be my banner and I will plant it on the council tier one day when I declare peace between all three races." Alador spoke with such certainty that Henrick could only nod in wonder.

"We will leave tomorrow. I hope that is enough time for you to prepare." Alador turned and strode from his father's study. He did not wait for an answer.

Alador made his way to his room. His visit with the High Master of the Blackguard had gone well. The man seemed relieved to hear of Aorun's death and was sympathetic to Alador's situation. He did not question the High Minister's decree that Alador be given an additional fortnight away from the guard. Alador deliberately did not mention to him that the fortnight was to learn spells or visit dragons. Instead, he gave the leader a rather plaintive tale of how the High Minister was allowing him to go home and seek to reconcile with his family on Daezun ground.

Alador reached his room and let go of the tension with a sigh. The day had been a tense one so far and now he could finally have a moment alone to process everything. He opened the door to his room and stopped in the doorway. Several of the light stones had been covered, creating a soft soothing tone in the room. Keelee was there on his bed and dressed in a revealing gown. Her long black hair was not braided and fell around her in a silken curtain. She looked up at him with those large, shimmering eyes that would have once drowned him in desire. She flashed him a hopeful look.

Alador stepped in and slamming the door shut. "What are you doing here?" Alador snarled in a low, hissed voice.

"Well, you sent Mesiande home…" she began, wringing her hands in her lap. She did not move from his bed though her eyes fell to her toes. "I know you are angry…"

He roughly pulled her off his bed bringing a shriek of surprise and fear from her lips as he glared into her gaze. "Damn right I am angry. You lied to me. You knew I was waiting for that case and you hid it. You're a lying bitch and... What the hell are you doing here?"

"I… I am your bed... servant," she stuttered out. Her eyes swelled with unshed tears.

The thought of her in his bed sickened him. "No longer. I release you. I don't want a wench I cannot trust anywhere near me." He did not let her arm go as he glared down at her.

"I... have nowhere else…" A single tear slipped down her cheek as she began to speak.

He cut her off. "Not true. I happen to know that Sordith fancies you. Why, I cannot fathom," his voice was cold and mocking. He tapped her chest as he continued. "Your heart is as black as your hair, because if you had cared a single bit for me, then you would not have continued to hide it." He grabbed her chin to stare into her eyes. "Why DID you hide the case?" he demanded.

"I... was afraid that you would cast me out for whoever was sending it." Her voice took on true panic. "Luthian had commanded me to bring him news of anything unusual so… I took it." She hastily added, "But I never gave the tube to him." Her voice held a bit of hope that this would make a difference. Her hands moved to his chest, her eyes pleading with him to understand.

Alador was not moved by either her posture or her tear-filled eyes. "Why not? You had it. He'd have paid you well for it." Alador's gruff tone did not ease though he did let go of her chin.

"I don't know. I just felt something really bad would happen if I did. I've learned to trust my dreams and feelings like that." Her own words were desperate whispers, her eyes begging him to understand. She put a hand to his face.

He brushed her hand from his face roughly. "The fact you didn't give him the case is the only reason I won't kill you. However, Keelee, I'll never trust you. Return to Sordith; I gift you to him." He pushed her back from him and the closeness of the bed hit the back of her knees forcing her to collapse down onto it. Alador added. "He'll see to your keep and well-being."

"You are sending me to the trenches?" she clutched the bed cover on either side of her, her knuckles white.

"No, Keelee," he sighed out in exasperation. "I am sending you to the Trench Lord, who actually gives a damn what happens to you. I suggest you don't betray him as you did me." He picked up her cloak from the end of the bed and tossed it to her. "Get out!"

Keelee caught the cloak and stared at him. Her face was white and her eyes wide as the tears slipped free and flowed down her cheeks. "Please…" she begged softly.

"Don't make me throw you out of the caverns, Keelee," he snarled. "Go to Sordith."

Keelee turned and fled from the room. She did not close the door and her echoing soft sobs did nothing to appease the anger that Alador felt at finding her in his room. He sat on his bed and flopped backwards, his hands over his face not only to hide from his own pain and frustration, but also to shield the soft scent she had left in her wake.

He had not needed that interruption in his thoughts, as he was playing a dangerous game; one that not only risked his own life, but everyone he cared about. He groaned at the thought of Keelee and her ability to distract him. His plans required focus, and the last thing he needed was distraction.

He felt no sympathy for her. She had chosen her path: he might have kept her close if she had not betrayed him. He lay there for some time, just trying to regain a sense of peace and balance.

When he finally calmed the anger that had overtaken him, he changed into the armor of the Blackguard. Alador was thankful that Sordith had sent it around so quickly. He felt safer with his armor donned and his sword again on his belt. He set out to find Jon.

It took him a bit of time to find him as some of the rotations in class had been changed since he had last been here. A member of Jon's sphere directed him to Jon's room. He found the door and knocked lightly, realizing he had never been inside before this.

"Come," the bland voice called, reassuring even from the other side of the door.

Alador opened the door to see Jon's feet on his bed. The way the bed was situated behind the door, he did not see all of the death mage until he had fully entered the room. Jon looked up at him with that face that held no emotion. Alador realized he had rather missed Jon and his cold quips.

"About time you crawled out of under the Trench Lord's skirt." Jon sounded irritated. He did not look up from his book, a sure sign of Jon's displeasure.

"Hey, I nearly died," Alador pointed out, a little hurt by the cool reception. "Give a man a chance to heal." Alador glanced around the room. The walls were covered in chalk drawings of a woman dressed in armor. She reminded him of a dragon in many ways: actually being depicted with a dragon in some of the drawings, and in others with a strange, green, flowing spray from her hands. Some of the drawings were explicitly sensual.

"I gave you a chance to heal, but that damn rogue of a nursemaid had you so closely sealed in that I couldn't even get news if you were mending or not," Jon said, affecting indifference and still not looking up.

"Yeah... Sorry about that." Jon had not moved from his position on the bed. He was sitting up with feet crossed before him. Alador indicated the end of the bed. "May I?"

"Suit yourself." Jon continued reading as if intent on ignoring Alador.

Alador sat at the end of the bed, facing the drawings. "Careful Jon, I might think you missed me so much you are fighting back tears of joy at having me to yourself again," Alador teased. "Perhaps I should offer you a hug." He smirked at Jon, hoping playful words might soothe the mage's displeasure.

"The moment you do, I will fill your mouth with the vilest concoction I can imagine," Jon murmured with his curiously menacing monotone, still not looking up.

"Who is this on the wall?" Alador asked, hoping to draw Jon out with a change of subject.

"The dark goddess, Dethera," he answered, finally looking at the wall. "She won't stay out of my dreams. Lately, they have been incessant." Jon sighed and frowned. "They have been so intense that I have been talking to a couple of men who have returned from guarding in the North." Jon looked at Alador, the intensity emanating from him suddenly concerning. "Did you know that there are no black dragons in the bloodmines?"

Alador looked back at Jon in surprise. "No, I didn't know that." He moved to sit cross-legged on the end of Jon's bed. He was truly puzzled as to why that would be. "Maybe their eggs are harder to reach," Alador offered as a possible solution.

"I don't think so." Jon closed the book and set it aside. "It would be to her advantage if other dragons fell by mortal hand. Dethara seeks the souls of mortals and dragons alike. The more war there is, the more power she holds from the souls of the fallen." Jon looked at the drawings on the wall. "What if she is telling the Lerdenians where to find the other nests?"

Alador blinked in genuine surprise. "The gods created the dragons, why would one sacrifice almost all of them?"

"Power," Jon stated with a menacing coldness. "Maybe she is not content in just being 'one' of the gods," Jon suggested.

"Isn't this the goddess you serve?" Alador was growing worried.

"Yes and no." Jon admitted. "An odd predicament. I do not condone the sacrifice of other flights of dragons, and yet the one from whom I draw power appears to be doing just that. I did not choose the black sphere; it is where my powers manifested," Jon blandly pointed out. Jon looked at him for a long moment. "I have asked to be assigned."

Alador was deeply disappointed. He had hoped to involve Jon in his plans. Now he was learning that Jon, bound in duty to his goddess, might very well be forced instead to oppose him. "Why?" he asked.

"I am going to see for myself," Jon answered. "I am going to the bloodmines. It was easy to get the assignment as very few volunteer."

Alador tensed as he felt Renamaum shift in him angrily. "How can you go guard that atrocity?" he growled.

"I have a decision to make, my friend. It will not be an easy one." Jon caught his eye with deep seriousness. "I will either follow the path of my Daezun blood and look for weaknesses in the mine to help bring it down, or I will follow my Lerdenian blood and goddess to protect her will," Jon made this announcement so simply that the horrific impact of it took a moment to sink in. Jon took a deep breath. "I can do that best by seeing first hand what occurs within those hidden walls."

Alador knew that few were aware of the way to the mines. Having a man inside would be a benefit. In this case, depending on Jon's decision, it could also be devastating. "If you decide the bloodmine abomination is Dethara's will and that you will follow her, when next we meet..." - Alador swallowed hard - "it will be as enemies." He felt true sadness at having to admit this.

"Indeed, that's true. I make you this solemn vow: whatever my decision, I will never kill you," Jon stated with cold bluntness.

Alador chuckled nervously. "Why is that not reassuring?"

"Because you know there is a lot I can do that won't kill you, I suspect," Jon casually stated. He shrugged. "I know you hate the mines, and I know from our talks that you wish it to end. I hope that if we meet on the field of battle, it will not be on opposite sides." Jon paused looking back to the drawings on the wall. "But this decision is one of faith and moral code. It is not one that I can make based on a brief friendship. It will define the man I will become."

Alador felt a sense of sadness. He knew Jon well enough to know that he was not going to be able to convince him to take another path. "Then I ask that whatever you decide in the future, you guide me to a few guards I can place a basic trust in before you leave." He looked up at Jon hopefully. "Apparently my judgment of what is trustworthy is tainted."

"I do know a few mages that hate Luthian and all he upholds. I suspect they will be willing to help in any matter that opposes the High Minister. I will give each one a paper with Dethera's mark and tell them to seek you out." Jon's offer was solemn and sincere. He swung his feet off the bed and sat to face the wall.

"When do you leave?" Alador asked.

"In two days." Jon seemed completely unaffected.

"I will be sad to see you go," Alador admitted.

"You will just be sad not to have anyone to save your ass when they come calling with swords and daggers." Jon's attempt to tease and his brief smile were hardly humorous.

"That's true," Alador admitted with a frown. "But you've truly been a friend, and I don't have many of those."

"Must be that winning personality you have," Jon grinned again ever so slightly. His voice was dripping with sarcasm.

"Yes, it must be that." Alador chuckled. "I leave tomorrow to take care of another matter that, unfortunately, I cannot share till you decide your path."

"So tonight is our farewell," Jon pointed out.

"Yes, yes it is." Alador smiled at Jon. "Let's go grab dinner and a farewell drink."

Jon swung off the bed. "That is the best thing you have said since you got here."

The two men left Jon's room. The evening was spent on lighter topics, good stiff drinking, and a couple of willing bed mates.

Chapter Fourteen

Lexital were strange creatures that could carry a single rider because of a natural dip in their strong necks. These unique birds had a curved beak with what looked like the sail of a boat rising above both beak and eyes. Their necks were long and serpentine, moving side to side as they steered through the sky. Their eyes were red and trimmed in aquamarine, and their wings varying shades of blue with a ridge of red that seemed to arch out mid-feathers. This was especially noticeable in flight.

Alador's lexital landed gracefully beside his father's own bird. The flight had been exhilarating and terrifying all at the same time. He had only had a few minutes of instruction. Fortunately, his lack of skill was redressed by the lexital's inclination to follow her mate rather than test his skills. It also did not help that he was still suffering the lasting effects of his farewell to Jon. They had stayed up far too late and drunk far too much mead.

Alador unbuckled the saddle harness and slipped shakily to the ground, eyeing the great bird with amazement. He held the reins in his gloved hand, petting the lexital with the other to show his appreciation for its compliance.

"A bit unnerving the first time, as I said." Henrick spoke with amusement . He came around wide to make sure the bird could see him

"Yes, a bit. However, I see why you like flying. The view was indescribable." Alador was still caressing the lexital's head, while the bird was happily letting him loosen the shafts on her crest's pin feathers.

Henrick smiled. "I do love the feel of the wind on my face. However, do note that the higher you fly, the colder that wind becomes." Henrick held his hand out for the reins. "Here, let me tether them. They won't fly any closer to Keensight's cave. I have tried, and they have panicked every time."

Alador handed them to him and stepped back from the bird. He did not even want to imagine what a panicked lexital was like. "So, we walk from here?" He looked about. They were in Daezun lands, judging by the terrain. It was the familiar rock and scrub brush that he knew so well. To the east of him, hills rose up, covered randomly in rocks as if the gods had tossed them down. Some of the boulders appeared larger than a dragon.

Henrick was tying the two birds to a larger bush with a solid base. "YOU walk from here," he stated in an amused voice, glancing over at Alador.

"You're not coming?" Alador looked at him in surprise. "You said you'd take me to him."

"I have brought you to him." Henrick gestured up at the hill rising up beside them. "However, he said if I joined you at the cave, he would finally eat me, and this time I don't think he was playing." Henrick looked at Alador with obvious concern. "You don't have to do this. We are only an hour's flight south of Smallbrook. We could fly up there and I could sneak Mesiande to you. You could make things right with the girl," Henrick offered. "I am not sure you are well enough for this, son."

"I told you not to call me that." Alador glared at him, his response snarled in an almost feral manner.

"I am not going to stop just because you have some fool idea that I lied to you. I will say it one more time. I have never lied to you." Henrick sighed in defeat. "Maybe the dragon can knock some sense into that thick skull of yours."

"I know you used a spell on my mother." Alador's accusation seemed to be solely centered on this one statement.

"I have never said I didn't," Henrick stated. "It doesn't mean I don't care for her or enjoy her company. It doesn't mean I don't give a damn what happens to the child born from the pleasures of that night." He glared back at Alador.

Alador shuddered at the thought, not wanting to imagine his mother in that way. "It was a use of dark magic, a magic may I remind you that you said was a violation of all the rules of magic." Alador glared at him, the accusation still strong in his voice.

Henrick threw up his hands and sighed out in defeat. "I don't want to fight with you when I may never see you again. Please. What is done is done. You exist because of that night. You should be grateful."

"Grateful that I am the result of a dark magic used in violation of a sacred trust from the dragons themselves?" Alador continued to belabor this point. "That might make the damn dragon eat me in itself." He looked up at the hill. "Which way do I go?" he demanded.

"Alador, a glamour spell doesn't subjugate the will of another." Henrick grumpily stated. "It merely makes the one casting it a little more appealing. Your mother was free to choose as she wished. I did NOT compel her." Henrick's tone implored Alador to understand. "Besides, I have changed a great deal since the day you were conceived. May I point out that it was nearly thirty turns ago?"

"As you said, what is done is done." Alador said with a terse finality. "Now, which way do I go?" Alador repeated the question, not looking at Henrick.

Henrick watched his son for a long moment before turning in defeat to get a pack off his own lexital. "There is a path just across the stream near that large tree next to the cliff face." Henrick pointed it out before continuing. "It will take you up the hills and on into a hidden valley. Within that valley there is a lake. Find the stream that feeds it and follow it to its head. You will see a beautiful waterfall and if you look up then you will see the cave." Henrick brought him the pack. "It is a half day's hike to the valley, and maybe another two hours to the cave."

Alador had been listening intently to Henrick's instructions. He eyed the indicated tree that Henrick had pointed out as he absently took the pack. "Will you be here when I am done?"

Henrick nodded. "I will wait here for three days. If you are not back by then, I will come looking, and if I don't find you, well, then, I will assume that Keensight has eaten you." Henrick smirked slightly. "I would prefer not having to make that apology to Luthian. Sorry, I let a dragon eat him. I am not quite sure how I would explain that..."

Henrick sighed: it was clear that his stubborn son had stopped listening and his attempt at humor had failed. Alador had nodded tersely and strode off, heading for the tree. He was determined to speak to Keensight, now more than ever. The mage needed the help of a dragon, and Keensight was the only one that either he or Henrick knew how to find. He only hoped the dragon had not decided to take off for a couple of weeks rather than speak with him. As he moved to part the brush heading out of the small clearing they had landed in, he heard his father call after him.

"May the gods be with you; and for once, watch that tongue of yours!" Henrick's tone held true care and concern.

Alador just smiled coldly as he moved on, not looking back. He was done watching his tongue. If those that crossed his path did not want to hear what he had to say, they had best not ask. He made his way across the stream, keeping an eye on the tree that Henrick had indicated. Everything he had planned, everything he needed. now depended on winning Keensight over to his cause. He found the path and began the climb. When he was high enough, he looked back to reassure himself that Henrick had kept his word.

Sure enough, he could see Henrick moving about the clearing setting up a tent. A part of him still wanted to trust his father, but he could not get Luthian's words out of his head. His father had known what he was about when he entered his mother's circle. Alador could not find it within himself to let go of that painful fact and move on. He had managed, after Sordith's scolding, to let go of some of the other wrongs that he had held Henrick accountable for. This one continued to haunt him.

He rolled his shoulders and shifted the pack to a more comfortable position before continuing to follow the trail. It was faint in places, and in others there were rock slides that had obliterated it altogether, making the climb more difficult. More than once, he was forced to backtrack to find the path again. In addition, the higher he climbed, the more biting the wind became, no longer constrained by the small vale below. He pulled his cloak about him, securing it more tightly to keep the wind out. The cold did not bother him as much as the cutting edge on the wind.

While he made his way up the path, his mind raced through the hundreds of ways he could approach this dragon. Apart from Henrick, he had never heard of anyone who had spoken to a dragon. Even in the old tales, there were no actual instances of Daezun and dragons communicating after the Great War. He knew that they had communicated all the time before the great betrayal of the pact.

Alador was so lost in his thoughts that he failed to notice his cresting of the hill. Below him the winding path made its way to a valley floor with a beautiful emerald lake. There were prang and korpen milling about and seemingly quite at ease. He was surprised that a valley this close to a dragon's cave had so much wildlife. The climb down to the lake took a lot less time, and soon he was following its shoreline. It took about an hour to find the stream that fed it.

He realized, as he made his way up the stream, that it was beautiful here; peaceful, in fact. The wind was still. and for a moment Alador wished that he could hide here. The birds were singing their evening songs as the sun sank behind the hill. Fish jumped as he made his way up the stream, and more than once a prang just stood and watched him pass. Clearly, nothing had hunted here.

He could not see the cave yet, but he doubted Henrick would send him on a fool's errand. It took another hour of winding through bracken and heathery scrubland before Alador came to the cliff face at the other end of the valley. Here, there was a beautiful waterfall feeding the stream, and Alador's eyes followed it up...

There was the cave.

Making his way along the cliff face, he could see no path up to it. How, by the gods, did Henrick get up there? He guessed his father had more magical means that Alador had yet to learn.

The mage cursed softly as he studied the face. It was not quite sheer, as there were hand and footholds, but the rocks looked slick from the spray of the falls. He had climbed such cliffs with Gregor many times, but he was out of practice, and there was no one to share a rope with if he slipped.

He finally chose a route that looked the safest, set his jaw, and began to climb. If he didn't start now, then it would be too dark to make it. His fingers were burning before he was halfway up. Cursing, he shifted his feet to find enough purchase and took the weight off them for a while.

From here on up, the rock was badly shattered and the wall almost dead vertical. Alador carefully tested the integrity of each hold by banging it first with a loose rock, avoiding any hold that moved. The last part turned out to be the hardest: there were few hand holds, and by the time he pulled himself up onto the ledge over which the cave towered, his fingers were sticky with blood, the gloves shredded on sharp rocks.

He flipped over onto his back, his nerves frazzled, his entire body aching and his hands stuck in a claw-like position. He lay there panting with the exertion and watching the sunset above him. The sky was turning a beautiful red, dotted with golden clouds at its edge. He closed his eyes, content to lie there until he smelled a strong odor of musk, sulfur and burnt wood.

He opened his eyes warily. There, looking down at him, was the largest head he had ever seen. It looked ten times bigger than it had in flight. Keensight was staring down at him with those great lavender eyes. The red of his facial scales were dulled with black soot and a small wisp of smoke drifted up as he breathed out.

Alador's heart began to beat at a frantic pace as the beast opened his mouth. He was certain he was about to die, lying there on the doorstep of the great red dragon. To his immense relief, it merely spoke in rasping, guttural tones. "Why didn't you take the stairs?"

Alador lay for a moment in shock, taking in the words of the great beast and trying not to be sick from the overwhelming stench of sulfur. He coughed a few times then sat up and carefully looked over the edge. "There are stairs? WHERE…?"

"Behind the falls..." The dragon turned and casually lumbered back into the cave. A strange huffing sound emanated from the beast. Alador was fairly certain the sound was akin to mortal laughter. He groaned and fell back as he realized that of all the ways he had planned to introduce himself to the dragon, flat on his back after climbing to the cave the hard way was not one of them.

Cursing Henrick for leaving out that small, but very important, detail, he pulled himself up and followed the dragon into the caverns. On the bright side, Keensight had not chosen to roast him or eat him on sight. That was encouraging in the short term...

The dragon had merely walked up the stream that fed the fall into the dark depths of the cave. However, Alador had to pick his way along a path on the edge that would have been dry had the dragon not splashed its way through. He felt for his center and used a cantrip to fashion light into his hand so he could see. Alador realized that he'd been forced to learn all those cantrips because they had their uses. He followed the dragon further into the depths of the great cavern the beast had claimed as its home.

At last, the cavern opened up, and he found he was able to see better. Keensight was moving along the walls puffing small bits of flame onto torches. Alador watched, not willing to speak until spoken to, silence seeming a smarter move than words at the moment.

His eyes were drawn to the largest mound of gold and medure he had ever seen. It was dotted with other bits of jewels and fine, mortal-made items such as bejeweled silver goblets. He continued to survey the pile, seeing that there were weapons, crowns, jewelry, refined medure and unrefined chucks of the same ore. Such wealth was beyond his ability to calculate.

The dragon finally dragged its large form to the pile of treasure. He watched in awe as the dragon climbed onto the mound and wiggled into it as if it were a bed of feathers. The flickering torches created dancing lights on the walls of the cave as the light reflected on various items in the huge pile. The sound of skittering metals mixed with Keensight's loud breath. Alador jumped when the dragon finally spoke again.

"Well, don't just stand there like a hatchling; you came to speak to me. Now, let's be honest. I might kill you - actually, it is quite likely." The dragon made that strange huffing noise. "You can try to convince me otherwise, but I am quite hard to convince." The great beast laid its head down onto its forefeet, the movement sending medure and jewels skittering down its sides. "I also expect an apology for that arrow. It took forever to get it out of the back of my throat." He raised his head and scratched at his neck as he let out a menacing growl.

Alador swallowed hard and slipped off his pack, finally tearing his eyes away from the mound of treasure. He set it on the ground at the edge where the cave opened up, then with slow, measured steps made his way in front of the dragon. Alador was very aware that Keensight was watching him closely the whole time. He appeared larger in size than he had when he had assaulted the village, and he had appeared enormous then.

Alador had expected the dragon to want an apology, and he had decided he would not give him one. He had to show the dragon that he was not weak or fearful. He met the dragon's gaze boldly "I'm not here to offer an apology," Alador declared, "but to receive yours." The mage crossed his arms as he stood and planted his feet in assured defiance before the great dragon.

The dragon raised its head with obvious surprise, and the spines along his back became rigid. "Me?" Keensight pointed to his chest with a claw that was nearly half as long as Alador's height. "Apologize? I will remind you that you were the one with a bow." The dragon shook its head from side to side. "I am not sure if you are brave or just stupid."

Alador moved forward as he began to speak. "I will remind YOU that you assaulted Smallbrook without provocation and killed six of my kin." Alador began to count out the damage on his fingers, his voice increasingly accusatory. "You nearly destroyed half the town by flame. And, had I not shot you, you would have killed many small ones as well. The village of Smallbrook is due compensation for your temper." Alador held his ground, though his heart beat with genuine fear. "Oh, and don't let me forget that I hold your best friend's geas and that my death will draw a final line under his."

The dragon let out a great snort of disbelief and soot flew from his nostrils. When it was done settling, the only part of Alador that was not black was his eyes. He looked down at the covering and back up at the dragon. At least it had been soot and not fire.

The dragon fired his answer right back. "And your village is the one who disturbed my friend's place of rest." Keensight glared at him. "He should have been left in peace."

"Then you did not know Renamaum well." Alador dusted off some of the soot. "He planned for his stone of power to be found. He invades my dreams. He has forced me by magical means to a task that I cannot complete alone, even with his powers vested within me." Alador bravely took a step forward. "You were his best friend, but he still told me where to shoot to stop your attack on Smallbrook."

"I should burn you where you stand for your insolence," the dragon hissed, rising part way up from his position on the pile of treasure.

"You could. That would end each of our complaints," Alador agreed, crossing his arms defiantly again, his eyes challenging Keensight as he began to offer an alternative in a slow, vengeful voice. "Or… you can listen to what I've to say, and get your revenge on those that slew Renamaum, your mate, and took your hatchling." Alador cast out the only bait he had.

A strange tense silence fell between them. Alador was afraid to make the first move and the cave echoed with the rasping breath of the beast. Each stared at the other; neither one spoke nor made a sound. Finally, Keensight hissed out a long breath of fire that flared towards Alador. He dove for the floor sure that Keensight had chosen the first option. He rolled to the side, watching the dragon closely, finding his center in case he needed a shield…

Finally, the dragon plopped his head back down into the pile. "What do you have in mind?"

Chapter Fifteen

Alador smiled. Revenge was a powerful motivator, and Henrick had hinted that dragons might hold on to a slight for as long as they lived. The death of the dragon's mate and the stealing of his egg were far more than a slight. "We take out the council-sponsored bloodmine."

The dragon harrumphed, rolling its great eyes. "We have tried that. It only results in the death of the dragons chained and then the stealing of more eggs. If that is all you have to suggest, then I am better off eating you instead." The dragon's tone was arrogant and dismissive.

"You have never had help from within the mine before," Alador pointed out, clasping his hands behind them. They burned from the scrapes and cuts in them, but he needed to stay focused.

"Now we are speaking on things that interest me. Go on," the dragon grumbled. He suddenly lifted up his head and shouted. "Oh, wait!" The dragon's bellow interrupted Alador as he opened his mouth to explain.

The sudden increase in sound rattled pebbles on the floor and dust fell from the cavern roof. The suddenness of it had made Alador jump in surprise, snapping his mouth shut. He eyed the dragon with concern.

"I have forgotten the manners Henrick taught me. Let me get you a chair." The dragon heaved its bulk up and swung around as if looking for something. "I know it is here ... somewhere..." As he moved, the huge ball-like end of his tail swung about, and had Alador not ducked, he would have been impaled on its lethal spikes.

"Really, it is no bother, I am fine." Alador called out with concern, more worried about the damage the dragon could do looking for the chair than the need to sit.

"No, no. A proper host sees to his guest's comfort. Ah, here it is." The dragon turned back around, forcing Alador to duck under the tail again. Keensight's 'chair' turned out to be a throne. He lumbered over with the throne in his mouth and sat it carefully before his treasure pile. "There you go. Have a seat. After all, you did decide to climb a wall rather than get wet."

Alador stared at the throne in amazement. It was covered in the richest red material he had ever seen. The elaborate scroll work was craftsmanship the like of which he had never seen before. It was gilded with the finest gold-leaf and set with glistening rubies laid out in unique patterns. "Where did you get this?" he asked in awe, moving to trace the patterns and touch the fabric.

Keensight made his way back to his indent in the pile. "That old thing? I found it in a tree house. It was so shiny that I could not resist borrowing it."

Alador chuckled. "Did the owner mind that you borrowed his chair?"

"I don't think so. He was rather dead at the time. He had had the audacity to shoot at me," Keensight answered, looking pointedly at Alador.

Alador ignored this barb as he cast a cantrip to clean the soot from his body before he sat on the throne. It was indeed a comfortable seat; the previous owner must have loved his comforts. He felt odd sitting on a throne before a dragon in a cave. It was a scene that less than a turn ago, he would never have envisaged, let alone calculated the likelihood of it ever coming to pass. "Shall I continue?" he asked the red beast politely.

"One moment, let me get comfortable. Mortal men are so impatient." Keensight huffed as he writhed and rustled his body until he was settled once more. "There, please continue." The dragon propped his head up upon his right claw.

"I propose to ensure a group of men loyal to the pact and the Daezun people are on guard duty the night that we agree to assault the mine. This will enable the dragons to free the fledglings with minimal risk. My men will ensure that not a single spear thrower is on duty that night. We will take on any guard who tries to resist the attack." He put one hand to his chest and gestured to the dragon. "Your… um… *companions* will be able to release the dragons and set them free." Alador was careful to use more formal language.

"I see three problems with your plan…" Keensight's tone, however, was one of discussion rather than dismissal. His guttural utterances were surprisingly easy to follow, as he spoke slowly.

"I am listening." Alador had never seen the mine; Keensight had.

"First, the dragons on the ground will never have learned how to fly." Keensight slightly expanded his wings for emphasis. "They have not been taught anything of their true nature, so they will need to walk out. Secondly, given that my '*companions*' as you called them are accustomed to killing any mortal in sight, they will not be able to discern friend from foe. To be honest, some may not even care to discriminate: killing them anyway just to be on the safe side."

"I had given that possibility some thought. I hope you can select for this mission only dragons you can trust not to kill those that are assisting them. Your human allies will all be wearing a blue tabard with Renamaum's image emblazoned on it," Alador suggested. "Our donning of them could be the signal to attack."

The dragon's great head extended towards Alador, his scent overwhelming. "You take a great risk proposing such a plan, given your Guldalian blood. You directly descend from the one who first broke the pact."

Keensight's gaze was unnerving; silently Alador cursed the fact that the dragon's gaze could cut to his very soul. He was convinced he would never become used to it. "I was once told that one's bloodline does not determine who one chooses to become. I would like to believe that is true. I can't make amends for what was done before I came of age, but I can make a difference in my lifetime. I would see the pact restored."

The guffaw that rolled out of Keensight made Alador's heart race. "A lofty goal for a mortal... You are up against turns of betrayal and hatred," Keensight reminded him.

"I know that. It is a three way dilemma. The Daezun lost the war that was to make the Lerdenian's pay for their crimes against the dragons." Alador leaned forward on his throne. "But the Daezun people have not forgotten the old ways. Why... in Oldmeadow they have planted apple trees above their town for the dragons' pleasure…" *'I have to convince him,'* Alador thought. *'One man and one dragon… We can make the difference, but only united.'*

"You don't say?" Keensight sounded strangely amused.

"You said there were three problems," Alador said, changing the subject. "What is the third?"

"The eggs... The dragons will want any remaining eggs, and they are buried deep in a cave. A bronze could manipulate the stone to get to them, but not without risk of breakages, and maybe breaking them all." Keensight had calculated the risk and was clearly not optimistic. It was a serious stumbling block.

Alador had to admit that the dilemma of the dragon eggs had also been perplexing him. "How big is a dragon egg?"

"About half your size, some a bit smaller," Keensight replied.

Alador sighed. "So a single man couldn't carry one out in a battle without serious risk to the egg." He ran a hand through his loose hair. "I see no way to release the eggs safely without first killing or subduing every guard present."

"Is that something you are willing to do?" Keensight asked, still watching him closely.

Alador thought about Jon. If Jon chose to side with his goddess and guard the mine, he did not know if he could kill him and he doubted Jon would subdue easily. Then again, he could decide to be true to his Daezun cultural roots, and not use his considerable striking force against his friend's objectives. He weighed his thoughts and concerns carefully. "Yes," he finally answered. He sincerely hoped that Jon would come down on his side.

"Now... I see…" - Alador swallowed down his hesitation - "...a problem." His words were drawn out as the harsh realization washed over him. Alador frowned, realizing that he could not just subdue the guards and deny any culpability to his Uncle. "The bodies of the guards who perish will be examined for clues as to what actually happened. There can't be any evidence of Daezun involvement, nor can any be allowed to escape."

A hardness formed within him as he buried his remorse for the men who would die obeying orders. "In the future, I plan to remove the High Minister from power. For the time being, my hands must appear clean of any involvement in this… enterprise."

"I have kin who prefer Lerdenians toasted," Keensight rumbled. "I will take care of any evidence. Scorched ground tells few tales."

Bile rose in Alador's throat as he realized his plans went beyond just freeing the dragons from bloodmining: an idea, a purpose that had seemed noble whenever he had thought of it. He was planning coldly to end the lives of men and women, some of whom he had trained with in the Blackguard.

"You have gone pale, boy, and your heart rate is up," Keensight observed. "Don't you have the stomach for it?"

Alador did not even want to think about how the dragon could sense that. "It is one thing to think of a noble goal and another to realize the steps that must be taken to reach it," Alador murmured. "It bothers me to know that I must kill my own kind to free yours."

"If it did not, I think I might have a need to kill you here before we start. War is harsh, Alador, and comes with a high cost: not only to the men who fight such wars, but to those who command them as well. A man that can send a group into battle knowing they will die and do so without conscience is headed for certain death, or on his way to a brutal dictatorship." Keensight's tone was slow and teaching; it held no censor. "A true leader sends that order with true regret for the men he will lose; but even in the face of his grief, he sends the order anyway."

"And if he cannot give the order?" Alador looked up at the dragon. His way of sharing things was oddly familiar. Maybe it came from spending too much time with Henrick.

"Then he is not a leader that men will follow long," the dragon answered coolly with a smile - which was eerie, as it looked far more like the precursor to a snarl. It was unsettling to see so many teeth.

Alador nodded. "I will need time to arrange things so that I have the people I need in place."

"I will as well. I will have to pick carefully those that will fight by my side and not end the mortals that aid us." They both fell silent.

Alador mulled over their conversation before moving on to the next point he needed to discuss. "I have a question for you..." Alador picked at his leathers as he tried to decide how best to ask it.

"Only one…?" Keensight sounded bemused and Alador swore that the dragon was trying not to laugh. The magnificent beast hauled himself up to sit on his haunches.

"Well, one to focus on at the moment," Alador corrected. "Have you ever seen a black dragon in a bloodmine?"

Keensight raised his head as he considered the question. "No. No, I've never seen a black fledgling."

"A friend of mine suggested that the Black Flight - and maybe even the Goddess Dethara - are in league with those running the mines. He went on to suggest that the Black Flight is providing information on where to find other flights' eggs." He looked up from his leathers to the dragon, and his eyes grew wide with alarm.

Keensight was rising onto all fours, his eye narrowed into mere slits. Every spine on the dragon's back had risen. His wings had expanded as much as the space around him allowed, and they twitched with the fury in his tone. "If this turns out to be true… they will ALL die! I will help hunt down any and every dragon involved in such a heinous betrayal of our sacred heritage," he bellowed. Fire spat in short bursts from his mouth as rage overtook reason.

Alador's hands sprang to his ears as he stared at the furious beast. He shrank back into the shaking throne, afraid the rocks peppering him were just the beginnings of a cave-in. He watched in horror as the dragon's tail hit the wall, dislodging even more of the ceiling.

Alador shouted out. "You are causing a cave-in! Calm down!!" Dirt and rocks rained down from the ceiling, a large boulder rolling past his chair. It seemed likely that Keensight would bury them both…

…but seeming to hear him, Keensight drew in his wings and tail. Only when the dragon had calmed somewhat, and the dust had settled, did Alador dare to speak again. "I only brought it up because you might not want to tell any black dragons what we are about." Alador eyed the clearly still angry dragon.

"I had never… I should have…" Keensight snarled, barely able to finish his own thoughts. "If it is true, it changes everything…" The dragon's nostrils flared and smoke billowed from them.

"Please don't roast the bearer of bad news." Alador was feebly trying to pour a little humor on an inflammable situation. However, the dragon must have taken him seriously, for it plopped down into the pile of treasure, sending stones and slips rattling everywhere.

"My apologies." Despite the attempt to remain calm, Keensight's rage was snarled out in his words. "It is just that I know of one of the Black Flight who knew where my mate nested. If he betrayed her to the egg-hunters, I will kill him. I will make his death so slow and so painful that he will regret ever being hatched." Keensight's anger rumbled the pile.

"I know how it is to be betrayed by those you trust. If this is true, I'm very sorry." Alador was honestly sharing a familiar pain. The two fell into silence.

Alador was unsure of how much time had passed. He did not press the dragon, and he was considering their exchange as well. So far, it was going very well, all things considered. Well, discounting the fact that his words had almost ended in a collapse of the dragon's cave.

It was better than he had dared to hope: Henrick had made it sound like this would be an impossible task. He kept an eye on the angered dragon, watching his tail flick angrily back and forth, sweeping jewels and medure in its wake.

Suddenly Keensight lifted his great head, startling Alador out of his own deep reverie. "I must leave for a short time. There is an area against the east wall partway down the flight of stairs I told you about. Henrick makes himself at home there." He slithered his incredible bulk off the pile, starting a treasure-slide as he headed for the entrance. "I doubt he will object to your making use of it. When I return, I will bring a meal." Keensight called back as his tail was disappearing: "Do not touch my bed."

Alador eyed the enormous pile of treasure Despite its size, he suspected that Keensight would know if a single jeweled cup went missing. He slowly pried his aching body from the chair, realizing he could use some water and a nap. The exhausted young mage made his way to the wall of the cavern that the dragon had indicated, and sure enough, there was a flight of rickety wooden stairs fixed precariously to the jagged, glistening rock…

Taking a flickering torch from a sconce on the wall, he made his way down the treacherously slippy stairs, and came to a small area recessed into the rock, just where

Keensight had said. It had obviously been kitted out for human comfort: there was a bed, a desk and a small bookshelf, though the books appeared mildewed and untouched for some time.

He could see a small pool of water in a hollowed rock a little farther down, fed by the spray of the falls. Carefully he descended the rest of the stairs and moved over to the small pool. Eyeing his hands, he pulled off the shredded gloves, wincing as some cuts were reopened by the removal of the leather caked in dried blood.

He bathed them carefully, then called on his magic to form strips of linen. He frowned at the strangeness of magic while carefully bandaged his hands: it was odd that he could make it rain, call lightning, create linen, and yet he could not heal his own wounds.

He made his way back up to the ledge and fell onto the bed. The covers were just out of reach of the spray of the falls, but still had drawn moisture from the damp surroundings. He dried the blankets with a simple cantrip, and then pulled the rough blankets over himself. Alador had no idea how long Keensight would be gone. He had left angry and with an obvious purpose. Alador was unsure if mentioning the absence of black fledglings was to his advantage or not. However, if Jon's suspicions were true, then any black dragon was a danger to their plans.

He really was exhausted. Taking into account the many days in a sickbed, and the climbing of that cliff face… Alador snorted with frustration: a cliff he had not even had to climb. He could not help wondering if Henrick had left that small detail out on purpose. He made note to punch his father when next he saw him. The warmth of the covers, the lulling sound of falling water and exhaustion finally combined and Alador fell asleep.

Chapter Sixteen

Alador was uncertain how long he had slept by the time that he heard the dragon return, the noise of his movements carrying over the sound of the waterfall. He stretched and groaned as every muscle in his body seemed to protest such simple movement. Pulling himself out of the bed, Alador formed a bit of light in his hand to illuminate what the torch, long burnt out, no longer did. There was no light coming through the water, indicating it was still night outside the cave.

Making his way up the fragile stairs carefully, he tread lightly so as to not make a sound, as he was not certain what mood the dragon would be in when he made it to the top. He realized, as he made it to the top, that it was unlikely he was sneaking up on the beast.

Carefully, he peered into the cavern, searching the large room. Keensight was once more nestled on the top of his mound. A table had been set by the throne and a steaming carcass of prang was draped across it. He could tell that the dragon had not bothered to skin it before he cooked it. The mage shook his head with a bit of a grin. At least the dragon was trying to be hospitable.

He moved across the cavern floor feeling the eyes of Keensight follow him as he made for the table. "Thank you for dinner," Alador politely said.

"You're welcome, I know your kind prefers kills for food dressed out, but with these…" Keensight held up the huge talons, "Skinning them really isn't that easy. I was able to remove its insides. I like that part best anyway."

Smiling at the words of the dragon, Alador pulled his knife from his boot and used it to pull away the skin. He then carved off a healthy piece of meat. It was still too hot to eat, so he set it aside on the table to cool. The smell of scorched hair was mingled with the roasted meat, dampening the appeal somewhat.

"I hope you have regained your temper?" He watched the dragon and attempted to hold no sarcasm in his tone. He flopped down in the throne, still eying the dragon with a bit of concern.

"It was a fact that I should have seen myself," Keensight growled. "That a mortal had to show me the obvious is irritating at best." He shifted with that irritation and a bowl rolled free of the pile then spun at Alador's feet, the slow wobbling stop drawing the mage's eye.

"Yes, well I would guess that even the purest of dragons are not perfect," Alador offered almost absently, watching the jeweled bowl come to a stop. He looked up as Keensight raised his head and slapped his right paw onto the pile making Alador flinch.

"I would not go that far," Keensight protested.

Alador cocked his head and for a moment, he was sure that he had just hurt the dragon's feelings. "Let me rephrase, you were probably too close to the problem to observe such a fluid detail. I'm sure the fledglings in the mine are changed often," Alador offered, so as to soothe the ego of the arrogant beast. Keensight let out a low growl, and Alador realized that he had just picked at the grieving wound of the dragon. The only reason that the fledglings would have changed was that they were unable to offer viable blood any longer.

"Yes, yes, that is likely it. I was too close to it to see." Keensight grabbed at the morsel of balm, but his voice held the pain of the reminder. Silence rose between them as Alador was attempting to eat the hot meat and

Keensight was absorbing their conversation.

After a long while, the dragon sniffed and his long neck stretched toward the table where the prang rested. "You going to eat that?" Keensight eyed the prang hungrily as his tongue snaked out as if to taste the very air emanating from it.

Alador had not found Keensight's way of cleaning and cooking the prang very palatable, so waved towards the steaming carcass. "I've carved off a piece more than enough for me, so if you wish the rest, by all means, it's yours." He did not have to offer twice.

It was rather ominous to see a large dragon lunge in your direction, even if it was for the steaming meat at your side. It felt as if he had barely uttered the words before Keensight was gulping down the prang, and he was being pelted with scattering medure. When the dragon was done eating, he settled backwards into his pile to watch Alador. Alador felt as if the dragon was following every morsel to his mouth as he picked at his own steaming piece.

"Why are you still here?" the dragon asked gruffly.

"You told me to stay downstairs, remember?" Alador grinned at the dragon mischievously before speaking a bit more seriously. "I was unsure if we were done. Times and such were not arranged," Alador pointed out. He took another bite, having to work at chewing and keeping the burnt hair-flavored meat down.

"How much time will you need to prepare your part?" Keensight asked, clearly considering the matter.

"I was thinking we would move at the first full moon following the showing of early spring flowers," Alador suggested.

"Easy enough to mark," the dragon nodded in approval. "Then it is settled. You may finish your dinner then return to Henrick."

"You know that Henrick awaits me?" Alador looked a bit surprised.

"That mortal builds a big enough fire for any dragon to find," Keensight harrumphed, and smoke swirled up from his nostrils.

"Well, he does dislike being uncomfortable." Alador grinned. He toyed with his meat, knowing he had one other matter to address. He was not sure if the idea was brilliance or stupid and he took a deep nervous breath. "However, our business is not quite done."

"It is not?" Keensight tipped his head left and right.

"There is still the matter of compensation to Smallbrook," Alador stated casually as he ate from his cut. He very deliberately did not look up at Keensight.

Keensight let out a snort of smoke and soot. "You are not serious?" Keensight sounded totally taken aback.

"I am." Alador stated with a full mouth and paused to finish chewing. "The High Minister of Lerdenia seeks to push the Daezun into starvation through me. I'll need to capitulate to his demands to buy time to find a way to truly unseat him." Alador took a deep breath and continued. "Given this, I think the best way you could make amends for damage done in anger is to either part with a bit of your bed, or you could help make sure villages under his onslaught have meat."

Keensight looked around at his precious pile and back to Alador. "Your insolence and disrespect are boundless," he growled, and Alador was sure that strange grimace on the dragon's face was a pout.

Alador looked up at him. "How have I been disrespectful? I have offered alternatives for the damage done." Alador held out both his hands, palms up as if weighing matters. "I have offered my own life and the lives of many who revere dragonkind to free your young." Alador stood up and moved to the edge of the massive mound.

"I would think a simple request to repair the damage you did to an innocent village is very respectful." He turned his back on the dragon bravely, despite the pounding of his heart and moved to the back of the throne, partly to have something to hold to still his shaking hands, and partly to put something between him and the agitated dragon whose tail was twitching much like a cat about to pounce on a field mouse.

Keensight glared at him for the longest time. Alador leaned against the throne, his heart was racing so loudly that he was sure that Keensight was more than aware of his apprehension and fear.

"Are you sure you are not part dragon?" the dragon finally hissed.

"Is that possible?" Alador asked curiously, his fingers white from clenching the throne.

"No! But you bargain as one, and you are as arrogant as one," Keensight blustered. "You are just like your sire."

Alador's eyes went cold and hard as he made eye contact with the dragon, cold rage flooded through him. "I am nothing like my father," he said slowly.

Keensight snorted with amusement, "Denying a truth doesn't make it false. You are just like him. Calculating, brash," Keensight paused and pointed a talon at Alador, "and I bet you have that same damn temper."

Alador worked to rein in said temper before he proved the dragon right. "He lies," Alador argued simply, as if this was a defense. He held the dragon's gaze. The dragon's eyes held amusement and Alador's still held indignation.

"So do you," Keensight pointed out. "Otherwise, you will never get your half of your plan in place, and you would not cave into the demands of the High Minister to buy time."

Alador stared angrily at the dragon as he moved around the throne to the pile. Totally forgetting Henrick's warning to hold his tongue, he snarled up to the looming head above him. "Henrick didn't tell me I was part of some breeding plan." The mage spat out with disdain "He used magic against my mother to ensure he was in Daezun furs."

The dragon shook its great head. "You are a fool to think that you are exempt from the very crimes you press upon your father. You just told me that you will cast spells against your own people for a greater cause." Alador was so close to the dragon's maw that he could see a remnant of a prang hoof stuck within the dragon's teeth. "Sometimes the means are justified in the great scheme of things, boy." Keensight lowered his head as he spoke, the snort of amusement from Keensight's nostrils sent Alador's unkempt hair backwards.

"Don't call me boy," Alador snarled. He did not like Keensight's words. He didn't want to admit he was doing the very things that he was mad at Henrick for doing, and Keensight was not the first to point out that he was acting just like his father. Alador rubbed his jaw absently, remembering Sordith's solid blow.

"I will quit calling you boy when you quit speaking as one, not discounting the fact that I have lived many of your lifetimes." Keensight raised his head up, peering down at the angered youth.

"You…" The dragon moved over Alador as he had the prang before gulping it down. His words were terse and cold, "want me to trust you, trust many dragons to this cause, and yet you speak like a fledgling who has been denied his favorite toy." Keensight did not move further as he countered Alador's rants "It does not gain much faith on my part to hear you hold a grudge against a man who, at least as long as I have known him, watched over you with true care."

Alador shifted uncomfortably as the truth of Keensight's words solidified the truth of Sordith's. He finally offered his last excuse for the abuse he had been throwing Henrick's way. "He doesn't even know how many small ones he has. Just recently, I met one of my half-brothers that he didn't even know existed." Alador stared at his feet.

Keensight laughed in that strange huffing manner. "I don't know how many hatchlings I have created," Keensight pointed out. "You going to tell me you have checked every wench who has warmed your bed to make certain you did or did not father a child?" Keensight gave that weird noise that could only be a laugh.

Alador turned a deep shade of red bringing even more of the rumbling noise from the dragon. "I see. Too few so far to have such a care." Keensight continued, "Boy, I have known Henrick for some time now. He is also on a mission of his own, and one he is not yet free to tell you about. I do know he has a genuine care for your well-being. So I suggest you take a step back and make sure you are not flinging the very mud you stand in. You may do more damage than you can fix."

Alador sighed as he clasped his hands behind him. Great, he thought, now I am getting the same lecture from a dragon. Perhaps they all were right, maybe he was expecting his father to be some paragon of virtue like some raptured small one. Had he put Henrick in a category that did not allow for mortal failings? Alador kicked a piece of medure back into the pile of treasure absently as he considered this. Given his love of female attentions and food, was Henrick even capable of being the father that Alador had always longed to have in his life? He also wondered if Henrick had been hanging out with this great beast too long; the two took a similar tone.

"I will consider your points," Alador conceded putting his hands out in surrender. "However, you have avoided the topic of recompense to the Daezun." It had not been lost on him how successfully Keensight had pulled him off that topic.

Keensight let out a huge exasperated sigh. "I still feel I was not in the wrong. Renamaum's bones were disturbed… violated." Keensight's tone was almost pleading

"A gift of the Gods, and a practice long standing of the People. One, as a flight leader, you would be well aware of," Alador pressed.

"Who said I was a flight leader?" Keensight said, sidestepping again.

"Renamaum," Alador replied.

Keensight paused then leaned down and sniffed Alador. The dragon's drawing of breath was so strong that his hair flew the other direction, filling his face. "You can speak to him?" Keensight looked at him curiously.

"More like he speaks to me, but I suspect my thoughts and words are not lost on him. It's like a piece of him lives in me. Especially when the same thing makes us angry," Alador admitted. "I don't suppose you can tell me more of the nature of a geas stone?"

"Generally, yes, but Renamaum's would have been different." Keensight rubbed his nostrils with a great paw.

"Oh, why is that?" Alador leaned forward.

"The Gods give a dragon a gift when they come of age. Renamaum did not receive a single gift, but one from each of the Gods. He told me that one of them was that he would not truly die, or something close to that." The dragon waved a claw in almost a dismissive manner. Keensight then arched his back, stretching before he spoke again. "So his death stone would hold more, proven by the fact he guides you."

"So that is not normal to a geas stone?" Alador asked in surprise.

"No. Geas stones are rare to begin with, as it requires a single wound for the blood to flow into a large mass." The dragon shifted backwards towards his indentation in the mound. "It also requires a highly skilled dragon in matters of magic. Some dragons do not fully explore their potential in magic, preferring a more natural, simple life. However, usually there is a simple impression of what must be done, and once it is done, the drive disappears," Keensight explained. Keensight laid his head down on his paws and closed his eyes.

When the dragon did not speak further, Alador called out. "Go on." Alador was relieved to finally get some educated answers into the matters of his magic.

"If Renamaum speaks to you, then a piece of him still lives. If this is so, then all of his magic still lives, not echoes of it pressed into a stone," Keensight continued.

"Wait, what does that mean?" Alador tried to piece together the difference in his stone and a usual geas stone.

"It means you were not gifted with a bit of a blue dragon's magic." Keensight eyed the Daezun mage. "You were gifted with a blue dragon AND his magic. I doubt you have scratched the surface of what you can do." Keensight closed his eyes again.

Alador stared at him wide-eyed. "You are saying that Renamaum lives in me somehow, with all his powers and skills?"

There was a long sigh as if Alador was trying the dragon's patience. "Yes, that is what I am saying. You are likely as much a dragon in skill as your limited mortal form will allow." Keensight frowned. He raised his head as if considering something then added in an offhanded manner. "Maybe I should kill you. It could drive you quite mad, I suspect. Yes, It could. Having any crazy thoughts or ideas?"

"I came to see you after I stuck an arrow in your throat," Alador pointed out. "Many would consider that a bit crazy."

"Yes, that is probably enough evidence. We should probably put you out of your misery before you become miserable," Keensight said solemnly. "Why ... you could become a danger to those around you. One should always get rid of a possible threat while the threat is only possible.

Alador frowned at the sudden riddled speech of the dragon. Realizing the dragon's tactic, he smiled with amusement. "You are just looking for a reason to avoid making a choice of compensation." The beast was rather good at redirection. "How can I learn more of what Renamaum gave me?"

"Well, I cannot teach you. My skills lie in another area," Keensight admitted with a snort of frustration.

Alador noted that the dragon did not acknowledging the statement of avoidance. "What of Pruatra? Does she still live?" Alador felt a sudden sense of urgency to know that answer and the words spilled out his lips before he could bite them back. "The eggs she was sitting when Renamaum died, what of them?"

Keensight's head cocked sideways as he surveyed Alador. "So you do lay in there, my old friend." Keensight's sad tones were not lost on Alador. "Pruatra lives, as do the two fledglings. Much time has passed, and they have each had their own blessing. A female and a male that would have made you proud."

"Could you arrange for her to come?" Alador's eyes filled with tears, and for the first time, he felt that the dragon had risen up and truly taken control. It was a sense that he had only had hints of in the past. He was aware of the words and feelings spilling out, but it was as if he was behind bars, unable to exert any control.

"I do not know if she will come, but if she will, I will have her meet you by the lake when the boy departs," Keensight offered.

Alador felt a sudden release and took a deep breath. "Okay, that has never happened before," he muttered. He sank down, as it felt as if his legs would not hold him, and his hands were shaking.

"I doubt it will happen often, for Renamaum was ever a respectful beast. Wise beyond his turns, with hopes for mortals that seemed impossible." Keensight seemed a bit melancholy.

"Pruatra can teach me?" Alador again asked hopefully.

"If you and Renamaum can convince her that he rests within you, I have no doubt she will teach you," Keensight said..

"Can you go fetch her now?" Alador asked with growing hope and excitement.

"I am not your carrier pigeon, boy. I only returned from flying a fair distance. I intend to sleep till the morning birds sing. Then, and only then, will I go and speak to Pruatra." Keensight plopped down and rolled about shoving treasure left and right as if trying to find a more comfortable position before continuing. "She would not take kindly to a male dragon invading her lair in the dead of night, and she is not a female I ever plan to cross," Keensight firmly stated. "I suggest you find your bed as well, unless you plan to sit in my chair, staring at me as I sleep.

Alador nodded. It was a clear dismissal and one that he was not going to ignore. As he started to move away from the large dragon, he realized that once again Keensight had sidetracked him. He turned back. "I will leave you to your rest when you have given me your recompense," he challenged boldly. He set his feet firmly with arms crossed.

"You are like a hatchling with a bone that it just will not give up," Keensight growled out without opening his eyes.

"Nevertheless, I expect an answer. You and I both know that the villagers that perished in your fires were innocent of any harm to you," Alador pressed.

"Fine," Keensight snarled as he raised his head. Alador could see the remnants of fire when the dragon flared his nostrils.

"Fine is not an answer. A bit of your bed or meat through the winter?" Alador pressed.

Keensight eyed his treasure pile with frantic consideration of what he could bear to release. Alador could not help but grin, because the dragon acted as if Alador had asked for a piece of his wing as he nuzzled and touched various places on his pile.

"Well?" Alador pressed.

"Damnation, mortal. I am thinking." Keensight spat a bit of fire at Alador..

It stopped just short of Alador, but he was fairly

certain that his eyebrows were now truly curled from heat. He had gambled the dragon would not hurt him, so he still stood cross-armed, waiting for the dragon to make up his mind.

Finally the dragon slumped down. "I will take them meat as there is a need," he morosely answered.

"Good enough." Alador nodded. As he turned away, he could not help but smile in amusement. Leave it to a dragon to agree to hunt all winter rather than give up a few slips of his treasure. For some reason, it helped to build a bit of trust more than if the dragon had given over a part of his bed.

He made his way back down the stairs and crawled fully into the comfortable bed. He pulled the covers over his head to keep the gentle mist from his face. He did not fall asleep right away as he had hoped, however. Keensight's words about his father haunted his thoughts for a long while before he finally fell asleep.

Chapter Seventeen

Alador slept peacefully through the rest of the night with no dreams or nightmares to disturb his sleep. The sound of falling water had been comforting. He would have slept longer, but eventually, the damp of the fine spray sank through the pile of blankets. Even then, he stayed where he was, merely using a cantrip to dry them before nestling once more in their depths.

He felt surprisingly safe here. The fact that a dragon with jaws and a gullet so large they could swallow him in one gulp was lying in the chamber above him did not cause him any alarm at all. He rather liked the beast. He was everything Alador had always dreamed dragons would be.

Keensight had a sense of honor. He was arrogant and very possessive of his treasure hoard. He was intelligent, and skilled in the ways of magic. Alador wondered whether life would have turned out more favorably for him if he had been blessed with a father such as Keensight.

However, the dragon so affectionately in his thoughts seemed to lack the patience Alador had been told his kind had in abundance. "And I was told dragons sleep excessively long," Keensight called. "Are you alive down there?"

He groaned as the guttural tones bellowed down to him, and uncovered his head enough to shout back: "I'll be right up!" He pulled the blankets back over his head in annoyance.

"Oh good, because I went and got bacon and bread from Henrick, and if you don't get up here, I may be forced to eat it out of a sense of obligation to my stomach." Keensight could be heard lumbering off.

Alador chuckled and threw back the covers. He had no doubt that Keensight would devour his breakfast as promised. He saw to his own needs and drank from the pristine falls before hurrying as fast as he dared up the creaking stairs. He stepped into the cave to see the table now held a variety of breads, cheeses, and - as promised - there was bacon.

"I know for a fact that Henrick did not bring all of this with us." Alador sat down in the throne and began devouring the food before him. He was actually quite hungry.

"Well, umm…" - Keensight lumbered up onto the pile before continuing - "I might have stopped by and borrowed a bit from a neighbor," he confessed.

Alador paused in his eating to study the fare laid before him. He gave a small private smile of amusement before looking up at the great beast and grinning. "I do not think you know what 'borrowed' means."

"I surely do," Keensight responded defensively. "It means to relieve your neighbor of something he is not using." He sounded almost hurt. "Why… these paltry provisions were just lying on a shelf for the taking."

Alador wiped his mouth with the back of his sleeve. He picked up a large pastry and waved it at the dragon. "That is called 'stealing', Keensight. The 'shelf' was probably for mounting a display of goods for sale at a market." Alador eyed the dragon, certain that he knew damn well the difference between stealing and borrowing. "Borrowing means you intend to give it back."

"Well, I hardly think anyone would want their food returned after it has passed through my digestive system,"

Keensight answered with a toothy grin. At least, Alador sincerely hoped that was a smile.

"No, I am sure they wouldn't want it back after you were through with it." He shook his head, chuckling. "Did you at least leave a slip or two behind for their trouble?"

"Why would I do that?" Keensight protectively eyed the pile of slips and unrefined medure that made up the bulk of his bed.

"Because without payment and without return of said borrowed item, it is stealing." Waving the large piece of pastry at the dragon, Alador grinned in triumphant amusement as he ate the pastry. "How did you get into a pastry shop anyway?" Alador eyed the large dragon from nose to the twitching ball at the end of his tail

"Well, the door was a little on the small side in my opinion; so I…" -Keensight paused as if searching for the right word - "***expanded*** it for them," he admitted.

Alador almost choked on the sweet pastry as he tried not to laugh. "So you ripped out a piece of their wall?" Alador started to laugh outright. "I hope this was a Lerdenian neighbor and not a Daezun one."

"Of course... Daezun hardly ever make more than they need. Lerdenian people seem fond of excess." Keensight eyed Alador from head to toe. "I do not see you complaining, given you are filling your mouth with my ill-gotten gains," he huffed indignantly.

"Damage is already done..." Alador shrugged and popped a bit of cheese in his mouth.

Keensight snorted. "When you are done eating, you may show yourself out." Keensight flopped down into his glittering pile, medure and slips clinking noisily down the pile.

"So eager to get rid of me already?" Alador frowned. "I still have questions."

"Ask them. When you are gone, I will begin investigating this suggestion that the Black Flight is involved in the abomination of the bloodmines..." Keensight was deadly serious as he closed his eyes and laid his massive head down upon his front paws.

"Can you teach me to travel by magic?" Alador asked. "It'd make everything I need to do that much simpler, and easier to hide my involvement as well."

"I could, but we do not have time." Keensight paused as he lifted his head, tilting it as he considered. "Tell Henrick I said it is time to give you the medallion. It will do what you need done, and he will have the time to explain the risks thoroughly." Keensight was inspecting his talons.

"Is Pruatra going to meet me by the lake?" He was not sure about successfully navigating two different dragon meetings on his own. He picked up a roll while keeping his eyes on Keensight.

"I do not know. I broke it to her that Renamaum now resides in a mortal's body. She was a trifle… displeased." Keensight paused, and Alador felt more than a twinge of perturbation. "I am not sure if she will come or not." Keensight stuck the talon he was examining right between his teeth as if searching for something...

"Great," Alador said with heavy disappointment. "The last thing I need is one more angry female in my life." He tossed down the roll he had been about to take a bit out of.

"'Di'n't inherit yor 'ather's charm, eh? Now dat's a shame." Keensight gargled out with his talon still in his mouth. Suddenly, a little bone came flying out. "Ah, that's better."

The frustrated young mage just shook his head. "No! I don't have any of Henrick's charm," he freely admitted. "I seem to have inherited more of what my mother calls my 'korpen-in-the-wash-yard' tendency: blundering everywhere, knocking things over, and ending up with a woman's broom between my eyes." Alador sighed. He knew, dressed as a mage, he cut a striking figure in Lerdenia, but back home he was scraggly and pale compared to other Daezun males.

The dragon laughed. It was easier to recognize now. "That is a well-painted picture, boy."

Alador smiled but returned his mind to the questions he had for the dragon. Part of him wished he could just stay here exchanging words and quips. He could see why Henrick enjoyed his meetings with the dragon.

"If she is there, any ideas on how I should approach her?" Alador asked, his concern was evident.

"Well given your vivid description, I would suggest... carefully." Keensight laughed at his own humor.

"Yes, very helpful. Seriously…?" Alador pressed in quick response.

"I suspect that Renamaum will help you there." Keensight sobered slightly. "I could sense him yesterday, so it is likely, as they were mated, that she will sense him as well."

Alador nodded. He hoped this was the case. Given that he had no idea how to appease the damage he'd done to his relationship with Mesiande; appeasing an unhappy, large, blue dragon was hardly likely to be on his list of skills. Alador wondered if there were similarities in the behaviour of a displeased dragon and a displeased Daezun female.

"I guess I should be off then." Alador stood up, having eaten his fill. "Is there… Can we talk again before we take the bloodmines?" Alador hurriedly added: "…to ensure that our plans are melded well?" He sighed, hoping that Keensight had not picked up on his wanting more than just plans to meld.

"Of course. Henrick's medallion will ensure that you have that ability. However, I do suggest some form of announcement before you arrive. You might catch me at my most charming and, well… you seem to be an impressionable lad." Keensight seemed to be quite amused with himself today.

Alador shook his head with amusement and a soft chuckle as he moved to where his backpack still sat and scooped it up. He turned and stopped before Keensight. "Thank you for your hospitality and for your decision not to eat me," Alador stated solemnly. He bowed with a flourish.

"That decision can be reversed, if you fail me in the bloodmines," Keensight warned, pointing a sharp talon at him.

"I would expect nothing less," Alador said with a nod as he rose up.

"One last thing," Keensight turned his head so a full eye was on Alador. "Make up with your father. Too often in life, our last words spoken are the ones we regret when our loved ones have fallen." Keensight's tone held an edge of sorrow as he spoke.

Alador remembered that Renamaum and Keensight's last words had been bitter, but the sorrow seemed deeper. He decided not to ask and just nodded his head. He turned and left with a lump in his throat.

Returning the way he had come seemed much quicker. Of course, not having to climb a cliff face greatly added to the rate of return. He stepped through the falls swiftly and discovered that it was a colder day than when he had traveled here. The wind held the promise of snow, and the birds were quieter today. His breath formed outside his mouth in puffs of steamy clouds. He swiftly drew the drying cantrip up: it was not a day to be damp in the wind.

A sudden sound drew his attention and as he looked up he saw Keensight fly overhead. The dragon was impressive with wings spread in a full glide. He noted there were small rips and tears in them as the dragon passed by. Even so, the power behind each thrust and the snap of the wing in the wind was awe-inspiring. Their bodies looked too heavy to fly, and he wondered about the magic that enabled them to take to the air. He stared, watching until Keensight had disappeared into the clouds.

He made it to the lake and moved a bit more warily. He did not know where on the lake's edge he would find Pruatra, or if she was even coming. Alador checked the sky for any signs of a dragon at each clearing as he made his way back around the lake shore.

Stopping to chew on some jerky at the far end of the lake, he surveyed the hill rising above to find where he had made his way down. He sat down on a fallen tree and scanned the sky once more. The morning was serene with the lapping sounds of the water, the muted light, and the peaceful movements of korpen and prang.

"Is it true? Do you possess my mate's power, and does some remnant of him live within you?" A decidedly feminine voice questioned.

He was so deep in his scrutiny that when the voice spoke, he cursed as he rose and spun, lightening already forming in his hand. There, rising above the lake, was a giant blue dragon head. It was nearly as big as Keensight's, though it seemed more serpentine. The tones of her voice were more musical, without the guttural growl to them.

He immediately bowed low, letting the power ebb from his hand. "Milady Pruatra, a pleasure to meet you in person," he murmured. He felt a strange tugging at his mind. "I believe your mate would prefer to speak with you, rather than letting me talk." He found a way of responding to the pressure he felt inside: stepping back and letting go. He owed Renamaum this meeting. He did not like the idea that he was carrying the spirit of a dragon around, but at least he now knew what it felt like when that dragon asserted himself more directly than through dreams and warnings.

Pruatra moved gracefully through the water to the edge, staying just deep enough for her own safety, or so Alador assumed. "Prove to me it is true. Tell me something that only my mate would know," she insisted.

Alador smiled at her. He felt as if he was talking, and yet he knew the words were not his own. "When you were heavy with your eggs, a black dragon came to steal you away to his own lair. I fought valiantly for you, vanquishing my foe despite his youth and slick skills in the air. Yet, when the battle was done, your main concern was that he had ruined the fish I had brought for your dinner." Renamaum's haughty tones came through despite his use of Alador's diminutive vocal cords.

Pruatra made the same deep rumbling sound as Keensight had when he laughed. "Yes, I do remember that the fish was quite destroyed. But that could be a memory impressed upon the stone. Tell me something that is unlikely to have been impressed upon a stone, something more… intimate."

"You switch your tail just a little, back and forth, when you are sated." Alador felt himself blush, although the words came out of his own mouth.

Pruatra stared at him for the longest time. "How could you let yourself be… in a mortal body?" Her concern and grief were clear. She rocked back and forth making a strange keening noise that Alador did not understand, but obviously Renamaum did.

"Do not cry, my heart. It breaks me still, despite the passage of time. I told you of the blessings of the gods, and this is but one piece of what was foretold."

Alador listened uncomfortably. Why was it that so much was kept from him?

"But it is not even fair to look upon! It is as if a curse of ugliness was laid upon it at birth. Couldn't you have possessed something with more appeal?" Pruatra snapped out her displeasure, eyeing Alador with disdain.

"He is of the old blood. He has what is needed to see my greatest desire fulfilled: that this isle should find peace, and that dragons will no longer be hunted within the safety of this land." Renamaum's words struck Alador deeply. "Our time is short: I cannot speak through him for long; I weaken each time I do. Tell me of our fledglings?" Renamaum asked with a clear tone of hope.

"I will let them speak for themselves." The dragoness let out a strange shrill sound. Alador immediately searched the sky. Three dragons at once had not been not in his plans. He shifted within uneasily, but felt a wave of reassurance from the blue dragon that now held control of him.

Two younger dragons landed on either side of him. Alador's heart raced to be surrounded by such noble but daunting creatures. These two were a lighter blue, one slightly larger than the other, but both only about two-thirds the size of their mother. "They are magnificent," Alador breathed out.

Behind him, Pruatra splashed more up out of the water. "On your right is your daughter, her name is Rena. On your left is your son, Amaum. Fledglings, this Daezun is honored to carry the soul of your father: that his life's work may continue." Pruatra nuzzled Alador's head from behind gently, sending chills and water down his spine. "Your name, mortal?" Pruatra whispered in his ear, her breath damp and cool.

"Alador. I am pleased to meet you both." Alador could feel Renamaum's pleasure at seeing his fledglings whole and healthy He gasped as the dragon's emotions at seeing his small ones for the first time almost overwhelmed him. Alador slowly felt the dragon slide away. "He has gone," Alador murmured with sudden anxiety.

The one called Rena moved forward and pushed him a bit with her nose. "Let him out," she insisted with a growl. Her look could only be a displeased scowl.

"It does not work that way, Rena." Pruatra scolded gently. "This Daezun had no choice in the path he has been given. The most we can do to honor your father is to help him along the path."

Alador turned to face Pruatra. "I need to learn how to use Renamaum's power. There is more at stake here than just the dragons' fate. The leader of the Lerdenian people is a strong mage, and he intends to enslave my people, as well." He searched the head that was so close.

He longed to touch it, to feel what a dragon's skin was like, but he did not want to offend this newfound aid.

"That will take time," Pruatra warned. "Renamaum studied many turns to excel in the ways of magic."

"Then I need an intense lesson. I have about ten days, and then whatever I have learned is what I will have to complete Renamaum's geas." Alador put both his hands out to the side. "Please."

Pruatra considered carefully. "As it must be then. We can stay here; there are enough fish in the lake and other beasts to feed us for a time."

"This is a protected vale belonging to Keensight. Do you think he will mind?" Alador did not want to anger his allies before he had even established a good relationship with them.

"Do not worry about Keensight: he owes me a thing or two." Pruatra laughed in a knowing dragonlike manner.

"Then I just need to travel over the hill to fetch my father, I will need his help as well. He is a friend of Keensight's, so ..." Alador answered. "You don't have to worry about him," he promised hurriedly.

Amaum stepped forward with a deep bass tone that throbbed through Alador. "The mage with too big a fire…?"

Alador ran a hand through his hair, now wet from Pruatra's attentions. "That would be him."

"I will fetch him for you," Amaum said, wagging his tale with anticipation. "I like to sneak up on mages." The young male launched himself into the air.

"Now that, I wish I could see." He grinned at Pruatra.

The dragoness made her way out of the lake and flopped down. "Where do you wish to start, psuedo-dragon?"

Alador blinked at the title she gave him. He guessed, in a way, it was true. "Weather."

"You jump at the hardest of all tasks as your first?" Pruatra eyed him.

"It is the one I must master, as there is an immediate need," Alador answered.

"Well then, let us start where it will please us both. Rena..." She paused, looking over to her daughter.

"Yes?" The younger female moved up next to Alador. .

"Teach him to make it warmer. I could use a little sun on my wings." Pruatra laid her head down and stretched out in the grass as she closed her eyes.

Alador turned to Rena as she eyed him first left and right. "I hope you learn quickly. She gets a bit grumpy when she is cold." Rena sighed to indicate the severity of the consequences that might arise from her mother's 'grumpiness'. "Come, we will let her rest and work until my brother and your fire mage appear."

As she led the way, Alador smiled. He had hoped to enlist the help of one dragon. Instead, he had found four.

Chapter Eighteen

Rena turned out to be a very good teacher: she was patient and soft-spoken. He had never thought of dragons as individuals with personalities and quirks. In fact, he had always thought them as revered magical beasts, and the thought of sitting down and having a conversation with them had just never occurred to him. It would have been like sitting down to speak with a god.

Even after Henrick's tales of Keensight and their conversations, or even the dreams, a part of him had held onto a piece of his old way of looking at dragons. He now knew that he would never see dragons the same way again. He forced himself to pay attention as she began explaining the weather spell in a different way. Her first explanation of warming the air had confused him.

Rena sat on her haunches and, with a talon, pushed two stones side by side. "The air is filled with little stones that most cannot see. Heat is created when the stones get excited. They run into each other, like rubbing one's wing on the same spot over and over. Eventually, warmth is created."

Alador lowered himself to sit cross-legged across from her. "So like rubbing hands together to warm them when cold?" Alador asked.

"Yes, this is it. These air stones are your components for the spell." Rena looked down at him; even sitting, she was still a full man's height above him.

"How do you know the air is filled with these little stones?" Alador asked, looking into the space around him, confused as to how floating rocks, even small could not be seen.

"Do mortals not see the world around them?" Rena sighed with exasperation. "If you look hard enough then you can see them. These little air stones are important to any spell of weather. The problem is, so is the sun, and at certain times, the angle of Vesta tilts away from it. When that happens, the air is colder and the snows come."

"So if the stones are a component, then you must have them for any weather spell?" Alador eyed the two stones she had set side by side.

"Correct. So you must work with the other two aspects: the air stones and the water in the air," Rena said with approval. "To create a violent storm, you speed up the air stones creating heat in one part of the sky, and in another, you slow them down. This is the same way you can create wind, although at a lesser intensity than for a storm. To create a storm, you also add water into the sky."

Alador frowned. "Do I need to see the air stones to create a storm or calm one?" He looked up at the blue dragon who was sitting on her haunches still watching him.

"Yes. This is your first task. To learn what you seek, you must learn to see with more than your eyes," Rena tried to explain. "I cannot teach this. You must find it yourself. My Dame said my Sire could create a warm day for her anytime she wished it, or bring a cooling rain. If my Sire resides within you, then a part of you already knows how to see the air stones." Her tone sounded doubtful of his claim to hold a part of Renamaum.

She got up and lumbered off to join her mother in the patch of sun, curling up next to her. Alador looked back at the two females; Rena was still about a third smaller and the blue in her scales was lighter. Other than that, there wasn't much to tell them apart.

Alador looked back to the rocks on the ground with the trace of a frown. He did not doubt the dragon, but at the same time, he had always seen the sky as empty space when there were no clouds. What Rena suggested was that the sky was never empty.

He tried staring at a large rock in the distance, trying to see the air stones between him and the rock. All he accomplished was watering eyes and frustration. How did you see something that generally cannot be seen?

He was startled from his pondering as two large packs dropped beside him, then Amaum came skittering in, sliding across the dirt rather than landing in a direct descent. His slide sprayed dirt all over his sister, Rena.

Alador could not help but grin when Rena picked up her head with obvious disapproval. "When are you going to mature into a proper male?"

Amaum folded his great wings as he answered, "When it comes to you, little sister, never."

"I am the same number of turns as you are," she grumbled as she laid her head back down to return to her nap without bothering to remove the fine layer of dust and dirt.

"Yes, but you are still littler than me," Amaum smugly said before turning back to Alador.

Alador was amused by the exchange, having had similar ones with Sofie. He already liked these two siblings, and he was fairly certain that was independent of Renamuam's pride.

Amaum moved to Alador and smugly stated, "Your fire mage is in a bit of a temper. I decided to help place him in a better mood by carrying his packs. He should be here in a bit. He was bemoaning having to walk." Amaum flopped down close to Alador.

"Why is Henrick in a temper?" Alador was not late, and he doubted that Henrick was disturbed to meet another dragon.

"Well, his fire went out." Amaum stated, plopping his head down on his forefeet.

"He's a fire mage, I doubt that is a problem." Alador glanced over at the dragon and met his gaze; there was no doubt that the glimmer in Amaum's eyes was mischievous.

"What... what did you do?" Alador grinned at Amaum.

"Well, it went like this. It started to rain in a rather localized location, so he went into his tent," Amaum said holding up on talon. "Then his fire went out." A second talon went up. "This wind came out of nowhere and blew his tent off its loosened pegs." Amaum's amusement was barely contained.

Alador was trying not to laugh as he tried to picture the scene of this young male playing tricks on Henrick. "I see. Then what happened?"

"Well, he figured out by then that it was not natural weather, and so he started cursing you." Amaum stated with a huge grin that showed all his razor sharp teeth.

Alador sighed and rolled his eyes. "That was the last thing I need. We are already at odds."

"I figured this was the case and showed myself. You do, after all, carry my Sire within. I don't need your Sire damaging mine." Amaum eyed the hilltop that Henrick would be coming over.

"I appreciate that." Alador grinned at Amaum. "I wish I'd have seen his face when it suddenly rained on him."

Amaum just gave that toothy grin back. Alador shook his head and returned to trying to see the air stones. Amaum eyed the rocks in front of the mage then Alador.

"Trying to see air stones?" he asked.

"Yes. But I don't see how you can see with more than your eyes." Alador frowned down at the rock. "I can't seem to focus hard enough."

"That would be the problem: to see air stones you have to focus on nothing. You let your mind and eyes clear and you sense them, see them, feel them," Amaum answered.

"How do you focus on nothing?" Alador had a hard time following the way these two dragons explained things.

"You… well… I mean, in the distance." Amaum thought hard about how to explain. "Your common tongue is missing words sometimes"

"My common tongue? It's not the language of the dragons as well?" Alador blinked in surprise.

"Oh no," Amaum huffed. "Far too vulgar for a proper dragon."

"Well, what does a dragon speak?" Alador had never considered they would speak a different language than the Daezun and Lerdenian people.

"Draconic, of course," Amaum tipped his head. "Wish to hear it?"

"Yes." Alador was intrigued by everything that these creatures represented.

"Si charis ir kear ekess qe lae versvesh vur versel lae sia opsola." Amaum's voice took on an almost lyrical tone as the sounds rolled off his tongue with far fewer guttural tones.

Alador did not know what Amaum had said, but Renamaum must have, for a sense of pride welled up in Alador. Renamaum moved within him and Alador could not help but smile at the older dragon's reaction.

"I imagine that is a hard language to learn," he offered. "Whatever you said pleased your Sire."

Amaum sobered for a moment. "I can only hope so."

Alador felt a bit of discomfort at the change in mood. "So, don't focus, you say?"

Amaum nodded. "Look out, but look at nothing. You must quiet everything within you. You do not have to do that when you have enough practice, but the first time I saw the air stones I had to be completely still, aware of nothing but the air that touched me."

Alador decided to try again. He stared at the rock in the distance, then tried not to see it, even though he looked in that direction. At first, he saw nothing but a blur. He could feel the cool wind on his skin and the warmth of the sun. He suddenly saw movement in his vision. Alador tried to focus on it but lost it immediately. He let out a frustrated growl.

"Maybe it is just easier for dragons," Amaum consoled.

"I thought I saw them, but then when I tried to see them, to really look at them, they were gone." Alador shook his head at his failure.

"You cannot look at them. You must see them without seeing," Amaum repeated what Rena had said.

"That is silly; you can't see something without seeing it. It's a contradiction." Alador looked at Amaum with frustration.

Amaum let out a rumbling sound. "Yet you just did. You said you saw them until you looked at them."

Alador realized the dragon was right. He had seen the little flitting movements until he had tried to focus on them. "Well, shite," he spat.

The dragon just laughed with a deep rumble and went back to his napping. Alador kept trying. Every time he would get a glimpse of the flittering movements, he could not help but try to focus on them. Every time he would lose sight of them at that moment of realization that they were there. He continued until he heard a footstep. Alador looked up to see Henrick. He looked at the dragons who seemed unconcerned at the mage's sudden appearance.

"I thought I sent you to speak to a red dragon, not a family of blue ones." He clearly looked irritated. His hair was wild and unkempt, and his clothes were wrinkled and sweat stained. Alador could never remember seeing him in such a state.

"What happened to you?" Alador blinked, wide-eyed as he asked, though he suspected he already knew.

Henrick glanced over at the sleeping male that had curled up close to Alador. "It seems you have made friends who have a rather mischievous sense of humor." Henrick plopped down wearily beside Alador.

Alador was certain he saw Amaum smirk before he looked at Henrick. "Careful father," Alador teased. "You are starting to sound like a village elder. I thought you made this walk all the time."

"Not since I learned to use a travel spell," Henrick admitted. There was silence for a long moment before Henrick spoke. "It is father now?" Henrick asked.

"Don't question it and don't push it," Alador stated, looking off into the distance again. His tone was accepting and not upset.

A few moments passed again before Henrick questioned. "What are you doing?" Henrick looked at the odd expression on Alador's face.

"Trying to see air stones," Alador answered.

"Air stones…?" Henrick sounded confused.

"Has to do with weather spells; and don't ask! - it took me too long even to begin to understand, without having to try to explain it." He glanced over at the dragons, who all seemed to be content napping, and gave up, looking directly at Henrick instead. "I owe you an apology," he stated bluntly.

When Henrick started to speak, Alador put up his hand. "For once, Father, just listen. You are great at talking, but to be honest, you are crap at listening." He had the satisfaction of watching his father snap his mouth shut, though Henrick did look a little bit indignant.

"I am sorry I have taken my anger out on you. My image of an ideal father was moulded by Daezun decorum. I didn'ttake into consideration what growing up around Luthian must have been like - the lies you must have had to tell just to stay alive." Alador looked down at the two stones that Rena had placed side by side.

"I think I was angry that, if it were not for your magic, I could have had a Daezun father, and none of this would have happened to me. I could have grown up with Mesiande, become housemates and lived the quiet Daezun life." Alador took a deep breath, relieved that Henrick did not speak.

"But I realized that if this had been the case, Luthian would have eventually found another storm mage to cast his spell. I would have been without any power to save my people. Without Renamaum and you, the People might have well fallen into Luthian's trap to unify the isle." He looked over at Henrick. "If the Daezun fall, then there'll never be anyone to protect the dragons." Alador made that statement with firm conviction.

Alador was startled when Pruatra spoke behind him. "And that is exactly why we will follow you." She rose and lumbered around in front of the two mages before lying down again. Alador noted that she was not as graceful on land as Keensight. Her body was more elongated and her talons had webs between them, and her long tail reminded him of an oar with a single long line rising up and below the tail, much like small sails. Keensight's tail and back were covered in spikes.

Henrick and Pruatra's eyes met, and Alador swore that something passed between them. He did not miss the subtle shake of Henrick's head, nor Pruatra's slight nod. Henrick stood. "Greetings Lady Pruatra. I had heard tales of your great beauty, but in truth they fall far short. They pale in your glorious presence." Henrick swept an elaborate bow before the dragon.

"A slick tongue, fire mage, will not endear me to you. Pretty words are easily spoken and easily betrayed." Pruatra rose her head up. Alador swore that if there was such a thing as the Queen of Dragons, this one would be a candidate.

Henrick put his hand over his heart. "You wound me madam. Truer words have never left my lips."

"Says one who often says what he means but does not mean exactly what he says," Pruatra rumbled.

"Do you two know each other?" Alador was fairly certain he was missing something here.

"No!" both answered simultaneously.

Pruatra went on to explain, though her gaze still held Henrick's. "I recognize his type, be it in beast or mortal. A slick tongue, a charming demeanor and a quick wit...

Dancing about with such skill that he draws the feminine eye, and yet leaves a trail of hearts in his wake."

Alador laughed outright. "She described you perfectly."

"You slay me, madam." Henrick said with an obvious hurt tone. "I have only met two women who could tie my feet to a single abode. One is dead, and the other joined with my dear friend. How can one hope to find perfection when it has been lost twice?"

Alador looked at his father in surprise. This was a side of him that he did not know existed. "You do have a heart!" he exclaimed.

Henrick looked at the dragoness with a show of ire. "Now look what you have done: you've let the boy know I have feelings."

Pruatra shook her head. "I said nothing. You were the one who spoke," she pointed out.

"Damn dragon tricks," Henrick muttered and went stomping off.

Alador grinned after Henrick before looking at Pruatra. "Thank you. I don't think he would ever have told me that."

Pruatra looked at Alador, her mood sobering somewhat. "That is a man of secrets. I suspect there is much he has not told you for fear you will deny him. Give him time. Such males must come to the realization that the secrets they hold are the bars that bind them."

Chapter Nineteen

Sordith stepped out of the hall without Owen. He was leaving the man to watch over Keelee and the hall. The girl had returned in a high state of distress from the halls of the Blackguard. He did not know what it was about his brother and women, but it seemed he was the one who ended up consoling them. In this case, he smiled at the thought; the consoling had ended pleasantly.

He moved cheerfully down the stairs to the floor of the trench. Five of his men were sitting around at the base of the demonstration dais, a place that Aorun had often hung his vanquished from as a warning to others who disregarded the rules and whims of the Trench Lord. It lay empty today, as Sordith was more diplomatic in his leadership.

He eyed the men who were each at some small task, and noticed immediately that none met his gaze. "I will need two with me to inspect the miners' quarters," he commanded firmly.

Kester stood and stepped boldly forward. "I will attend you," he announced firmly. "Guarin will come too, won't ya Guarin." He indicated a decidedly weasely-looking man just behind him, who nodded a bit more reluctantly.

Sordith's eyes traveled over Kester. His swords were immaculate, and his armor had clearly been attended to recently. Like Sordith's own gear, the boots and leathers were shined to keep them supple and silent.

So, today would be the day, he concluded. He had known since he had killed and replaced the former Trench Lord, Aorun, that this day would come. There were always attempts on the new Trench Lord as the shuffle for power and place rippled down the ranks. He could tell that Kester was setting his sights high, just by the way he moved.

Sordith's eyes roved over the rest of those around the dais. Most were polishing weapons or seemed more interested in their boots than his presence. Yes, today would be the day that he had been dreading. He nodded to both men and boldly turned his back on them before striding off.

If there was going to be a fight, then he would choose a very public area: so there could be no doubt about who was Trench Lord. Kester was good with his blade and dagger; this could be a fight Sordith might lose - if he wasn't careful.

He purposely moved across the bridge to the side of the trench with more overhead exposure. A light rain was falling, creating run-off through the trench canal. He eyed it as he moved forward, very aware of the two men flanking him. However, he moved along the trench as usual, greeting people in his customary manner. He slipped trading tokens to various orphans and others without familial support. He suspected that Kester would make his move in the mine, where there was room to maneuver and drier conditions.

Sordith considered what he knew of the two men behind him. Kester had a good six inches on him in height, and nearly that in reach. The man was strong, and favored a slash and stab method of fighting. Kester was good, and in contests, often left with a purse. Guarin was the wild card. Sordith had not seen him fight much, and he knew the man was known for less than honorable tactics. He would be the one more likely to take sly advantage of an exposed flank.

Sordith eyed the widening area he was approaching. It was here that a short bridge had been built to prevent having to travel all the way to one end or the other. He considered the bridge with narrowed eyes as he approached it. It arched across the small canal, only about eight feet above the filth that ran below.

"Need to make a stop on the way," he called out to the men behind him. Turning his head to flash a grin at Kester, he moved to his right to cross the bridge. When he made it to the crest, he drew his blades and turned casually to face to two startled men behind him. They both took a step back.

"I get the feeling that we have unsaid words between us," Sordith stated casually. He planted his feet, making sure his stance was solid on the wet stone beneath him, and eyed both men's blades with a pointed look.

Kester grinned slowly as he drew his own sword and dagger. "I had planned to offer you a dry death." Guarin took a step backwards to give Kester more room, a little slower to draw his weapons.

"I prefer an audience," Sordith answered coldly. He eyed the denizens of the trench who were gathering on both sides of the canal in a wide arc around the three men.

Kester took advantage of Sordith's apparent distraction and rushed in, his sword slicing towards the Trench Lord's upper arm. Sordith had been watching his attacker with the corner of his eye, so was not caught unawares. He spun to the side to meet Kester's blade, but blinked when he realized that Kester had paused in his swing and altered its trajectory. He just managed to snap his sword to meet the freshly angled blow, and the sound of steel against steel silenced what chatter was left in the trench.

Sordith cursed as a stinging pain sliced up his right side. As the pain spread to his chest, he realized that by parrying the sword-thrust he had exposed his side to Kester's dagger. Staggering back, he swiftly found his footing and balance on the wet stone. Guarin had managed to dart past him during this swift encounter, forcing Sordith to meet attackers from both sides.

Kester pressed his advantage, launching his sword at Sordith's middle. The beleaguered Trench Lord managed to parry this blade with his left hand, the singing clash of blades echoing in the trench. Almost immediately he pivoted to meet Guarin's first strike with his right.

Kester stepped in swiftly, attempting to get another blow in with his dagger, but Sordith swept his right arm back while darting to his right, taking his attackers by surprise: the maneuver forced Kester round to his left, which meant his two assailants were now together and prevented by the narrowness of the bridge from mounting a simultaneous attack.

Sordith now commanded the width of the bridge. The only ways Guarin could have got behind him were by running the length of the trench to the next bridge or by wading across the putrid canal. The fumes off the filth made all their eyes water

Sordith and Kester then engaged in a deadly duel. Each blocked and parried as blow after blow rang round the narrow confines of the trench. Both were struggling to see in the constant drizzle of rain. The frenetic pace was wearing on both fighters...

Standing ready behind his more competent henchman, Guarin did not interfere for the moment and

Sordith was able to focus entirely on Kester. He was hard-pressed by the bigger man and barely managed to avoid a strike at his throat by crouching under the thrust. Desperate, he came up in a flurry of blades, pressing his treacherous assailant back. He got an opening and kicked Kester backwards, hope surging as the treacherous pretender slipped over on the slick stone of the bridge.

Sordith wasted no time in leaping past the sprawling Kester and going straight for Guarin: he was running out of energy, and these two could take turns. He needed to remove one or the other, and Guarin was the easier target. With a fierce cry he rushed at the slighter man, his swords clashing mightily with Guarin's. Guarin wasn't the swordsman Kester was and he was unable to respond as quickly. Sordith pressed him back and saw the blatant fear in his opponent's darting eyes. Feinting with his left, his right blade made it through Guarin's defenses and slashed across his thighs. He was able to get in another numbing blow to the man's right arm before he caught sight of Kester out of the corner of his eye; the big bastard was back on his feet, ready once more to launch into the fray.

Cursing, Sordith trapped Guarin's main sword with crossed blades, wrenching it from his numbed grasp and sending it flying. He grabbed the now empty, outstretched hand and jerked hard, sending the man stumbling past him and into Kester's path. Mouthing profanities of his own, Kester shoved his gibbering accomplice aside while attempting to recover a fighting stance.

Guarin completely lost his balance and went over the low stone wall into the seething mass of sewage and rainwater. Sordith heard him hit the stinking surface. He knew he was still alive by the splashing, retching and cursing coming from the center of the canal beneath his feet.

Kester lifted his blade and closed in, but now it was one on one. Sordith watched his opponent's shoulders and eyes carefully. Both men were panting with exertion, no energy left for insults or provoking banter. Sordith's skill was being sorely tested by the younger man. There was nothing he could do but fight on and hope that Kester made a mistake…

Kester's blade came at him, and Sordith crossed his swords, sliding them apart to divert it before attacking with three swift blows. Kester deflected them skilfully, spinning round and getting in another vicious stab to Sordith's side. The Trench Lord retreated, bleeding freely, his head beginning to spin.

Kester saw he had the upper hand and came in for the kill. Whirling, he caught Sordith's left hand and the hilt of his sword with such a blow that the blade shot from the wounded Trench Lord's grip and clattered to the flagstones. Grinning triumphantly, Kester raised his sword and put everything into a final lunge at Sordith's chest…

But he had underestimated his master and it was the last mistake he made. With sudden strength and ability that surged from deep within his genes, Sordith slipped sideways past the lunging blade and used the traitor's forward movement to drive his remaining sword deep into the man's gullet, severing his windpipe.

Blood gushed from the wound in Kester's throat, and he gurgled frantically, no longer able to breathe. Dropping both swords, he sank to his knees, clutching at his neck. In one swift movement, Sordith drove his sword through his opponent's chest, impaling his heart and stopping it in its tracks.

As the life drained from Kester's eyes, Sordith snarled between painful gasps of breath: "You... should have… brought… more men." He placed his foot on the dead man's chest and tugged the blade free from what had just become a bleeding piece of meat. He was severely winded, and his stomach was bleeding in two separate places.

He looked around wildly and spotted the weasel Guarin crawling out of the canal covered in blood, garbage and feces. Sordith retrieved his other sword and waited, blades held low as rain ran down them in bloody rivulets. Guarin made it to the bridge and, seeing Kester's bleeding corpse, tossed his blade aside.

Sordith eyed the man coldly. He would have killed him there and then, but he suspected that the wounds Guarin had suffered would fester from exposure to the filth in the canal. It would be a lingering, agonising death, almost certainly involving the amputation of a gangrenous leg - always supposing that Guarin lived long enough to endure it.

Sordith motioned to the blood-soaked corpse. "Drag that to the dais and see it properly displayed. Make sure that everyone understands the same fate will befall anyone who dares to make such an attempt in future." Sordith growled and motioned with his sword when Guarin hesitated. "NOW, or I will just kill you where you stand." The pool of blood around Kester was diluting in the falling rain, small red streams spreading down the bridge.

Guarin moved swiftly: grabbing Kester's hands and pulling the dead weight back the way they had come. Sordith stood motionless, blood spilling down his leathers, intent on not showing weakness. Only when

Guarin was far enough away did he choose to sheathe his blades.

He turned on his heel to stride to Madam Auries' haven of rest and recuperation. He trusted her to see to his wounds. The crowd parted wordlessly as the victorious Trench Lord made his way through.

It did not take him long to reach the brothel. Once inside, he leaned gratefully against the door jam with arms crossed, winking lewdly at the young women eyeing him. Here, he felt somewhat safe. He and Madame Auries had been friends for turns.

One of the girls hurried to his side. "May I see to my Lord's needs?" she murmured huskily, her eyes wide with awe.

"As much as that would probably be an hour well spent, lass, I fear the Madam will need to see to my personal needs today," he drawled. The girl noted the small pool of blood forming on the floor and her eyes widened.

Madam Auries hurried out of a nearby hall, one of the girls having already spread the word that the Trench Lord was on the premises. She hurried to Sordith's side, took one knowing look and put an arm around his uninjured side. She helped him towards her personal parlor.

As she passed, the Madam quietly gave firm orders. "Get me needle, thread, and hot water."

"And rotgut," Sordith added wearily as they left the main room.

"And a stiff drink for his lordship – bring the bottle," Auries called back as she led him away. Only once he was out of sight of all the other women did Sordith allow himself to let out a moan of pain. He accepted her help as she lowered him onto a settee.

"Here, lay back and let me have a look," she told him firmly. She deftly began to loosen his leather vest.

"I remember a time where you said that and we spent hours doing more than looking." He coughed and groaned as his attempt to tease fell flat. He didn't protest when she moved his hand from the wound in his side.

"By the Gods," Auries whispered as she traced the flow of blood from cuts in his leather armor. The severity of the wounds had been hidden by the confining leathers.

Sordith winced as she probed carefully. He coughed, then snarled out wearily: "No, by *an* idiot." He had planned to make light of the wound, but the adrenalin drained from him and pain claimed him. Sordith sank into dark oblivion.

Chapter Twenty

It took Alador two days before he could finally really see the airstones. Pruatra had shown her displeasure at his incapacity more than once, casting doubts as to whether Renamaum was present. When he was finally able to sense them - to truly feel and see them - he realized that they were everywhere. Rena had been right: there was no such thing as empty air. It was filled with constant movement.

The dragons each took turns working with him. Henrick sat by smoking his pipe, whittling, and watching. It was not lost on Alador that when he was working with one of the two younger dragons, Henrick and Pruatra were often deep in conversation. Rena was better at explaining mechanics, and Amaum was better at interpreting what was said using concepts that Alador could understand. The true lessons came from Pruatra, who pushed him to the point of exhaustion.

She had Alador speeding up the air stones, and then slowing them down. Often, she would have him speeding up half while slowing down another half to create wind. Soon, he learned how to choose what to speed up and what to slow down to direct the wind. Every evening, he would fall into an exhausted sleep.

He was famished all the time; he now understood why Henrick ate so much. The dragons were hunting for themselves, so they would leave Henrick fish or haunches to cook for the two mortals. There were rarely any leftovers. Alador ate between every lesson, feeling the drain on his own reserves every time he tried to do more than focus on a single task. He was pushed so hard that he was losing all sense of time; all that mattered was the next task.

He had just finished eating after such a session when Pruatra approached him. "It is time you made a true storm," she stated quietly. She drew her head high as she gazed at him confidently.

"I... are you sure? A simple rain or wind storm exhausts me." Alador rose to his feet.

"I am sure. Henrick tells me that you must soon return. We are running out of your allotted time." Pruatra dipped her head slightly.

Alador realized then that at least a week had passed. He sighed. A fortnight had not been enough time, he thought.

"All right... So, how do I begin?" He had learned not to gainsay Pruatra. Her answers were rarely confusing but her temper was short.

She turned in the direction of Keensight's cave. "Slow the air stones over the cave and bring the temperature down. Hold the slow air stones there."

"I... I don't really want to anger Keensight by bringing a storm down upon his cave," Alador stammered.

"He is not home," Pruatra stated.

"Are you sure?" He looked at Pruatra, wondering if he should question that.

"I am sure." She glanced at him with that familiar air of irritation.

Alador sighed. How had Renamaum kept this female happy? Her daughter had been right: she did have a quick temper.

"A lot of fish!" came the thought.

Alador just chuckled. He turned towards Keensight's cave and was able to swiftly cool the air.

"Good, now add water to the air," the dragoness firmly instructed.

Alador fed water into the air, watching a cloud form above the ridge. He fed it till he could sense a gentle rain falling.

"Speed up the airstones above us," Pruatra hissed, her tone condescending and cold. "But do not let go of the rain that falls over the cave."

That took all of Alador's concentration. The air around them slowly warmed from the fall chill it had held. His head began to throb as he held both activities in focus.

"Now, bring them together," Pruatra coaxed with a bit more approval. "Slowly now, bring the racing stones below your cloud. Let heat and cold combine."

Alador was so fixated on moving air stones that he did not at first notice what happened when the warm air slid underneath the cold rainstorm.

"Let the fast stones go," The dragoness voice held a touch of pride. "And watch."

Alador refocused on the actual sky rather than the stones, and watched as a big anvil began to form. The cloud began to darken. He let the storm go and watched as a few bolts of lightning flashed, then, slowly, it all began to dissipate, though they were assaulted by traces of the wind and rain. Its effects were impressive, although short-lived, because Alador had let go of the storm as instructed.

"To make a true storm, you will need to feed it longer, but I do not feel like being a target for lightning today." The amusement in her tone was not lost on Alador as Pruatra wandered off.

Alador stared in wonder at what he had created, and did not look away until only wisps of clouds remained.

He followed Pruatra over to the favorite spot she had chosen over the last few days and watched as she had stretched out. "What about a simple snowstorm?"

"Slower air stones, much water," she answered. "It will be harder when the sun is warm most days. The sun affects weather," she muttered with closed eyes, "and when it is higher in the sky, the air stones dance happily."

"Are dragons affected by cold, Pruatra?" Alador asked, a trifle concerned.

"Many hibernate when the air is cold, and sleep for longer periods of time. Red dragons, for example, seem to hate the cold. They will either sleep away winter or keep their caves warm with flaming rock piles," Pruatra murmured.

"Pruatra, if there are dragons living in the northern Daezun lands, you must warn them to prepare. It will be a hard winter there." Alador eyed her as he stood near her head, and he kept his hands clasped behind him.

This opened Pruatra's eyes. "How do you know this?"

"Because I will be the one delivering it," Alador declared.

"I did not teach you these things to have you bring harm to my kin or the People." She rose up as her face fins bristled out like miniature wings from her cheeks.

Henrick seemed to appear from nowhere. "Nor is it the boy's intent, Lady Pruatra. But some things must be done to bring about a greater good. Alador warns you now so that the warning can be passed. Dragons are far more immune to a hard winter than his own people. He will be warning them as well. " Henrick put both his hands out firmly. "Trust your mate; the boy cannot go against his own geas." He placed his hands upon Alador's shoulders, creating a united front.

Alador felt relief at Henrick's sudden appearance. He watched carefully as Pruatra slowly laid down her facial fins. "You know his plan? You agree, fire mage?"

"I do. It is a hard plan, but one that the leader of the betrayers will not suspect." Henrick's voice was soothing.

"You wear the skin of the betrayers; why should I believe you?" she hissed. Alador glanced back at his father, as the dragon had a good point.

"You don't have to believe me, Pruatra. You know Renamaum. As long as he has the power to manifest, do you not think he is guiding the boy?" Henrick squeezed Alador's shoulders as he kept Pruatra's gaze. "Well, except when they both lose their tempers at the same time, then neither one of them seems to have any sense," Henrick chuckled.

Alador frowned. He could hardly see how telling her that was helping, but for once he held his tongue. He had not meant to anger her, only warn the dragons to the northeast what was coming, so that then they could choose to hibernate or move to warmer climes.

Pruatra slowly settled, her face fins laying back but still quivering. "I do not like it," she grumbled unhappily.

"I don't like it either, Lady Pruatra," Alador finally spoke up again. "The woman I love, my family, will be the ones to feel the stress of extra mouths to feed as people move south. I will be warning everyone I can that won't carry my words to the High Minister." He moved out of Henrick's grasp and saluted the dragon. "I swear it."

"There will be death." Pruatra's stance was stamped in every word.

"Such is the way of war, Lady Pruatra. You know this better than any," Henrick gently offered. "But to do nothing, to let Luthian do as he wills, will mean many more deaths, and the increased hunting of your hatchlings."

"Why can't we just eat him?" Pruatra spat out, steam hissing from her nostrils.

"Another will just take his place. To effect real change, to really make a long-term difference in this battle, a ruler sympathetic to all races needs to be set securely in place." Henrick pushed his point strongly.

Alador blinked in surprise at Henrick. "I am just ending the bloodmining and getting rid of my uncle. I want no part in a grand war to grind the Lerdenians underfoot. Besides, Daezuns don't think that way. They work collaboratively to create a peaceful and content life, something Lerdenians seem to know nothing about."

"A good point, which is why it will need to be someone who understands both cultures." Henrick tapped his lip thoughtfully.

Alador shook his head. "Don't even look my way. That describes most of the Blackguard, and even yourself. I want no part of ruling the isle. I want a peaceful vale like this, where Mesiande and I can raise a family."

Henrick grinned at Alador as he clapped him on the shoulder. "I am not looking your way. I am just stating what needs to occur for real change. However, your footsteps are rather cast before you, and while you meander, fate keeps bringing you back to the path."

"No, Renamaum keeps bringing me back to the path, and when I am done with his geas, I will be free to tread my own path," Alador defended.

Rena sat up suddenly as if realizing something. "What if bloodmining is not my Sire's geas?"

"What? It has to be!" Alador spun around to look at Rena with a hint of panic.

"Did he tell you so?" Rena demanded.

"Well, not directly, no. He sent dreams," Alador said defensively.

Rena moved to Alador and pushed him slightly with her muzzle. "Dreams have many meanings. Are you sure the meaning you found was the one intended?" the young dragoness pressed. "Not so long ago, you saw yourself as a mere tool, a vessel. Now, you are a pseudo-dragon. Meanings change as facts reveal themselves."

"Wait, I never said I was a pseudo-dragon. I don't even know what that is! Pruatra called me that." Alador glanced at all of them.

Amaum chuckled. "He is rather dense at times. I would have thought our Sire would have chosen one more easily molded."

Henrick looked at Amaum. "More easily molded is more easily broken," he pointed out.

Alador felt as if he had lost control of the conversation completely, and in addition, they were indicating that he was missing some important point. "Well, what exactly is a pseudo-dragon?" he finally asked.

"It is not a true dragon, but has many characteristics of a dragon. They are seen as kin. Usually, because they are small, they are fairy mounts." Henrick moved between Rena and Alador. "In your case, you are slowly absorbing Renamaum. When he is completely absorbed, you will be as much a dragon in many ways as Rena or Amaum." His hand moved between the dragons and the young mage. "You are just smaller and, well, lack a tail and wings." This clearly amused Henrick as he grinned mischievously.

"Are you saying I am turning into a dragon?" Alador was in a full panic now.

Rena moved around Henrick and put a comforting wing about Alador. "You won't look like one," she offered shyly, "…if that helps."

"What will I look like?" He looked around at them all in genuine concern.

Henrick laughed. "As you do now, hence pseudo-dragon: you will still look like Alador, but you will also be dragon kin."

"When will this change start?" he asked with concern.

"It has been happening all along," Pruatra sadly added. "It is what Renamaum spoke of when he said he could not speak long. Soon you and he will be one."

"I won't be your mate, will I?" He looked a bit worriedly at Pruatra.

All the dragons rumbled. "Don't be silly; you are far too small and ugly to be my mate."

Alador breathed out his relief. While the ugly part stung a bit, he also did not want any large female dragon to insist on his being her mate. He only wanted one female, and she was not here.

Rena still had a large wing draped around him. "I don't think you're ugly," she quietly purred in his ear as she nuzzled him gently.

'Time to exit the wing hug', thought Alador. He politely stepped free. "You all think that Renamaum plans are more than closing the bloodmine?"

"Time will tell boy, time will tell." Henrick strode off to wherever he kept disappearing.

Alador watched as they all separated. Pruatra sank into the lake, followed by Amaum, as was their custom mid-afternoon. Alador realized they had left him with Rena and looked over as he heard her move.

Rena moved closer and sat on her haunches beside him. "You should try the storm again. Dame says you must leave in two days." She glanced at him in what Alador considered a suggestive manner, and appeared to flutter her eyelashes. "OR… we could get to know one another better."

Alador blinked in surprise and with more than a trace of foreboding as he realized what the dragon was suggesting. "Rena, your father lives within me. We are different species. I don't think us 'getting to know each other better' is a good idea, at least not any better than I know Amaum…" He was doing his best to sidestep her advance without hurting her feelings too much. "So, let's practice … for now." He turned his attention to the end of the lake and began again as Pruatra had instructed.

Beside him, Rena sunk into a pout, or at least, he thought it was a pout. He totally lost focus on the air stones as the realization struck him that another broomstick between the eyes was definitely in the cards.

Chapter Twenty-One

Alador went for a walk along the lake, needing some space away from the younger dragons for a time. Rena had insisted on staying close to him, and Amaum took great joy in teasing and playing pranks on his sister. While the two made him smile, it also made him miss home. They reminded him of his relationship with Sofie, and that brought up a sense of homesickness he had not felt in a while.

He stood staring out at the lake. The morning was crisp with the promise of winter. Alador could sense something different within himself since he had started casting the weather spell. There was this sense of strength and completeness that he could not remember having felt before when he cast his spells.

It had been less than two turns, he mused, since he was a powerless village outcast. How far he had come in that time: when he didn't even have the funds to buy an apprenticeship or leave home. Now he no longer had to worry about slips, and he had the power at his hands to bring a fruitful harvest or to destroy it completely. His mind moved to Mesiande's words about the man he was becoming. What kind of man did he wish to be?

He picked up a rock and tossed it into the still lake. There was no wind at the moment and the morning stillness had the lake looking like peaceful glass. The rock shattered the glimmering sheen, creating ripples that mirrored his thoughts. He was frustrated, and knew that he needed to quit acting like a child, but essentially, he had been one less than a turn ago. Like the lake, his peace had been shattered, and still the ramifications of the bloodstone rippled through his life.

"Renamaum, I know you can talk to me when you choose. Can you talk to me when the matter is not urgent?" Alador whispered to himself.

"*I can,*" came the internal response. The voice was reassuring and kind.

"Will you always be able to?" Alador continued to speak aloud. He looked around to see if any could observe him talking to himself.

"That will be up to you." Renamaum's tone and voice were clear.

"Up to me…?" Alador knelt down, resting on his own heels as he stared that the subsiding ripples. "How?"

"So far, you have been slowly absorbing what I was: my memories, power, and even some of my personality. You can continue to do so, or you can choose to allow me to exist within you. I will take no offense either way. You are well guided by those that are worth trusting."

Alador could picture the large dragon in the lake, gazing at him with calm assurance. "So eventually, you will, in effect, die if we continue as we have?" Alador struggled with this thought, mixed emotions swelled within him.

"All beings die," the dragon stated matter-of-factly.

"I thought dragons were immortal, though." Alador picked up another stone and tossed it in shattering the lake and making his mind image of Renamaum waver.

"Nothing is truly immortal; even the Gods eventually cease to be. We just appear immortal as we live such long lives."

"What is my geas?" Alador asked. Rena's challenge of his interpretation was worrying him. The dragon fell silent. Alador could still see the image so knew that the dragon had not totally withdrawn.

Alador pressed the matter. "Renamaum, you have forced me along a path I wouldn't have chosen; I've the right to know what it is you want from me," Alador said, and his angst was nearly palpable.

"Peace on the isle for all that live here: Daezun, Lerdenians and dragons."

Alador clenched his fists. "You ask the impossible from one who would still be a middlin if not for your stone. How, by the gods, am I to do that?" Alador wanted to strike out at something. Sheer frustration flooded through him. "This is… I can't do that!"

"Yes, you can. I have given you the power, and Keensight has ensured you have the means. You have but to trust him and Pruatra. You can and will do this," Renamaum insisted.

"If I refuse…?" Alador was panicking.

"Then you will die." Renamaum's simple answer was so emphatic that Alador dropped to his knees.

Alador did not speak to the dragon again, his mind racing with a million thoughts. Renamaum seemed to understand his need for space and receded to wherever he was living inside the mage. Alador sat on his knees, trying to shove fear out of his way. He would die if he attempted to fulfill the geas and he would die if he did not. The racing thoughts shattered the image of the dragon as he buried his face in his hands.

Henrick's soft step in the gravel along the edge of the lake drew Alador's attention. Henrick sank down to sit cross-legged beside his son. He picked up a stone to toss into the lake and looked at Alador. "And now you know," he said softly then tossed the rock sending ripples out again.

"How long have you suspected it was more than the mine?" Alador asked, looking up from his hands to his father.

"For a time." Henrick dug through the pebbles looking for another rock. "The interpretation that you had was plausible, but seemed a little shortsighted for the way Keensight had described Renamaum," Henrick answered. He tossed a second pebble, making cross waves in the ripples.

"How much did you hear?" Alador was not surprised to see his father; the man reminded him more and more of Sordith. They both seemed to show up when he thought none were about.

"Well, it was rather one-sided, but enough by your words and reaction to know he told you." Henrick pulled out his pipe and loaded it as he was speaking.

"He wants me to bring peace between Lerdenia, Daezun and the dragons. I could see maybe two, and that is doubtful, but all three…?" He looked back to Henrick.

"It is possible," Henrick answered. "A geas cannot be placed in the realm of completely impossible." He closed his bag of smoking herbs and placed it back into his belt pouch.

"Yes, but possible for me?" Alador searched his father's face.

"You have four dragons on your side. When was the last time you heard of that happening?" Henrick lit his pipe with a small flame from his finger. "Many would say that feat was impossible." He drew deeply on the pipe before he met Alador's gaze.

Alador had to admit he had hoped for one or maybe two. Having four agree to help with his cause was something he would not have predicted, and both dragons had indicated a promise of more to come.

"I don't even know where to start!" The panic in his tone was evident, as it was on his expression before he put both of his hands back over his face.

"That is strange," Henrick mused, then casually puffed out a smoke ring.

"What is?" Alador murmured between his fingers.

"Seems to me that you already have…" Henrick watched the floating smoke ring slowly dissipate. "You took down the stables. You just aligned with four dragons. You have a plan to take out the largest bloodmine. You are making decisions that will affect the Daezun as a whole, and yet sliding in the back door to make sure it minimizes harm." Henrick looked over at Alador. "I would say, my dear boy, you just need to keep doing what you believe is the next right thing to do. I suspect that it will all turn out in the end."

Alador was slowly musing over his father's wise words when he realized that Henrick must have spoken of that fateful night with Sordith. "Wait," Alador said as he lowered his hands. "You know about the stables?"

Henrick grinned at him. "It had you written all over it. The report of an attack on you the same night was brilliant. Who did you get to stab you, or did that happen in the stable house?"

Alador sighed. "We missed a guard and he got behind me. I am lucky to have lived." Alador subconsciously put a hand where he had seen the blade in his stomach. "Do you think Luthian knows it was me?" He scanned Henrick's face.

"Oh, he might suspect. The injury was a little suspicious. However, Sordith told me he went into detail with my brother on how Aorun planned the whole thing. I think he was trying to convince me of it as well." Henrick took another deep draw on his pipe

"Why didn't it work?" Alador pressed.

"Your questions about magic that takes one's will, combined with the fact that my favorite cloak smelled of blood." Henrick's nose wrinkled in disgust. "And as I said, it had your righteous sense of honor written all over it."

He gazed at his son curiously. "How by the Gods did you get them out of the city?"

Alador grinned. "No one wants to look in garbage carts. We smuggled them out during the morning rounds, covered in garbage."

Henrick laughed with delight to the point he had to wipe tears from his eyes. "Well played my dear boy. I would not have thought of that," he finally managed to acknowledge, though the chuckles continued.

Alador looked at Henrick in surprise. The older man did not offer compliments often, and that praise felt good, even though Alador had held him in disdain so recently. He looked back out at the lake. "I need you to be honest with me."

"I will if I can be," Henrick promised.

"What secrets are you keeping?" Alador moved in front of Henrick, blocking out the distraction of the still lake. "I need to know."

Henrick stared into Alador's eyes, clearly weighing his response. Alador did not miss a moment of pain on his face. "I cannot tell you yet. I will tell you this, though: not telling you right now is helping." He pulled his pipe out of his mouth and stared down at it. "I promise I will tell you the moment I think that not knowing is no longer helping."

Alador did not like his answer, but for now, he would accept it. "Have you ever lied outright to me?" He gave his father time to form his answer, and both sat quietly for a time.

Henrick looked at him finally. "Yes, I have lied outright to you about one thing: to protect the secret I will not tell you yet."

Alador gave a frustrated sigh as he threw up his hands. "I do not see how a lie or a secret will help me."

"What we do not know cannot be used against us. If Luthian learned what I keep for you, we would both be dead within days. It is… the nature of it is something you would not be able to hide." Henrick sounded a bit regretful.

"Tell me this, then. Does keeping this secret in any way harm my family or Mesiande in Smallbrook?" Alador looked worriedly at his father.

This time, Henrick did not pause. "No!" he said emphatically.

Alador breathed out slowly. "Then I will wait until you are ready to tell me." He did not like a secret between them, but at the same time, Henrick's honesty that there was a lie and a secret was more reassuring than a glib no would have been.

Both fell silent and neither looked into the other's eyes for a long moment. Finally, Henrick tapped out his pipe out and rose. "We should join the others."

Alador rose, too. "There is one more thing. Keensight said to ask you for the medallion, and to have you teach me to use it." Alador knew that his learning to travel was essential in order to carry out the first few things that he had planned to do for his people and the dragons. He would have to think more on the rest of it later. He would focus on the bloodmines for now.

Henrick pulled a chain from around his neck. The medallion slipped free as he pulled it forward and handed it to Alador. The medallion was black, and etched into it was a dragon's eye. In the pupil of the eye was a silver hour glass.

"This is beautiful," he murmured as he took and examined it. "How does it work?" He swore he could see the sand moving within it.

"Well, the work part is easy," Henrick said, watching the medallion as if he just parted with a best friend. "You imagine clearly where you wish to be and say the words I will give you; then you and anything you hold will appear there." Henrick's tone held an edge of warning.

"Your tone suggests there is a catch." Alador looked up at his father as the awe melted away in the face of his father's tone.

"If where you imagine has changed - such as a tree fell in a clearing for example - you could appear with it in you or you in it: a painful - and often deadly – outcome," Henrick explained carefully.

"So you need to imagine a place that you are certain will not have changed since you have been there last?" Alador had thought it was a spell, not a magical item.

"Correct. You must be certain. To go home, for example, I use my bedroom, and my servants have orders to leave nothing lying about nor to move any furniture, even to clean." Henrick's eyes were still locked on the medallion.

"This is important to you, isn't it?" Alador had seen that look before, but could not quite remember where or when.

"It is. Keensight gave it to me, and he received it from the Gods themselves when he sought a boon from them." Henrick blinked a few times then looked up.

"That is part of the secret, isn't it?" Alador touched his father's arm. "Keensight was that way with the items in his pile." He watched his father suspiciously.

"Yes, and I have said too much, so let us return to the others," Henrick gruffly answered with a hurried smile.

"Wait! What are the words?" Alador asked, still holding his father's arm.

Henrick smiled. "Persvek sia ricin, nomeno goawy si ocuir origato sia adon vur rasvimi qe."

Alador recognized the tones of it as the draconic that Keensight had spoken, though it did not roll off Henrick's tongue with the same ease.

"Keensight taught you draconic?" Alador sounded amazed.

"Some of the knowledge he taught me does not translate well to our common tongue. So yes, he taught me what I needed to know to do the things he wishes me to do for him." Henrick answered. "Let us go a phrase at a time." He repeated the first three. "persvek sia ricin."

Alador and Henrick worked for an hour on mastering the phrase before they returned to the others. As they walked back up the shoreline, Alador finally asked his father the question plaguing him.

"You said you learned what you must so as to complete Keensight's wishes…" Alador tucked the medallion out of sight. "Are you his servant?"

"I said he let me live, Alador. I never said that remaining Henrick Guldalian came without a cost." Henrick chuckled softly as he parted the brush where the three blue dragons waited.

Chapter Twenty-Two

The day to leave finally arrived, and Alador found that he was sad about it. The time spent with the dragons had been wondrous, every small one's dream and more. It had also been tiring, enlightening, and frustrating. He could not seem to shake Rena's constant attempts to flirt with him. He had finally gone to Pruatra, whose only advice had been that it was a phase that would pass after her next mating. This did not reassure Alador at all. He was fairly certain at this rate, the dragon would come calling for him when that time came.

He was sitting by the lake when the female in his thoughts strode up and plopped down beside him. "Don't you like me, Alador?"

He glanced over at Rena to see her eyes on him. They were excessively large at the moment, as well as tearful. "Yes, I like you very much. I think you are going to be a great sister to me," Alador offered in an attempt to deflect.

"I don't want to be a sister," Rena argued. "I think you are amazing and brave."

Alador scooted closer to her and put a hand to the side of her great muzzle. "Okay Rena. Let's think about this. First, I am mortal and you are dragon. You would never be able to mate with me or have fledglings." He waited for her to counter this most important point.

"I could go to the Gods and ask to be made a mortal," she quickly offered.

"You would not like being mortal Rena. Never to feel the wind beneath your wings, to die in a short time, as is the nature of mortals," he countered. "There are many chores to being a mortal that you don't have to worry about as a dragon, such as gathering water, or lighting a fire just to stay warm." He ran his hand over her nose crest gently.

"Then, you could go ask to be a dragon," she amended.

Alador sighed. "I do not want to be a dragon, Rena. I can't complete my geas as a dragon," he looked at the water rather than the dragon, letting his hand drop away.

"Then ask after," she stated huskily as she laid her muzzle against his leg. Her voice took on a pleading edge. "I love you."

"You have a crush, Rena. It is not love. I am just different, and that appeals to you." He looked at her and replaced the comforting hand on her head. He knew how it felt to be denied one you were in love with, and was truly regretting having to hurt Rena.

She raised her head, shaking loose his gentle touch. "I know the difference between a crush and love. I have mated, I am not a hatchling!"

"Then why aren't you with that male and your eggs?" Alador gently questioned.

"The mating didn't take," she snarled.

Alador winced. Again, he had blundered into another's wounds without thought. He sighed softly. "You can't be in love with me, Rena." He shook his head sadly.

She rose up indignantly on all fours. "I know it is love. I would die for you!" She hissed at him like a snake.

"May you never have to, Rena." Fearful of losing her support and genuinely not wishing to hurt the dragon, he rose up and hugged one leg. "I tell you what: we can have this discussion again after my geas is fulfilled - if you still feel this way." *'If nothing else,'* he thought, *'this would buy time.'*

"Do you promise?" She put her muzzle so close to his face he could feel the warm steam from her nostrils.

"I promise," he swore solemnly.

"You know a dragon can't break a promise, right?" she asked suspiciously. Her eyes closed tight as she reminded him, "And you are a pseudo-dragon, so that counts."

"I will not break this promise." Alador put his hand over his heart. "If you still feel the same way when it is all done, we will talk."

Rena heaved out a great sigh. "Henrick said to come find you and tell you it is time."

Alador squeezed her leg tightly. "If it is any consolation at all, Rena, I have truly enjoyed my time with you and your family."

"It would mean more if you had left off family," she said dejectedly, then turned and dragged her feet as she led him back to the others. Her head hung low as she plodded along.

Alador felt horrible, but at the same time, the last thing he needed was an infatuated dragon showing up at the worst possible moment. He had been careful not to mention Mesiande. He was fairly sure that a jealous female dragon was not a sight he ever wanted to see.

"You have no idea," Renamaum quipped.

"I don't want one. I am sorry your daughter seems to have taken a liking to me," Alador thought with true regret.

"What is there not to fall for? She is right: you are brave, and so far, you have the best parts of me."

Alador could feel the dragon's amusement coursing through him. "Do all dragons suffer from hubris?" he asked. "It seems to be a consistent trait." The internal conversation continued as they approached the others.

"Yes, so remember that, as you become increasingly dragonlike…," Renamaum cautioned.

"I will keep it in mind." Alador smiled. "We will talk more, I am sure," he quipped, and smiled at that thought as they entered the clearing.

Henrick eyed him and handed him one of the supply packs. "I had to send the lexital home, as letting it be a target for predators was not an option. You will have to use the medallion to return us to Silverport."

"Are you sure I have it down well enough?" Alador asked worriedly as he took the pack. Its weight took him by surprise and it fell heavily at his feet.

"Let us hope so. I really don't wish to be part of your bed." Henrick grinned at him, helping him don the pack.

Once he was encumbered, Alador turned to the three dragons standing side by side before the peaceful lake. The scene still struck him as surreal. He moved closer to Pruatra. "I will never be able to repay you for the help that you have given me," he told her, meeting each mournful gaze one by one.

Amaum took a step forward and bowed his head low. "You honor our father. Complete his geas, and the debt is repaid." Amaum's words held an edge of formality.

Pruatra nodded in approval to her son. "Well said," she seemed to cough out.

Rena looked at Alador. "We have already said our good-byes. I have your promise held deeply."

Alador nodded to Rena. He had best not put this off longer or he would stay here till the snow fell. Then again, the air felt cold enough that it was probably not long off. "I will visit again when the first buds form in spring: to fill everyone in on the details of the plan. We will strike the bloodmines at the new moon following. Until then, may the gods keep the wind under your wings." He bowed low.

Pruatra nodded as their gaze met. Alador felt a lump in his throat, but the dragoness said nothing in response. The three took to the air… It still amazed Alador that such large and heavy creatures could fly. His hair whipped about his face in response to their first few wing thrusts. He watched them until they were small blips, and then turned to Henrick.

"There is one more thing I would speak of before we go. I have a problem I cannot solve alone, and one I didn't wish to speak about till the dragons had left."

Henrick hefted his pack a bit up off his shoulders. "You have my attention and… curiosity."

Alador nodded and ran a hand through his hair, smoothing it from the recent tousling of the wind. "Renamaum has said that I have two paths concerning him, and both have their benefits and their costs. I truly do not know which way to go."

"I see." Henrick frowned. "What are the options?"

"I can totally absorb him and truly become a pseudo-dragon. I will, in effect, know all he has ever known," Alador sighed. "But he will cease to exist. Or I can let him live inside me, gaining what I can that will not dissolve who he is, and he can counsel me."

"I can see the benefits of both. What costs do you see?" Henrick tapped his lips considering.

"Well, if I absorb him, then Pruatra and his children will lose him a second time. I don't know if I could bear to do that to them. And if I did, what if they no longer wished to help me?" Alador looked down at his feet.

"Yet if I let him go on living within me, I know there are things he feels strongly about. What if something I have to do to complete his geas is not on a path he foresaw? If that happens, he could assert control, or at the very least be a distraction in a critical moment."

"It seems to me that you already know what your choice should be," Henrick answered gently.

"I know, I know; but… I don't like it." Alador frowned. "It's just that I gain from either choice, but at a price."

"The choices a man must make when facing war are never without cost: never entirely good and right, but hopefully least bad and wrong." Henrick took his son's hand and clasped it firmly. "I swear to you, I will follow you to the very end. I know Pruatra feels the same way, so I have a suggestion…"

"What is that?" Alador looked at Henrick in amazement.

"There is a shape-shifting spell that only lasts about an hour. I can find that spell for you. Let Renamaum take his form one last time and bring proper closure to his family," Henrick eyed his son closely as he let go of Alador's hand.

"That is even possible?" Alador returned his father's gaze with deep concern.

"Yes, for a short time." Henrick answered. "Renamaum would know how much time he had, and he would make good use of it."

Henrick was right: Alador knew that he had to absorb all of Renamaum or he would never complete the geas. He could feel that in the very depths of him. This suggestion from his father would at least allow some dignity and closure. "Then find the spell. We need to make this happen soon. I am leeching Renamaum away piece by piece..." Alador was worried about the reactions of the three blue dragons. Renamaum could explain it much better.

Henrick nodded. "I will get everything ready." Both men shifted uncomfortably in the emotion-filled silence.

"Okay, so how do I bring you with me with this thing?" He pulled the medallion from beneath his tunic and looked at it.

"We just have to be in contact," Henrick answered, moving closer to Alador.

Alador then understood why Henrick had insisted on his putting the pack on: he needed both hands free - one to hold the medallion and the other to grasp his father. He closed his eyes and pictured his bedroom at his father's house, choosing a space well away from any furniture. When he felt centered on his view of his room, he whispered the words…

A strange sense of movement and magic washed over him. The feeling was both exhilarating and a bit nauseating; much like falling in love for the first time, he mused. When the ground felt solid under his feet once more, he slowly opened his eyes. He hoped to the gods that he had not just put them somewhere else or in anything. He slowly smiled as he realized they were both safe in the unoccupied part of his room.

"Well done, son." Henrick smiled down at him. "You are stronger than even I had given you credit for. I cannot imagine what you will be able to do when you have fully taken in Renamaum's gift."

"That was amazing," Alador whispered.

"Dragon magic usually is." Henrick pulled free of Alador, who had not yet thought to let him go.

"Henrick…" Alador was unsure of how exactly to ask this question.

"Yes?" Henrick took off the pack.

"Are you under a geas from Keensight?" Alador asked. "Is that a part of your secret?"

Henrick looked to his feet before finally looking up at Alador. "In a manner of speaking... Ask me no more, boy. All you do is beg lies from my lips. I cannot tell you more right now."

Alador eyed the obvious regret written on his father's face. "All right. It… I just felt some similarities in what you said yesterday. However, I will ask no more for now," he promised.

Henrick nodded. "I will leave you to sort this stuff out. Have a servant carry off what you don't think you need or want. When will you see Luthian again?"

"Isn't there some big ball tonight or tomorrow?" Alador asked, considering his father's question carefully. He shrugged the pack to the ground.

"I believe that it's tonight. I didn't think you cared for such pomp and circumstance..." Henrick looked at Alador almost hopefully.

"Well, I am not due back to the guard until tomorrow. I think it's time that I made an entrance in my own right, rather than traipsing after my uncle in the shadow of his power and position," Alador mused.

"What do you mean, exactly?" Henrick's look changed from hope to one of concern.

"I think I will publicly claim my birthright as his heir." Alador was amused by the look on his father's face.

"Oh, now I am going! I need to make sure I arrive before you. I want to see the look on Luthian's face when you claim your position as a right, rather than a result of his largesse." Henrick put his hands together as if praising the Gods.

Alador smiled. "I think that Luthian needs to see that his 'storm mage' comes at a price. I can't see a better way of making that clear in the public domain. He has already claimed me: so it is time I took my place as a Guldalian."

"I had the perfect robes made for the next ball. I'll let you see to the packs…" Henrick turned and hurried off make himself more presentable.

Alador chuckled. He had no idea that Henrick was so fond of such public events. He had not seemed that fond at the dinner they had been forced to attend; maybe he just did not like his brother's dinners, Alador mused. Alador had never been to a ball, but he understood that there was dancing. He forced away the image of Mesiande the night of the trader's feast and the homesickness that welled up within him. He had been forced to endure a few lessons from a dance master, insisted upon by both Henrick and Luthian. He knew he could pull off one or two of the simpler tunes.

He turned and moved to his balcony, looking out over the city and off to the forests. Now, what to wear? It would need to be more spectacular than anything that Luthian had created, or at least comparable in excellence. It needed to make a statement of his sphere and his power. He sat staring off into the woods until finally an idea came to him.

He moved to his closet and changed into the black leather pants that signified membership of the Blackguard. Moving to the mirror, he then formed a dark blue, pleated knee-length tunic cut away at the front from the waist down, showing his uniform pants and shining boots beneath. The tunic had sleeves at first, but he removed them so as not to become too heated when dancing. Over that, he created a full-length robe of silver, the sleeves draped slightly giving him freedom to move. Smiling, he added a significant detail to the back of the robe: a light blue panel on which was woven a large image of Renamaum, standing out proudly in a filigree of intricate silver and midnight blue threads.

He surveyed himself in the mirror. Even so, the image was not quite complete.... The young mage added a hood to hide his drab brown hair and the odd white stripe, forming it to drape all the way down to his shoulders. He added a circlet to hold it in place with a shimmering blue stone. Turning in the mirror, he smiled. Even in Silverport he had never seen a mage so bedecked before, but then, he had never been to a ball, either.

Alador carefully removed each layer, not wanting to have to form them again, and laid them out on the bed. He called for a servant and had him go through the packs with him. There was nothing in there he had any use for, and he suspected Henrick of landing him with a task he couldn't be bothered doing himself. He grinned at the thought, whereas not a month before, it would have angered him. Dirty and famished, he ordered a bath and a tray of food, then sat down to plot on how to present himself tonight.

Tonight, he would claim equal partnership with Luthian: a lie he would repeat a thousand times. Tonight, he would declare it for the first time before all of Silverport's ruling mages. He smiled coldly. Dorien, his oldest brother, had told him to keep his enemies close. He could not think of a more fitting place in which to transform himself into the kind of skilled courtier that his father presented himself as. It would be harder for

Luthian to make him disappear if thereafter he gained in popularity and surrounded himself with support.

The steaming bath arrived and he sank gratefully into it. He realised he now understood Henrick in a way he never had. The memory of the cold words he had thrown at his father made him wince. By being a flirt and a gallant in court, Henrick had made it harder for Luthian just to do away with him. Any removal of Henrick would have to be made to look like an accident, or appear to have been carried out by other hands.

The game that this city played had just got a bit more interesting. It was like the game he used to play with Terent: sometimes, you had to sacrifice pieces to win. However, the sacrifice had to be subtle: anything too obvious betrayed your intentions and against another skilful player often ended in a loss. He saw no difference in the game of politics that the Lerdenians played. Their game pieces were alive, but they were game pieces nonetheless.

Chapter Twenty-Three

Luthian stood near the dais of the main hall. The tables for banquets were cleared away, and instead, small tables of titbits and drink were set about. Benches lined the walls for those that would become tired of standing. His own corner was set up with comfortable chairs, far from the dais, as that was where the musicians would play from to project the music. Satisfied that all was as it should be, he nodded to the servants to let in the guests arriving early.

He moved to greet each as they were announced. Eventually, there would be too many, but he always tried to have a morsel of conversation with those that had chosen to come early. He was surprised to see the Trench Lord, Sordith, was one of the early arrivals. He moved to welcome him with an outstretched hand. It always pleased him to see the concerned looks by others when he and the new Trench Lord were of one accord.

"Good eve, Lord Sordith." Luthian offered his arm and Sordith clasped it warmly. "I hope you are finding the transition to power is going well."

"Well, other than that strange riot that erupted right after you left my hall..." Sordith eyes met Luthian's in a manner that let the High Minister know he was aware of the causes, "...things have been very quiet. Shipments have been coming as expected, and I have managed to reduce the overcrowding a bit." Sordith held his hand against his stomach.

"Oh?" Luthian looked at him in surprise. "How did you manage that?"

"Upped the wages of the miners and offered to let them build homes in the mining excavations that have petered out while providing them with furnishings at cost." Sordith smiled. "Production in the mine increased almost immediately by ten percent."

Luthian pondered this for a few moments, then slowly smiled. "So by investing a few slips up front, you increased your yield significantly. Wise man... I think I am going to like working with you." Luthian's tone held true admiration. If the man could improve conditions in the trenches somewhat, there would be fewer souls willing to throw away their lives in an uprising.

Yes, he mused, he would have to keep Sordith around for a while. "I think I would like to have you at council meetings. I will have my convenor send you the proper passes and times." He spotted another member of the council that he needed to speak with before the man was in his cups. "Now, if you will excuse me."

Sordith bowed, but not as low as usual, wincing slightly. "Anything to be of service, my Lord."

Luthian moved past him, intent on the council member. His mind was still on the Trench Lord, however, as the man's physical discomfort had been obvious. He'd been severely injured lately, Luthian mused. How had such a man risen so quickly in the trench? He could only put it down to that quick mind, for he did not seem to be the archetypal warrior: it was usually a man of the sword who rose to the top of the dung heap in the lower city. However, he had clearly emerged the victor from a power struggle of the trench, and that could not be ignored.

Luthian approached most members of the council over the next half hour. By far the majority were pompous fools easily led by their greed and sloth, but there were a few that he had to be careful of: men who would swiftly take his place if he faltered. He was ever aware of their movements, their bed mates, and even their preferences in particular habits and pleasures.

He was surprised when his brother was announced. The High Minister had expected Henrick to miss this ball, as he and Alador were supposed to be in some remote area practising. Had the two weeks ended already?

"Henrick Guldalian, Mage of the Fifth Tier and Master of the Sphere of Fire," the doorman announced.

Many eyes were drawn to the handsome mage's appearance. Luthian's eyes narrowed as his brother almost immediately seemed to command the attention of the women present. Henrick seemed unaffected by the attention. Unlike his usual entrances, Henrick made straight for his brother, only stopping to give polite nods of greeting.

Luthian picked up a goblet from a nearby table as his brother approached him. He handed it over, choosing to speak first. "I had not expected to see you," he admitted, his tone only loud enough for Henrick to pick up. He looked at Henrick curiously.

Henrick took the goblet with a smile. "Ah yes, well, Alador was quite insistent we make it back in time for your gathering." Henrick snagged a plate of sweetmeats from a passing servant and set it close by before responding. "You do not often host such socially significant events." Henrick popped one of the meats into his mouth as he glanced around at the swelling crowd of finely dressed mages.

"Oh..." Luthian looked about for Alador, "Has he arrived? I did not hear him announced."

"He was taking a frightful time dressing, so I left him behind. I didn't want to miss the first dance. You know how I love to avail myself of the opportunities it presents." As they spoke, Henrick was busy catching the eyes of different women and toasting or nodding to them. He didn't seem to distinguish between bonded and unbonded, as far as Luthian could tell..

"Yes: you hardly miss a dance if you can help it," Luthian chuckled before taking a deep sip.

The two men stood side by side in silence; each watching the crowd carefully until the music started up for the first dance. Henrick excused himself and set his glass down. Luthian made his way to his corner of choice. He usually did not dance, finding it demeaning to be on the floor apparently indistinguishable from the other nobles of the city.

The High Minister smiled and shook his head as he watched Henrick make for the very desirable widow, Lady Thoren. The woman's green dress sank so low between her breasts that Luthian was unsure how she kept them within it. Probably some small cantrip in place, for he had no other explanation as to how she curtsied so low and still maintained even a minimal amount of decency. He smiled, considering dispelling such magic, but decided it was not worth his time. Besides, how many mages would such a spell disrobe? He chuckled and returned his attention to Henrick.

It was rumored that Henrick and the widow had been seen on more than one occasion slipping from some social event in one another's company. Luthian could not blame his brother: the woman would have been striking on any man's arm. He smiled into his cup. Luthian would not have to worry about his brother's antics much longer. He was merely waiting for his usefulness to Alador to wane before he had Sordith assassinate him.

Luthian was watching the door more than the dancers. He was alone in his corner for now. None would ask to join him, as it was well known that Luthian only wanted the company of those he personally invited. The only exception to that was Henrick. Luthian glanced at the entryway again; surely the boy could not have taken that long dressing? When the music fell away from the first dance, Henrick joined him.

"You should have waited for him," Luthian scolded unhappily. "Maybe he does not plan to attend, after all," Luthian complained as Henrick sank into one of the chairs.

Henrick just nodded to the door. Luthian turned to see a hooded man, dressed in layers of blue and silver, step up beside the doorman.

"Announcing Alador Guldalian of the Third Tier, the son of Henrick Guldalian and heir to the Guldalian line. Master of the Blue Sphere." The staff hit the floor and the doorman stepped back.

Much of the talking had stopped at this announcement, and whispers filled the air. Luthian stood wide-eyed at his nephew's bold proclamation. He glared at his nephew then swiftly turned and nodded to the musicians to strike up the next song. Luthian turned back to watch as his nephew arrogantly strode into the room.

"Did you know he was going to do that?" Luthian turned on his heel to glare at his brother.

"Yes, I did!" Henrick applauded softly as he caught Alador's gaze. "The look upon your face was priceless, and worth every ounce of trouble the boy has been to me." Henrick picked up a goblet and toasted his brother.

Luthian was furious and he gritted his teeth tightly in an attempt to get a hold of his own anger. He should have intervened at this bold proclamation. The half-breed had just publicly declared himself Luthian's heir, and short of creating a huge scandal, Luthian was forced to accept it, either until he had his own son, or until he found a way of discrediting his jumped-up nephew. The problem with that, though, was he needed Alador's spell-casting powers to bring his own plan to fruition. He had been outmaneuvered by a half-Daezun, and a youth, to boot.

"I should roast you where you sit," Luthian hissed angrily.

Henrick waved his hand indifferently as he swallowed his wine. "I told you, anytime you are ready. I think you will find I have learned a few things since we last came to blows." Henrick sat the glass down and rose to his feet. "On that note, I think I will find more pleasant company and leave you two to speak."

Henrick passed Alador, and Luthian did not miss the wink that Henrick gave the boy. He watched Alador approach and forced a welcoming smile to his face. His corner was now the focal point of the ball, though some had moved to the dance floor when the musicians had struck up their tune.

Alador offered his uncle his hand and Luthian clasped it in welcome. He blinked in shock as Alador pulled him close to offer him a familial hug. "It is so good to see you, Uncle."

Luthian pulled free as soon as he was able. "A bold move, boy, and one that could easily have ended your miserable existence. How dare you declare yourself my heir without consulting me!" he hissed so only Alador could hear.

"Now, now, ***Uncle***... we both know you don't have a son. Henrick has so far claimed no other son with the full-blown powers of an *exceptionally* strong mage. So who does that leave? And it isn't as if the title of 'High Minister' is part and parcel of your personal estate…"

Alador was the picture of innocence. A servant approached very hesitantly and offered a goblet of wine to Alador while darting glances at the clearly irritated High Minister. Alador took it with the calm assurance of a High Minister in waiting.

Luthian stared at him for a long moment then sat down. He crossed his legs and indicated for Alador to sit in the chair close to him. "You had damn well be able to cast that spell," he snarled quietly as he watched the swirling movement of the dance floor.

Alador took a long drink before answering. He shifted to get comfortable in the chair as he too watched the colorful array. His answer, however, was just as serious as Luthian's own tone had been. "I can cast your spell," he stated behind the cover of the goblet.

Luthian also took a drink and nodded to a passing fourth tier mage before asking: "With control…?"

"I can control it as long as I can see the area it is intended to hit. Once I am no longer present, the storm will do as it wishes." Alador smiled at a young woman who had been staring at him.

"When can you start?" Luthian eagerly licked his lips.

"After the first natural snowfall," Alador answered. "It is easier to cast, and will last longer after I am no longer present, if the natural conditions favor the spell."

"That should be soon, if it has not already occurred." Luthian sat the goblet down and leaned forward with obvious excitement.

"I foresee a problem, Uncle." Alador set his own goblet aside and looked over at Luthian.

Luthian did not wish to hear of problems; he wanted solutions. "And, what is that?" he demanded.

"How will you explain my two and three day absences from the guard?" Alador studied his uncle.

Luthian had not considered that. The lad had not been in the guard a full turn yet. He was hardly going to be considered for an assignment. *'Unless…'* he thought, *'the boy tested out as a mage.'* "I will lift the ban on testing half-Daezun. You declared yourself a master of the blue sphere. I hope you weren't bragging. If you can pass a fourth or fifth tier test, then I can have you assigned to me," Luthian declared. "I will just need to get it past the Council."

"Why, Uncle," Alador looked over in feigned surprise. "I would never have thought of that. You continue to amaze me." Alador met Luthian's calculating gaze evenly. They both were silent for a long moment.

"Liar," Luthian chuckled. "I am going to regret teaching you the way of Lerdenian politics, I can see that already."

Alador just smiled. "By your leave, Uncle. I have been in the wilderness with no one but Henrick, who is quite full of himself. I would love a pretty woman on my arm for a few hours before I report to the guard."

Luthian nodded as his gaze swung to Henrick. "Alador, do you have a use for him? - your father?"

Alador stood and turned to look Luthian directly in the eyes. "Any use that I had for Henrick is long since past." He glanced over at his father. "He is a stuffed dandy with hardly a thought beyond his own pleasures. He withholds critical knowledge and... I suspect he works against you." Alador's tone took on a bitter edge as he looked back to Luthian.

"I am sure there is some long mission I can set him to complete that will take him out of our way. Perhaps some ambassadorial position on the mainland..." Luthian smiled and waved Alador off. “Go! Enjoy yourself. After tonight, you and I have much work to do.” Luthian dismissed his nephew with the hint of a smile.

After the boy had wandered off to walk the edges of the dance floor, Luthian sent for Sordith. It did not take long before he had the Trench Lord sitting beside him.

Sordith slid into the indicated chair. “You have need of me, my Lord?”

“Do you remember that matter we spoke of, the problem I needed... removed?” Luthian’s eyes found Henrick swirling another matron around the floor.

“Indeed, you had bid me wait,” Sordith acknowledged, having followed Luthian’s gaze and swiftly looked away.

“Do not stay your hand any longer. I would see it done within a fortnight.” Luthian picked up his goblet, which had been filled by attentive servants when he was not looking. He took a sip as he glanced at Sordith.

“I will arrange it as soon as possible,” Sordith answered with a nod. “It will take some time to find an arrangement that will not seem too premeditated.”

“I do not care about the details, just see the matter closed.” Luthian was watching his nephew. The boy had led some shy wallflower onto the floor. He had to admit that it did not take the boy long before he had the young woman gazing at him with an admiring smile on her lips. Alador was gaining his father's way with women and Luthian's skill at politics. He knew that could be dangerous in the longer term.

“Is there anything else, High Minister?” Sordith asked politely.

“No, no. Go enjoy yourself.” Luthian waved dismissively. His mind was racing with the facts he had learned and the swift changes he would need to make. He did not even register the shallowness of Sordith's bow as his mind leaped ahead.

Alador declaring himself in the way that he had could be used in Luthian's favor. As High Minister it behoved him to be seen as the kind benefactor, slowly uniting the isle. Allowing half-breeds to test would be a first step into showing an increased acceptance of Daezun with magical capabilities. Yes, he could use this to his advantage. He sat mulling the situation over for some time before he realized the second set was done. There would be others who craved the privilege of being seen in the High Minister's corner. He had social duties to complete.

Chapter Twenty-Four

Alador moved away from Luthian with a self-satisfied smirk. He knew that he had caught Luthian off guard and that, short of provoking a round of even greater gossip, Alador had fairly tied his hands. Things had gone exactly as he had hoped. He had freed up testing for half-Daezun, and he had no doubt he could test at least to the fourth tier. His magic was only getting stronger with each passing day: gifts from Renamaum as the two were slowly merging.

He made his way around the dance floor, stopping at the far side. He was not surprised to see that Sordith had already been beckoned to his uncle's side. The last few words that they had spoken were almost certain to incite the attack on his father. They would have to coordinate with Sordith to make the attack appear solid, or Sordith would lose positioning. He and Sordith had most of the details worked out as to how this attack would occur. They just had not bothered to fill in Henrick yet. He smiled at what Henrick would think when they did share this minor element of the grand plan.

He spied the young woman that he had nodded to earlier. She still had not taken to the dance floor, so he moved his way closer. The musicians were starting a number whose movements he recognized, so he approached her carefully. She reminded him of frightened fawn. As he approached, a woman who could only be her mother, abruptly stepped in front of the young woman.

"Lord Guldalian, how pleasant to meet you…" Her voice filled with ingratiating charm. "I am Lady Muntain and this is my daughter, Lisvette." She pulled the shy and clearly horrified young lady forward.

"A pleasure to meet you both..." He bowed low. "I came to ask Miss Lisvette if she would take the floor with me."

"She would be delighted." Lady Muntain literally shoved her reluctant daughter into his arms.

Alador caught her and helped her regain her balance. He offered his arm which she hesitantly took, and he led her on to the floor. As they began to dance, he smiled at her, murmuring: "Charming woman..."

"I apologize for my mother," she began with obvious embarrassment.

"Think nothing of it." Alador interrupted. "I am quite familiar with the embarrassing situations an overbearing mother can create for their reluctant offspring." He regaled her with some of his mother's more embarrassing moves and statements. At first, the young lady laughed demurely while remaining on her guard; but before the dance was half over, she was contributing her own little quips mimicked from her mother. Alador enjoyed the dance thoroughly, and was thankful it was one that had allowed them to talk.

When the music ended, he kissed her hand gallantly and noted the flush of color that filled her cheeks. "I regret, M'Lady, that I must return you to the dragon that guards your virtue," he teased as he took her arm gently to guide her from the dance floor. He noted her immediate frown and felt a moment of regret that he must return her. Despite her preference not to return, she let him guide her and properly whispered her thank you for the dance. Alador just smiled as they approached her brash mother.

"Thank you for the honor, Lord Guldalian…" Lady Muntain began.

Alador gave her a withering look. "Your daughter would fare better in this gathering if you allowed her own charming personality to win admirers, rather than thrusting her upon men in hopes of a profitable match."

He faced the dumbfounded Lady Muntain squarely. "Try loving the child you raised, and stop treating her as a commodity expected to bring you a rich return. I found her quite delightful." He smiled at Lisvette before turning to glare at her mother. "Her mother, rather less so if I'm honest." Before she could sputter a response, Alador turned away, winking at Lisvette as he did so. She mouthed him a silent thank you.

As if his attentions had raised Lisvette's profile in the eyes of the other men, Alador noticed a flock of other young mages approaching the young woman. Well, at least he had maybe helped one person here tonight. He felt the dragon's amusement as well and smiled with genuine pleasure.

He made his way to a table where his father was regaling his small court with tales designed to cause gales of laughter. He unfortunately chose the moment when his father was explaining a certain explosion of apple mead all over the tavern keep in Old Meadow. He blushed with embarrassment as he realized that Henrick had not left out the fact that he had implied that Alador was his lover rather than his son to the Oldmeadow villagers.

Henrick did not seem to notice his son until those listening to his tale were looking behind him. He saw the glare in Alador's eyes. "Speak of the serpent, and thus, he appears." He toasted Alador with a hint of mischief in his eyes.

"Telling stories again, Father? You know, eventually you will lose track of what was real and what makes for a better telling," Alador said to mitigate the impact. Those about the table chuckled softly. "Why, one might think you are getting old, and soon we will all hear how you had to trudge your way to Daezun lands uphill, in a snowstorm, both directions." Alador picked up a fresh goblet and saluted his father as those about them laughed with delight.

"Your son is quick of wit as yourself, Henrick. Better watch out, or soon you might find your son has gained the higher ground," quipped one man at the table with a chuckle.

"The day the boy bests me, I will give him my manor," Henrick declared boldly.

"Ah, then I shall begin packing my things to move in," Alador challenged with a grin.

"If the women can't bring me before the bondsman, I doubt you will find your way to best me in a battle of wits, BOY..." Henrick drew out the last word for effect. The gales of laughter drew Luthian's gaze, and Alador toasted him from across the room.

The musicians moved to take a short break, ending the set of dances. Servants were bringing out new rounds of food and restocking the small tables around the room. Conversation was loud and laughter sounded here and there as people mingled and gossiped, telling their own tales…

Alador spotted a woman who drew his eyes. Her manner was elegant, and her silver gown glistened in the lights as she moved. In appearance she was almost his female equivalent: her dress trimmed in blue filigree and thread. He tugged on his father's sleeve and indicated the woman. "Who is that?" He had not seen her at any of Luthian's dinners that he had been forced to attend.

Henrick followed his gaze and smiled. "That is the elusive head of the Healing Sphere. Her name is Lady Aldemar. Many a man has gazed on her with longing, but to be honest, I have never seen her leave with a single one." Henrick took a slow, calculating drink.

"I think I shall try my hand." Alador knew without a doubt that if he could get that woman on the dance floor, they would make a striking pair. Her hair was as white as snow, and she had woven into it threads of silver that made her hair seem to glisten as she moved. She was a striking woman by any standard, regardless of her more advanced age. If Alador had to guess, he would say she was more his father's age.

Alador moved through the crowds milling about. He was forced to stop and give polite acknowledgments, but given that the musicians were just now returning to the dais, he had time. When he finally made it to her side, a cluster of men and women were gathered about her. Unlike other groups he had passed, this one held a more serious tone. He was not going to be able to mimic his father's charming ways with this lady.

The circle fell silent as Alador approached and he could feel immediately that this was a group of mages who held his family name in disdain. He bowed very low. "I apologize for being forward, Lady Aldemar. I wished to introduce myself."

"I think you made sure, Lord Guldalian, that we all know who you are." Her obvious cool tones created a frigid tension in the circle.

"Yes, a fact that displeases my uncle, you can be sure." Alador let a small warm smile grace his lips. "I fear he did not know such an announcement was coming." He glanced over at Luthian who was now watching him closely. Had he stumbled into a circle that Luthian feared?

The lady followed his gaze and looked back at him. "He did not know?"

"I fear not. I know how much he dislikes rumours that he hasn't started himself, so he will shortly be hard at work undoing what I chose to do this night. You, however, do not strike me as a rumour-monger. I wondered if you would dance with me, that we might speak?" He looked apologetically at those about him.

"I think… I would be delighted." Lady Aldemar quietly answered. "If you all will excuse us, I will return shortly. What is said at this table is not to leave it." Her look was not lost on Alador and her words made it clear that this was an order of some sort.

The musicians were just starting up a tune, so Alador offered her his hand, which she gracefully took. The two were the first to the floor and, fortunately for Alador, the steps were ones he had learned. He managed to keep up with her graceful movements. The dance had many moments when they were apart, but there were also moments when they turned with hands held palm to palm. It was in these moments that they spoke.

"You made a bold move to declare yourself, a half-Daezun, Luthian's heir," she stated.

"Bold moves make visible what others do not see. They also make quiet disappearances harder to arrange," Alador explained.

She smiled as they parted. When their hands touched again, she asked. "What is it you want of me, Lord Guldalian?"

"Well to be honest, when I first saw you, I merely thought how striking your appearance with me would be.

Tonight, for me, is about making a statement. But as I approached, I found the seriousness of your table far more interesting," Alador admitted.

"Are you always so honest?" she asked as they parted.

The response had to be delayed while the number called for a changing of partners and it took a few moments before he had her back again. "No," he answered. "This city does not allow a man the luxury of complete honesty. I can tell by your manner, however, that you hold my uncle somewhat in disdain, and that in itself is refreshing."

"I assure you, I bear the High Minister no ill will," she replied cautiously.

"I would think one of a healing order would find it hard to bear anyone ill will. It does not mean you have to like an individual, or agree with the methods he employs to gain his ends," Alador countered. He was frustrated as the dance parted them again. Alador could feel the many eyes upon them and smiled. He had chosen his dance partner well. The dance would end soon, so he pushed to make his point.

"I could use a friend in this city, my lady. I do not ask to be a paramour. I need a friend I can trust. I sense in you someone who would give sound advice and keep a confidence," he pressed. He hoped he was right, but there was something about her.

"I might just be better at being false than the rest," she pointed out.

"You might. Then my uncle will be very interested in the content of this conversation. I guess, by the end of tomorrow, I will know if you are a skilled Lerdenian player or a person of real merit." The music ended and

Alador bowed low. He offered her his arm to escort her back to the table that he had stolen her from.

"I find your candor refreshing," she admitted.

"That would be new. I am often scolded for my outspoken tongue." He flashed her a charming smile. "May I call upon you?"

"You do not know where to call," she pointed out.

They reached the table and Alador kissed her hand gallantly. "I am quite sure that if you truly wished to grant me this boon, you could send me word within the Blackguard." His eyes met hers over her hand. "Enjoy your evening, Lady Aldemar."

The lady sank into a deep curtsy, making those about them draw in a surprised breath. Alador smiled, realizing he had just won a few more moves within the court of his uncle's little empire.

He took his time returning to his father's side, taking the opportunity to acknowledge the many who stopped him, curious to know more. He was careful to give no indication of any word that might compromise Lady Aldemar's standing or honor. His main goal had been achieved: the two had commanded attention. Not only had they made a striking couple, the fact that she did not take to the floor often featured in conversation as Alador passed through the differing groups.

Henrick handed him a goblet when he returned to his father's side. "Well played. Whatever did you say to her to get her to dance with you?"

Alador murmured softly to his father. "I used a tactic foreign to this court." He sipped the goblet as he looked around.

"What is that?" Henrick was truly curious as he turned to face Alador.

"The truth," Alador answered, grinning into his goblet.

Henrick looked a bit puzzled by that, but just nodded in response. Alador looked across the room and saw that the lady in question was watching him, so he ever so slightly toasted her, bringing a smile to her lips. "Doesn't Luthian dance?" he asked.

"Oh, I think he will now." Henrick chuckled.

Alador looked at where Henrick pointed with his goblet. Sure enough, Luthian was moving his way through the crowd to Lady Aldemar's side. "I guess I will find out tonight how well the truth worked," he muttered into his glass.

When Luthian reached Lady Aldemar, Alador could tell by her expression that she was shocked. His soft whisper brought a concerned look to her face, but then she nodded and offered him her hand. All eyes were on these two, more so than when Alador had danced with her. Luthian led her on to the dance floor and nodded to the musicians who started up a slower tune. Soon the floor filled around them, but Alador's eyes were on the couple.

Unlike in his own company, the lady's posture was rigid. Her body language, as she moved perfectly through the steps, spoke volumes. He could tell that she had no desire to be on the floor with his uncle. He doubted anyone ever denied the High Minister a dance, especially if, as Henrick said, the man rarely took to the floor. *'Well, this will be interesting,'* he thought.

It was then that the doorman's staff hit the floor to announce a late arrival. Alador's eyes casually swept over the doorway and swiftly returned to it. His eyes widened and his face paled, as there standing in the doorway, was the woman on Jon's walls.

Her black dress showed more skin than it covered. It fell in waving strips of black, a veiled shimmering shadow of movement. Her gleaming complexion was in sharp contrast with the deep, shimmering black against flawless alabaster skin. Her face shined with a beauty he had never seen. The lady's eyes were darkened and her lips reddened to draw the observer's gaze.

"Lady Morana, Mistress of the Black Sphere and Guardian of the Rites"

Alador felt Renamaum recoil within him. He had never felt anything like what happened within him at that moment. Alador trembled and clutched his goblet tightly as emotions boiled through him. He forced a barrier of magic between him and the dragon within. The wine in his goblet began to steam and bubble. It was as if Renamaum was attempting to burst free from his internal confines. Despite the shield, rage poured through Alador as he fought to contain the blue dragon. The hand gripping his goblet turned white.

Beside him, Henrick cursed softly. "We have to leave," he whispered. "Meet me at the manor as soon as you can extract yourself." Henrick grabbed his arm. Alador barely noticed the grasp as his vision swam, still attempting to gain the upper hand over Renamaum. "Alador, I mean it. Get out of here quickly. She might be able to sense Renamaum," he hissed.

"He can sure sense her," Alador managed to squeak out.

"Then you know who that is?" Henrick pressed.

Alador nodded. It was Dethara, the Goddess of Death. How was it that she was here? How was it possible? He turned to ask Henrick, but the man was gone. He took a deep drink trying to keep Renamaum in check.

'Stop it, damnit,' he thought quietly.

"Betrayer…! Vile, lying, poisonous snake…," came the returned, snarled thought.

"You will give us away. Go to wherever you hide within me. Go deep, Renamaum, very deep," he commanded desperately.

Alador watched the woman as she glided into the room as if she were the High Minister, herself. She made her way across the dance floor, dancers parting as she moved. It was then that Alador's eyes found his uncle. His uncle stood still, Lady Aldemar at his side. Luthian's face was pale and his eyes were wide. At that moment, Alador knew that his uncle also knew who this was.

Renamaum must have listened, because Alador was able to find some semblance of a center. He watched as Lady Morana moved through the dancers to Luthian. The music faltered to a stop. Silence descended on the room at this strange entrance and the High Minister's response. The only sound was the tapping of her shoes, the heels on them higher than any lady's slipper he had ever seen.

"Ah Luthian, it has been too long. When I heard you were hosting a ball, I decided I must come for a visit." Her voice was silken and pitched so all could hear her words. "I was MOST disappointed not to receive an invitation..." Though her words held a husky sense of chastisement, her movements were all sensual. She rubbed her arms then her bare sides as if she were cold. "The mountain cities are so cold this time of season." Lady Morana looked around, fully aware that everything had come to a complete stop. As if she had not meant to, she waved to the musicians in a soft command. "Please, do not stop on my account." She took his hand, effectively cutting Lady Aldemar off his arm.

Morana flashed Lady Aldemar a look of clear dismissal. Alador noted that the woman did not take offense. In fact, Lady Aldemar escaped swiftly to her table. His eyes switched back to Luthian to watch as Lady Morana whispered something in his ear.

Luthian waved to the musicians to continue and the two began to dance. The floor had largely emptied by this time and so all eyes were on the striking couple. The lady was clothed completely in black and the High Minister in a matching black trimmed in red. The only contrast between them was the white of Luthian's hair and the black of Morana's; somehow it made them that more striking.

Alador decided that now was the time to leave. The last thing he wanted was Luthian to decide to introduce his heir to the Goddess of the Black Sphere. He feared what she could discern at a mere touch. Alador could not risk her learning of his friendship with Jon. He set down his goblet on his way to the nearest servants' door, not pausing to become drawn into the whispered conversations.

Once outside, he began sweating despite the coolness of the air. *'Why was she here?'* His thoughts swirled as he dodged bowing servants. Cursing softly, he emerged outside the manor, magically transforming what he was wearing to darker thicker clothing to hide him better in the crisp night. Swiftly he made his way to the stairs, nodding to the guard at the top of the steps.

The faint sounds of music still played from the hall behind him: a haunting melody that seemed foretelling and ominous. One thing he was clear about: when he had last glanced at Luthian, he was certain that there had been fear in the High Minister's eyes.

He could not help but feel as if he has been outmaneuvered. How did one outplay a goddess? He could feel Renamaum seething within him. By Luthian's body and expressions, even the High Minister had been unprepared for that swift turn on the game board.

'Regardless, things just became much more complicated,' he thought bitterly. *'Much more complicated, indeed.'*

Glossary

Blackguard – an elite army of half-Daezun and half-Lerdenian who have shown the capacity for spell-casting. First school of mages established on the isle.

Blood-mining - The practice of feeding a chained dragon to full health then cutting it so that its magical powers and blood meld into the ground. The mixture is harvested and planted into dirt in a nearby mine to congeal into bloodstones. Process takes a minimum of one two turns.

Bloodstone – A magically embed stone created from the magic and the blood of a dragon. These combine into a hard substance that can be drained or used for item enhancements.

Circle- In an attempt to control birthing and population, Daezun use this ritual for coming of age, reproduction and celebration of high summer.

Daezun – A shorter stocky race proficient at mining and other trades involving the use of hands. Daezun cannot cast spells. They revere the dragons and the Gods.

Geas – an obligation or prohibition magically imposed on a person. In this case, the geas was established to whoever harvested Renamaum's bloodstone.

Korpen – Korpen had originally been slow moving pests that traveled in herds and are now domesticated for farm use. Their massive heads had double, vertically-oriented horns. The upper horn curved forward from behind the head, while the lower emerged from the head itself. As a protection from predators such as dragons, the spikes along their backs were almost impenetrable. That was useful to the miners as well: korpen were strong and a great amount of weight could be attached to each spike

Lerdenians – Lithe and lean, many have white hair due to magical drain. Most Lerdenians are capable of some spell casting.

Lexital – These unique flying creatures had a strange curved beak with what seemed to be like the sail of a boat rising above both beak and eyes. Their neck was long and serpentine, moving side to side as they steered through the sky. Their eyes were red and rimmed in blue. Their wings were varying shades of blue with a ridge of red that seemed to arch out mid-feathers. There was a natural dip in this neck right before the body that could carry the rider.

Medure- Medure was a hard metal that glistened with flecks of blue; it was difficult to find and harder to work. Used as currency in rectangle pieces.

Panzet – large birds with long legs, prized for their long purple feathers. Often used in comparison for those who have a focus on appearance but lack intelligence.

Prang – A local herbivore, their white and brown coats made it easy for them to blend in with the dead foliage of the cold winter months. An adult prang could weigh up to two hundred and fifty stones – too large for individual families. A prang's up-swept and back-curving horns could be used in medicine for headaches and eyesight.

Slips- Another name for medure that has been formed into currency. These are small rectangles of the medal with a small hole in one end so that they can be strung into strings of one hundred.

Trading Tokens – Smaller form of currency for day to day items. There are fifty trading token in a single slip.

Trench- A below ground level area carved out with a central canal that takes the city sewage out to sea. Many denizens of Lerdenian cities that do not have spell casting abilities are forced to live there in abject poverty.

Turn – How the denizens of Vesta measure time. A turn is approximately eight earth months and is measured from winter to summer solstice.

ABOUT THE AUTHOR

Cheryl Matthynssens is a mother of four and a grandmother of four. She graduated from Western Washington University as an English Education Major with a minor in Psychology. She later went back and received certification as a Chemical Dependency Counselor.

Combined with a love of helping others, there has remained a strong passion for all things fantasy. An avid reader, RPG player, and as her family calls her – a computer nerd, Cheryl has never given up her writing or desire to share her art with others.

She has six prior books published at this time. Many are available in hard, electronic and audio formats through Amazon and Audible.

Children's books:
Not an Egg!
How the Dragons Got Their Colors
Once Upon a…Wait!

Adult Novels:
Outcast
The Blackguard
Magic Scorned – Sorceress Chronicles

Cheryl also has a blog and website. You can contact her through those sites at dragonsgeas.blogspot.com or http://dragonologists.com/

Dedication

This book is dedicated to Robin Chambers, an outstanding author in his own right. Robin has taken the time to work with me to improve my style and technique as he shared his love for my creative vision.

He has his own series that I highly recommend. The Myrddin's Heir series is a blend of magical intrigue and adventure. His work not only entertains, but it leaves you with things to ponder and it encourages personal growth. Written with three distinct messages, they are so subtly interwoven that they only add to his timeless work.

Robin believes in being read and so all of his creative treasures for e-book is only .99 cents. I am currently working my own way through the series and I do not think he will be able to write them as fast as I am reading them around my own writing.

So with special thanks and tribute, I dedicate this book to Robin Chambers for being willing to take time out of his own busy schedule to mentor and guide me on my own path in creativity.

21696426R00156

Made in the USA
Middletown, DE
08 July 2015